The WATER WOMEN

Other Titles by Bonnie Blaylock

Light to the Hills

The WATER WOMEN

A Novel

BONNIE BLAYLOCK

LAKE UNION
PUBLISHING

Published by Lake Union Publishing, Seattle

www.apub.com

EU product safety contact:
Amazon Media EU S. à r.l.
38, avenue John F. Kennedy, L-1855 Luxembourg
amazonpublishing-gpsr@amazon.com

ISBN-13: 9781662535666 (paperback)
ISBN-13: 9781662535659 (digital)

Cover design by Emily Mahon
Cover image: © Lee Avison / ArcAngel Images; © ilbusca, © enotar, © Katsumi Murouchi / Getty; ©Maizephyr / Shutterstock

Printed in the United States of America

For Samantha

Roll on, deep and dark blue ocean, roll. Ten thousand fleets sweep over thee in vain. Man marks the earth with ruin, but his control stops with the shore.

—Lord Byron

Allegra

Sardegna 1910

Chapter 1

When Allegra gazed offshore at the dark and roiling sea in storms like this, the ocean seemed almost sentient. The waters bucked and jumped like the wild horses that roamed the center of the island, reckless hooves flying. Rain needled Allegra's face as she tilted her chin skyward for a deep breath of salt air. No solitary swim today, then. The sea's spectacular turquoise churned to deeper hues, midnight blues and violet far offshore. It was a siren's call, but she knew the current's pull would be too strong, even for her.

Allegra had arrived earlier than the others. They'd celebrated her sister Ella's wedding until late yesterday, full of dancing, eating, and music. Her ears still rang with the laughter and bells jingling on the horse's bridle as Ella and Gus had ridden off to their little cottage a short distance away. Ella was the first of their family to leave, although she wasn't the oldest. The house already seemed strangely quiet with her absence. Accustomed to her large family, Allegra hated to think what it might be like to live there without her sisters. They were so close, and especially so in the work they did. Wedding or no, it was the first moon of May, their traditional gathering day, marking the beginning of another season of harvest from the sea. Like the others, Allegra anticipated this day all winter, waiting for the sun to warm the water while the mollusks and other creatures rested beneath the darkened waves. The first moon of May was as much a celebration as her sister's wedding had been. More so, since it meant a dozen women would meet again regularly at the water's edge, chatting and laughing, flitting about like a flock of sandpipers, glad to be free from weather and work that had kept them indoors since late autumn.

As the wind picked up, a trio of white gulls fought against it, pushing for the refuge of the rocky cliffs jutting from the surf. Allegra followed their impulse and hoisted her basket of tools across her back as she turned toward the shore's rim of craggy stone. Pocked with small grottos, most too small to be called proper caves, the rocks absorbed the buffeting Mediterranean waves casually, having resisted them for centuries. Allegra avoided the slippery algae and hidden urchins as she picked her way into a dry nook just large enough for her to shelter in while she waited for the storm to pass and the women to arrive. The fishy odor of dried seaweed wasn't so overpowering here, and when she stepped out of the wind, quiet enveloped her like a blanket.

Allegra sighed deeply, brushing damp locks from her face. Between foraging for food and the all-consuming work of collecting and weaving the byssus, spare moments came seldom. Her family and their close community of neighbors depended on everyone bearing their share, a work ethic Allegra's mother had ingrained in her early. She sorted through the items in her woven basket, strung with buoys and an anchor weight to hold it in place on the ocean's surface: various knives that she'd strap to a belt for her dive, a glass jar for collecting the byssus, a small net and diving spear (if she happened on an eel or octopus that might do for dinner). All in order, clean and tidy.

Her island of Sardegna was charming and somewhat insulated, wild and untamed in many ways, but despite Allegra wishing it so, the place she called home wasn't beyond being drawn into the world's politics. She wondered if people everywhere in the world struggled like they seemed to in Italy. Some of their mezzadri, or sharecropper, neighbors found themselves tending smaller and smaller plots of land, scarcely enough to feed their families. There was talk of families scraping together what they could and striking off for better prospects in America.

Allegra's family, she knew, would never consider such a thing. Granted, it was hard to find essentials for the pantry, but they were lucky. Lucky they'd been trained to find and use what the land and sea provided. Lucky their fathers and brothers knew how to throw nets and set traps on the ocean floor to keep them fed. There was another reason they would never emigrate: her family's chief concern had always been caring for the *Pinna nobilis*, a unique giant mollusk that rooted itself in the waters of their cove. As long as there had been memory, she and the women of their Hebrew sisterhood carefully cut the keratin threads the mollusks produced and wove them into fine cloth, ornaments, and tapestries: the byssus. It was their sacred oath and duty, passed through generations and guarded through the ages. It bound them to one another, this skill and the honor of carrying its knowledge, and they gave it as a gift to a world that seemed bent on turmoil.

A break in the sky. The sun pierced through the clouds, parting them like a curtain. On cue, the ill-tempered gulls took flight, eager to resume their endless glide back and forth across the cresting waves, searching for an unwary morsel. Allegra rose, too, lifting her long black skirt trimmed with its traditional red and green and shaking the damp from its folds. A peal of laughter from down the beach reached her ears as she climbed back down the rocks. A group of a dozen women walked toward the shore.

"Lora!" Allegra called and waved, and her oldest sister waved back with a wide smile, beckoning Allegra to join them. For a moment, Allegra pictured Ella raising her arms as they lowered her dress over her head before the ceremony and the unmistakable thickening of Ella's waist that clearly signaled a child on the way. A twinge of concern pricked at Allegra's stomach. Two women in their town had died last year giving birth. Children always brought risk.

The dark clouds had already blown several kilometers offshore, receding with the tide, and Allegra shielded her eyes against the sun. Her heart filled with anticipation as she trotted toward the group, and she batted away her momentary concern over Ella. She stripped off her white outer apron and unbuttoned her vest to ready herself for the sweetest part of the day: their collective swim.

They'd dropped their baskets in a circle behind the familiar rock formation and without hesitation began stripping down to their thin cotton undergarments. Although she'd never seen one, Allegra imagined they must resemble a flock of penguins, donned in their traditional black and white garb. Each region of Sardegna had its own variation on the costume, a slightly different waistcoat style or a wider embroidered trim, but the flash of red panel in the folds of the black skirts, the sun-bleached white of the shirts and trim on their caps were the same. It was yet another tradition that linked them and set the people of Sardegna apart from the Italian mainland.

"Watch the waves just past the drop-off," Allegra said. "That storm current dragged seaweed in, and there could be jellies."

"Last sting I got stayed red for two days." This from Danetta, one of the older women, who rubbed her arm in memory of the pain. "Stick with me, Gabriella. I'll show you what to look for." Allegra smiled when the shoulders of the youngest among them relaxed.

They helped one another undress, arrange supplies, repair equipment, and sharpen knives against their whetstones. Then, as if conducted by an invisible maestro, they all stood together with their arms outstretched toward the sea. The cool water hissed against the sand and lapped between their toes. In an odd, singsong mixture of Hebrew, Italian, and Nuragic, they repeated the names in their lineages, paying homage to the mothers and grandmothers who'd spun the byssus thread for centuries.

Something always stirred in Allegra's heart when they did this. She loved being counted as part of this unbroken line, each link connected to the ones before it and the ones after. She imagined their craft, this divine gift, stretching into the future, like the ocean reaching to meet the horizon. The thought made her feel safe somehow, secure in the thought that a part of her and her work would always continue.

Lofty thoughts for a morning swim. With a final prayer of service and pledge to offer this gift where it was needed, they waded in and floated their baskets out past the cresting waves. The women bobbed for a moment in pairs as they breathed in, and one by one, their dark heads disappeared beneath the water like seals. Allegra filled her lungs beside her sister Lora, and with a deep breath and curve of her back, dove to join them.

Chapter 2

The women naturally fanned out across the grassy seabed, inspecting the field of mollusks that grew offshore in a protected lagoon. Allegra noticed Danetta and Gabriella together. Danetta demonstrated how to twist the wrist just so, to wrest the shell from the mud where it was implanted. The warmer days and warming water had softened the mud enough to pry the shells loose without damaging the mollusks' feet. These mollusks were large, a bit over three feet at their height, and it took some strength and maneuvering to budge them from where they'd dug in.

Allegra witnessed Gabriella surfacing two or three times before Danetta went up for her first long breath, and she smiled to herself. It had taken Allegra months to build up enough lung stamina to stay under for more than two minutes. Her mother had led her through practices at home while they did other chores, teaching her to use busy hands to keep her mind off the air demand. It was much easier to hold her breath above water than below, where she had to overcome her mind's distrust of lingering in a place where breath was impossible.

Allegra hoisted shell after shell to the surface, where she used her short knife to cut the filaments that fanned out from the bivalve's clamped halves. This was the byssus. She was careful not to lose a bit of the dark-amber fiber, placing each piece in her basket as she cut it. Once she'd harvested thc threads, Allegra dove again and nestled the mollusk's base back into the muddy lagoon bottom so that it could live on.

Closer to shore, the seabed changed from mud to sand, and Allegra noticed a subtle circle of white spots in the sand near a rock. She drew the three-foot spear from her belt and hovered above the pattern to make sure. A slight movement of the sand confirmed her suspicions: a flounder lay partially buried, its gills sending up the barest disturbance of sand. Her well-aimed spear pierced the base of its head, and she pulled it flapping from its hiding place. A school of sargos darted away in a flash of silver, startled by the movement.

"Brava, Allegra." Her mother praised her catch as they swam toward the shore, and Allegra beamed. Contributing to the family table was an added benefit of their diving—and a necessary one because the byssus brought no income. It was part of their vow that it couldn't be used for personal gain.

Allegra and Lora compared their harvests on the shore as they dried off and dressed. Lora was four years older and, Allegra thought, the prettiest of the three sisters and the responsible one. Ella was more like an ocean breeze, apt to waft in and out quickly, her attention easily stolen. Ella sparked fun and laughter, splashing in the water, hanging on to someone's basket to be dragged in to shore rather than swimming herself. If pressed, Allegra might label herself the quiet one. Pretty enough, tall and slim, with muscled arms and long, dark hair that hung most often under her cap or scarf in a thick braid down her back. She worked hard. At seventeen, she sometimes wondered if she'd marry or have children. It took a patient sort of man to marry a weaver woman, one who knew where he stood when the seasons changed and the days grew warmer, when most days between May and September, he'd wake to find his wife already gone to the shore, tending the byssus rather than his breakfast.

Allegra and her sister linked arms and set off toward home, the flounder she'd snagged still flapping in her basket.

"What do you think Ella's doing?" she asked.

"They're on their honeymoon, sciocca. What do you think?"

Allegra pushed Lora sideways with her hip. "That's not what I meant. Do you think she misses the first harvest this morning?"

Lora shrugged. "I think Ella's mind is elsewhere."

"I'd be sad to miss it. Even for someone like Gus. I still can't believe Mamma agreed to have the wedding so close to first moon."

"*We're* here," Lora replied, as if that made up for their sister's absence. "Anyway, Ella hasn't taken the water oath yet."

Allegra stopped suddenly, jerking Lora backward with her. "You think she won't?"

Lora pulled her forward again. They'd almost reached the small footpath that led to their home beyond the cliff face. "It'll have to be her choice."

"Did she say something to you?" She glanced out at the waves breaking against the shoreline, the gulls squawking overhead, and the line of laughing women laden with baskets walking behind them toward their own homes. It was all she'd ever known, and she loved it entirely.

"No," Lora admitted. "But Ella's married now, with babies soon to come."

"Mamma's married." Allegra glanced at Lora. She said nothing about her suspicions or concerns that Ella might already be carrying.

"Yes, but Mamma is a maestra. You know how Ella is. She'd just as soon go cliff jumping with friends as swim with us in the lagoon."

"We're water women," said Allegra, as if that settled it. Her papà was a pescatore, and her brothers would follow. Just as the sheepherders knew their trade and the bakers theirs, families inherited the land or business and learned the skills, the younger generation placing their feet in the treads of their fathers and mothers. Allegra's father appeared at the top of the path and smiled at them. He reached out to take their baskets.

"Flounder," he exclaimed. "And still fresh." His large, warm hand rested on Allegra's head, and for the second time that day, she felt complete, the ground solid beneath her and her task predictably set before her.

The muscles in her arms and legs ached pleasantly, evidence of a day well spent. Ella would return to them soon enough, she believed, and when she did, Allegra wouldn't feel her absence so keenly. As it was, her thoughts kept returning to her sister repeatedly, like a tongue drawn to the cavity from a lost tooth.

Chapter 3

That spring, Allegra, Lora, and their mother spent the long, warm days diving and swimming most mornings. Afternoons passed with careful rinsing and drying of the byssus threads, a task that had to be repeated until every trace of salt and bit of sea life had been washed away. After drying in the sun, the strange alchemy of the process transformed the limp amber threads into soft, fine strands of priceless sea silk. Hung in the windows of their studio, the fibers caught the light of the Mediterranean sun and glinted pure gold.

Ella was conspicuously absent, endlessly busy with the demands of her new husband and household, or so she claimed. Allegra found herself growing impatient with her sister, disappointed in her wayward heart.

"Ella used to start the weaving," she said, frustrated when her inexpert fingers fumbled at the loom. "She was going to teach me her trick of securing the first threads so they wouldn't slip."

Her mother nudged her to scoot over on the stool. "It's not hard. Let me show you." She took the comb from Allegra's hand and placed it where the weave would start. "Lay it flat here with one hand and use the other to coax the threads down where you want them."

Allegra rested her chin in her palm. "Can't you tell her to come help us?"

"You and Lora do fine work." Mamma's answer was encouraging but firm.

"Don't you care that she's not here?" Allegra pressed.

Her mother drew her hands from the loom and turned to face her. "Ella has a lot to think about right now. I do miss her being here, but she must make her own decisions."

Allegra protested, "A tradition of weavers for hundreds of years, as old as our first maestra, Queen Berenice, and Ella is too good for that?"

Mamma smiled, and Allegra felt a twinge of chagrin. Her mother was a maestra, the highest and most learned teacher of their craft. Did she think she could tell her mother something she didn't already know?

"You're here. And Lora's here. And all the other women in all the other families."

"You sound like Signora D'Ecco telling us to keep our eyes on our own work at school."

"Something like that." Mamma smiled. "Does it help you to worry about Ella? Your sister's a wife and, you may as well know, will be a mother soon." Of course, her mother had known. "She's got lots of time to make choices. The sea doesn't worry about tomorrow. The tides are for this day only." She handed the comb wound with byssus thread back to Allegra. "Your turn," she said, and nodded at the loom.

Not many months after that conversation, Allegra ran into Ella at the docks near the center of town. It had been some time since they'd seen one another, and Allegra was surprised at how different she looked. Ella carried a sack full of onions and garlic for a sauce she intended to make. Her sister was an excellent cook, Allegra allowed. The family had been invited to dinner at the newlyweds' home six weeks or so after the wedding, and her seafood fregola had been delicious. Proudly, Ella had shown off the saffron bulbs they'd planted in a corner of their garden, and the strands her husband had stored from the previous fall were still fragrant, the perfect ingredient for the dish.

"You know Papà would give you some of his catch," she said, as Ella picked over the fresh-netted brill and bream at the fish market.

"Probably, but Gus and I can manage."

Allegra thought about whether it occurred to Ella to wonder what she'd been up to, but why would it? Their days were governed by the byssus work, and that hadn't changed since Allegra was a child.

"Do you miss home?" Allegra asked.

Ella glanced up from the silver pile of fish. "I miss *you*," she said. "But we're not that far away. You act like we've moved to Roma when we're no more than a half hour's walk from you here in town!"

"I guess." Allegra tilted her head, sizing up her sister. Her face looked swollen and puffy, her cheeks flushed.

"You're asking about the byssus, aren't you?" Ella stepped past the stalls of fish toward the mussels and langoustines. "I do miss being together, but I have Gus." She shrugged. "You don't need me for the weaving."

"But it's your—"

"What?" Ella interrupted. "My duty? My calling?" She sighed. "You're as good as the rabbis, Allegra, at piling on the guilt. I think it will survive without me." Her ire was up, and she swiped at her brow in the heat. Was Allegra imagining it, or was her sister wheezing?

"So you're not going to take the oath? You're not going to weave?"

"When do I have time?" Allegra knew this was an excuse. Water women had managed to do the work and take care of households and children for centuries. Women balanced armloads, and when that got unwieldy, they learned to carry baskets atop their heads with an infant strapped to their torsos. She started to say so, but Ella stopped her. "I don't want to take the oath," she admitted, seeming suddenly weary.

Allegra was appalled. They were a community, a network. What one of them did affected them all in some way or other. What if everyone suddenly decided to abandon the byssus, to become . . . what, a teacher or sheepherder or miner?

"That's selfish," Allegra blurted. "How can you think that way?"

Ella paid for the small sack of langoustines she'd selected and fixed Allegra with flashing brown eyes as she stood with her hands on her belly. They were the same height, with similar features and childhoods, but apparently opposite thoughts. "Am I?" she challenged. "You want to weave because it suits you. You see the byssus as a thread, the unbroken line. That's fine. For you. For me, it feels like a chain, and I want to do something else."

"If the family needs you, it's your duty—no, your *honor*—to be there. It's more than just us. We put ourselves aside for something bigger." She struggled to put words to all she felt.

"Allegra." Ella softened and placed Allegra's hand on her protruding belly. Something swam beneath her hand, rippling and turning. "This *is* bigger."

A grin spread across Allegra's face as she registered the movements. What did she know about becoming a mother? About anything in Ella's life, really? She opened her mouth to voice a sheepish apology, but then Ella fell against her, the langoustines spilling out of her sack onto the market stones.

"Aiutami!" Allegra cried, catching Ella's weight and sinking to her knees with her sister's limp body.

Several women rushed to her side, one of them barking orders at a vendor to run for the doctor, another sending a young boy running for the midwife's house. Allegra held Ella's lolling head in her lap, unable to breathe as her heart pounded against her ribs.

"Someone get my mother," she heard herself say. "We need my mother."

~

Later, after she recounted how several of them had lifted Ella into the back of a fish vendor's donkey cart and run for the doctor, Allegra recalled odd details of the scene. Someone had gathered up the spilled langoustines and handed the bag to her, and she'd been confused. Were these supposed to revive Ella? What was she to do with them? Vendors' donkeys usually spent the market day resting in the shade, and this one had resisted the unexpected labor. Its loud bray rang in Allegra's ears as she ran alongside the cart, her sister's skirt having risen enough that Allegra was able to glimpse how tight the skin looked around her sister's ankles.

"She didn't wake up," Allegra told her mother. "I tried to make her, but she wouldn't."

The midwife's mouth was set in a grim line as she held Ella's wrist for a pulse. When the seizures began, the doctor had not yet arrived, and the midwife did all she could to help Ella. Allegra remembered it as if she'd been underwater the whole time, sounds muffled and far away.

"She had fish scales in her hair from the market." Allegra opened her palm, and there they were, five silver flakes crusted with salt. She'd plucked them from Ella's braid when the seizures had stopped, when everything stopped.

The doctor, by the time he arrived, could do nothing. Perhaps if he'd arrived sooner? Perhaps if she hadn't goaded Ella and tried to make her feel guilty about not taking the water oath? Perhaps, perhaps, perhaps. Allegra would never know, and she'd never meet the niece or nephew she'd felt kicking under her hand that same day. She couldn't look at Gus when he came, his hat in his hands. She couldn't face her mother's silent tears, or the way she pulled Allegra close to give her comfort, unaware that she may have been to blame.

Chapter 4

The maddening thing about losing someone close is that although time stills in the space of one moment for you, everyone else carries on. Nets are mended, meals are eaten, accounts are paid, and gardens planted as if your shattered heart isn't having to rebuild itself piece by piece. Byssus, too, carries on, and Allegra and the family who remained learned to find some measure of comfort in the predictable routine of their work.

"We're stewards," her mother said. "We steward the sea's offerings, the gift of our family, and we also steward our pain."

"How can we possibly do that?" she'd asked, in the time just after Ella had gone.

"It's what we've been given, and we can make something of it, as hard as it is, so it's not wasted. All these tears must be watering something."

Allegra sighed. "There have been enough to fill an entire well."

"We have to see what we can draw from it. Maybe not today," her mother admitted. "But something will spring from this if we let it."

Ella's absence constantly reminded Allegra how quickly ties can be severed. The loss of her sister became a sort of beacon to her, a warning to take care and treasure those she loved. She fashioned a delicate pouch made of byssus with a simple drawstring enclosure and placed in it a lock of Ella's hair and the five fish scales she'd kept from that day in the market. The family still had each other, their health, and work that needed doing. Though it sometimes made her grit her teeth, life marched forward, in spite of it all.

Fully a year after Ella's death, Allegra sensed herself growing around the stone of loss that seemed mortared into her heart. She still missed Ella, still thought of that day in the market and likely always would, but she was slowly learning how to bear the stone's weight as she went about her days. It no longer anchored her in place and restricted her breathing. She recognized pleasure again, able to enjoy the sun on her face or the brine of an oyster.

The small town of Sant'Antioco, where Allegra and her family lived, rarely saw tourists or visitors. It was on an island's island, a dot off the southwest coast of Sardegna itself. They called it Sardegna's beauty mark. Their community numbered only a few hundred, and those were families of farmers, fishermen, miners, and a few shopkeepers. Business owners lived in the town, and those who worked in the sea and fields made their homes on the outskirts. There was a small school and a church for the Catholics. If a boat sailed into the quay, its occupants would have a full view of most of the town and the homes of those who lived there with just a slight swivel of their heads. Allegra's family, along with most of the families associated with weaving the byssus, lived two miles or so outside of town, such as it was. They belonged to the small Jewish community on the island, their synagogue an informal back room in their neighbor's house. On holidays, they pooled their resources—a menorah from this one, candles from another. They were scattered in homes beyond the tide's reach, but close enough for a brisk walk to the byssus cove.

Although she knew practically everyone on their side of the island and some from farther afield, she was sure she'd never seen the boy she spotted knocking barnacles off the blue and white fishing trawler at the docks. Allegra was on her way to the small market with a list from Mamma when the image of the young man with the tanned back and dark curls stopped her in her tracks.

Muscled and wiry, he was waist deep in the harbor near the quay, holding his boat steady with one hand while scraping the hull with a wooden spatula in his other. He waved and called good-naturedly to the pescatori in the other boats motoring in. She put a hand up to shade her eyes from the sun and see better. Who was that in the water?

That, of course, was the exact moment the young man chose to toss his tool into the boat, launch himself up and over its side, and turn his face toward the market area. The wide grin that spread across his face told her he'd seen her obvious ogling—that, and the way he casually tipped his head to nod at her as he righted himself in the boat. Allegra dropped her hand and turned on her heel with a swish of her black skirt, disappearing into the safe and much less intimidating interior of the shop behind her.

Like many of the negozios that lined the main street along the quay, the windows of the dry goods store displayed small byssus weavings—handkerchief-size tapestries or light linen embroidered with the golden thread. Not for sale, they highlighted and honored the unique art of the area. Allegra stopped for a moment to admire the handiwork and catch her breath from the hasty retreat she'd made. A few different patterns reflected the light today. One of the weavers must have recently brought some for the display. Allegra could usually recognize the weaver by the subject matter. Some wove native fishes and boats, some focused on flora like the purple-flowered saffron or strawberry tree laden with gold and yellow ripening fruits, while others—like her mamma—were skilled enough to depict an entire story within a small square. Her favorite was a tapestry the size of a pillowcase that her mamma had woven over a span of two years: the night sky with constellations glittering in place over a moonlit ocean, with a gap in the heavens where the fingers of God's hand seemed to pry back the night to peer below. It was stretched in a wooden frame now, hung on the wall of their gathering room, above the loom where she'd woven it.

Allegra glanced at the list in her hand and remembered why she'd come. Flour, soap, and molasses, if it was available. She turned and searched the small shop for its owner.

"Signor Sanna?" she ventured. "Do you have any molasses in today?"

The man popped up from where he'd been bent behind the broad wooden counter. "Ah, Allegra. After something sweet?" He wiped his hands on the white front of his apron, stretched tight across his ample girth, and walked her to a tidy shelf in the back, the floorboards creaking beneath his tall boots. "Brought over from Roma just yesterday, so you're in luck." He handed her a glass bottle of the dark treacle, stoppered with a bit of cork.

"Perfetto," she said. "Mamma wants to make some small cakes, and she was hoping to add something special." The shop door's bell jingled, and Signor Sanna left her to the rest of her list.

As she headed to find the soaps, the unmistakable voice of the young man from the harbor reached her ears. She ducked down and peered around the end of the aisle. There he was, joking and chatting with Signor Sanna. He'd donned a shirt, its white linen collar damp where his dark curls still dripped seawater from beneath his long stocking cap. Even from her vantage point, Allegra noticed he stood tall, his lithe form as apt to haul in nets full of fish as dance the tarantella. As he spoke, his hands hastily buttoned the front of his mastruca, the familiar sleeveless jacket made of sheepskin.

"Buongiorno, Signor Sanna. Have you any seada?" he asked.

A sweet tooth, thought Allegra. She, too, loved the traditional pastry, fried and filled with lemon pecorino. Her mouth watered as she imagined the honeyed taste on her tongue. She found the soap and sugar and headed to the counter for her purchase while the shopkeeper wrapped the young man's parcel in thin brown paper.

"Found all you need, Allegra?" the older man asked. Nodding to the young man, he gestured to her. "If you will permit—"

"Of course, of course. Take your time." The young man smiled at her, fixing her with his merry nut-brown eyes.

Allegra nodded her thanks and paid for the groceries. She didn't risk casting a backward glance as she left the store. All this nonsense for a stranger, she thought, dismissing the flush that crept up her neck. He likely hadn't noticed her at all, and all her flutter was her imagination on a fool's errand. She quickened her steps on the path toward home, kicking up flashes of the red and green fabric in the panels of her skirt as she walked.

"Allegra!" She stopped and turned. She'd made it as far as the end of the quay and had been heading toward the edge of town. "Allegra!" he called again. It was the young man. He trotted after her, his parcel in hand, and closed the distance between them, not in the least winded. "Scusami," he said. "I heard Signor Sanna say your name."

She waited, her eyes drinking in his features up close. His fine, sharp nose; a jaw darkened by a few days' beard growth; brows that rose upward with an unspoken question.

"I saw you from the boat," he began. "In the water." The corners of Allegra's mouth curved with his display of nervousness. Perhaps she hadn't conjured the encounter after all. "Forgive me for chasing you," he backpedaled. "I've seen you before." He gestured back toward town. "Walking on the quay with others. More than once, walking into Signor Sanna's. But I was always working on the boat or had my hands full of fish."

She still hadn't spoken a word, and he tried another tack. "I wondered if you might like some seada?" He held out the parcel she'd watched the shopkeeper wrap. "I bought them to share with you."

"You don't even know me." She realized as she spoke that her words came across as rude.

He grinned at her. "But I'd like to. I've inquired." This surprised her. In their closeted hamlet, people talked, and no gossip had reached her about a handsome sailor asking after her. And he *was* handsome. When he smiled like that, his eyes sparkled and teased, so she couldn't help but smile in return. He swept his dark curls away from his face.

His brows rose again as he answered the questions she had wanted to ask while he unfolded the paper, revealing the golden sugared pastry, its sweet citrusy scent wafting out. "My name is Johann Renda. I've recently arrived from east of Cagliari. The capital is too much city for me."

Allegra had only been to Cagliari once, years ago, sailing two hours around the southern edge of the island to attend a wedding with her family. Compared to their slow and sleepy mariner town, she remembered the place as a confusing maze of streets and shops, constantly busy with people and carts. Too much city, indeed. She nodded.

"You already know my name, it seems," she said, and she picked a seada from the package he offered. "So you're a pescatore, then. Like my father and brothers." The seada was still warm, and a bit of the lemony cheese oozed out as she bit into it. She closed her eyes, savoring it. "Mmm, delicious."

She could see her response pleased him, and she was glad. Her sister Ella sprang to mind then, and a stab of guilt pricked her heart. Should she be allowed this pleasure? This—whatever this was—could go no further unless they had an understanding. It wasn't unusual for courtships to form quickly if families agreed.

"Why Sant'Antioco?" she asked. "Why not Corsica or elsewhere?"

"My father used to come here in his childhood to visit relatives. He told stories at dinner about how special it was." There was the grin again. "He made up things about mermaids and how beautiful all the women were. When I grew tired of the capital, I had to see for myself. I haven't seen a mermaid yet, but the rest seems true."

Allegra felt her face flame, and she dropped her head, hiding a smile.

"Would it be all right to walk with you?" he asked.

Allegra swallowed the seada. "That depends," she answered. "Did you notice the woven tapestries displayed in the storefront? If you've been here only a short time, what do you know about the women who weave them?"

"The water women?" He brushed an unruly lock from his face. "They're a sect, aren't they? A tribe of artists? Some say what they do is la magia."

Allegra licked her fingers, sticky from the remains of the sweet pastry. "Magic?" She pursed her lips. "I hardly think so."

"How do you know?" he asked.

"Because I'm one of them," she replied, searching his face. "Now, do you still wish to walk with me?"

Johann's lips curved into a wide grin, and he nodded. "Definitely," he said. "Lead the way."

Chapter 5

Thereafter, they began to take frequent walks together along the beaches and atop the cliffs. Allegra shared the traditions and expectations of water women with Johann. Sardegna itself was layered with customs and ways unmatched in the rest of Italy, so her stories of the weavers fit perfectly with the island's air of mystery. Allegra traced their line from the Hebrew queen Berenice, their ancient tutor and patron, through the Middle Ages, when the cloaks they'd fashioned had been worn by popes and kings. She recounted how, not so many years ago, her own grandmother had helped create the wedding cloak for Dona Maria Pia, the fourteen-year-old bride of the king of Portugal.

She told him the water women had always been different from the rest of the town's residents, but artists, as a rule, were often an odd bunch. Although now they were respected and honored because of their unique work, they hadn't always been. Being Jewish meant they were still sometimes perceived as strange, but that was nothing new. Although over time, many of them no longer actively and openly practiced the faith in the traditional ways, the townspeople always had and probably always would think of them as Jews. Perhaps because of their deep knowledge of plants and the mysterious language of the ancient Nuragic people they sometimes used when they sang (which even she didn't know the source of), there had been times in the past when their families had been labeled and marked with suspicion, called heathens or witches. But in truth, there was nothing magic about the beautiful weavings they created. As long as Allegra had lived there, she'd only experienced their island as home, a small, close community, its members linked by their shared love of the sea and working side by side.

Johann shared his love of the land, delighting in the long-haired sheep that regarded them with droll expressions as they passed by, outnumbering the island's human population by threefold. They parsed their common interests: music, the sea, a good meal shared, a solid day's work with their hands, and the roots of their faith. His father and two older brothers had been casualties of cholera, and his mother had remarried a widower and was now responsible for additional children.

"My sisters and their husbands are there to help her, but I'm the only one who remains unmarried," he told her. "I love the sea. Living on an island, I of course had sea legs before I could walk. I'd sail with my father and brothers. Papà would hoist me on his shoulders and announce we were off for an adventure, and I could think of no better way to spend a day. Pushing offshore in my boat in the mornings, not knowing what it will show me, what it might surrender to me from beneath—a thrill I'll never shake."

Allegra nodded. It was something she knew full well. "I love the morning dives with the weavers. The breathing, tending the mollusks, weaving the threads, caring for one another. We'll never be rich, you and I."

"A pescatore and a weaver." Johann laughed. "We'll have all we need." He clasped her hand as they strolled, the soothing melody of the sheep's tinkling bells carrying on the wind.

Over the course of the next several months of courtship, Allegra thought often of her sister Ella. She saw Gus occasionally in town, and she knew he had begun asking after another young woman. She didn't like to think that Ella was so easily replaced, but her mother saw it differently. Gus, too, had suffered and needed mending. Every heart beat differently. Though Ella had used her marriage as an excuse to leave the byssus work, Allegra believed she could honor both a husband and her water oath.

They delighted in each other's differences. In his spare moments, Johann was happy to walk with her through the pastures and along the seashore. Allegra pointed out this plant or that one as she placed it in her basket. She loved how he marveled at her knowledge and beamed with pride when he answered her quizzes correctly. He showed her the different types of clouds and ways to read the sky in both daylight and dark. While Allegra knew the sea, she knew only the shallow byssus coves and shoreline rather than the depths reached only by boat. That had always been her father and brothers' realm. But she and Johann sometimes sailed beyond the cove, out where the water deepened to a dark indigo blue. There, he'd map the world beneath the waves for her: here, a drop-off too deep to plumb; there, a cave and rocks where eels and octopuses loved to hide. He'd whip off his vest, shirt, and shoes, and dive in a perfect arc from the bow of the boat, resurfacing with gifts—handfuls of sand dollars, the mother-of-pearl shell of an oyster. Allegra leaned over the side to kiss him, his lips salty as the sea streamed from his hair.

Before the year was out, Johann had spoken to Allegra's parents, and the family had consented that they be wed. Through that winter, while it was too cold to swim and rougher seas curtailed Johann's trips out, they dreamed and planned their lives together. Johann had already begun building what would be their modest home, a block structure tucked into the curve of a cove off the coast, not too far from Allegra's family home. He made sure it would be sheltered from the coastal winds in the winter and that the eastern side would light with the sunrise. A simple stove and storage area for drying fish, octopuses, and whatever Johann would bring home. Shelves for Allegra's herbs and staples.

Allegra and her mother spent the winter tailoring the brocade and silk she would wear on the day of the wedding. Allegra herself wove the black orbace cape Johann would don. As her fingers worked the fine wool into its thinly knit form, her heart danced, and she couldn't keep from humming and singing softly to herself. She'd spent hours dyeing the wool before it ever touched the loom, boiling it carefully and adding vinegar, salt, and ash to fix the color until it was the perfect shade, the exact hue of the meurra, or blackbirds, flitting through the evergreen shrubs dotting their island. Painstakingly, she added a thick felt layer to waterproof the garment before declaring it finished.

Allegra's father set about borrowing a strong pair of oxen from a family that agreed to be paid with part of his weekly catch, and her mother and sister bent their heads together to whisper about how they would decorate the tracca the oxen would pull. The wedding carts would be full of color and whimsy if the two of them had their say. Both her brothers played the three-piped launeddas, and the house filled with their music while they practiced after the family's evening meal.

By early spring, the day had come. Johann's mother and sisters, with their children and husbands, had traveled to be there. Neighbors had kindly offered to help house them all for the week, and Allegra finally met Johann's family. They were a lively lot, pitching in to help with wedding preparations, make meals, and run errands. Johann was unlike any of them, Allegra thought, deciding he must have favored his father.

Before the procession began, the family gathered at the home Johann had built.

"May this home be blessed," Allegra's father asked. "May the hands that built it protect our daughter. May her hands work together with yours to build a happy and faithful union."

"May you be blessed with lots of children," her mother added with a smile, "bringing light and love to your home." Allegra couldn't help the blush that crept from her neck to her cheeks. If she was honest, she felt more than a little fear, remembering what had happened to Ella.

"May you grow together in wisdom, wealth, love, and abundance," her father recited as he raised a clay dish full of rice, wheat, salt, coins, and rose petals above his head.

Grinning from ear to ear, he dashed the dish to the ground, the auspicious ritual complete. The family scooped up handfuls from the ground and scattered them over the couple as they held hands and laughed. They climbed into the traccas, adorned with flowers, vines, and byssus tapestries depicting scenes from their island—fishing boats heavy with nets, herds of sheep in the fields, and of course, weavers at their looms. The notes of the launeddas drifted gaily around them as the procession made its way to the home of the rabbi, which functioned as a synagogue as needed. There, they raised a chuppah, and the rabbi united them in marriage, joining Allegra and Johann's hands with a silver wedding chain.

"I can't wait to start this life with you," Allegra whispered to her new husband as he opened the door to their home that evening. They were tired from the day and sated from the banquet her parents had managed to pull together despite the lean times.

Johann held her cheek in his large, warm hand and bent to kiss her, his eyes bright.

"A pescatore and a weaver," he said. "We may never be rich, but tonight I feel like a king."

Chapter 6

Aside from some unfortunate bouts of malaria in their first year of marriage, Allegra and Johann quickly grew into their own rhythms. Each morning, he enjoyed a breakfast of fish and bread that Allegra warmed in the small oven. Afterward, he placed a kiss on Allegra's forehead and flashed his bright smile as he bid her a good day. Then he left for the quay and his cheerful blue boat that danced where it was moored just offshore.

She'd sweep the floors, always sandy no matter how careful they were to leave their shoes at the threshold; do some light mending; and then head to her childhood home to join her mother and sister and help them with their tasks of weaving and dyeing. Some days she spent combing the landscape for a particular plant that was in season, gathering saffron or mixing dyes that would render the perfect shade of blue or purple. While there was no particular agenda or schedule, they each had their own goals for the day, and they whiled away the time chatting and singing until the shadows lengthened across the floor and Allegra took her cue to return home to make dinner for her handsome husband.

She treasured the predictability and the small pleasures of simple routines. Allegra didn't mind the repetition. It comforted her like a worn blanket, soft on the edges and frayed, just so. She loved lighting their lamp in the evening, laughing with Johann as he hung his vest on the peg by the door, a door he'd made with his own rough hands.

Another kiss as he returned from his day at sea, salt on his lips, his skin still warm from the sun.

Often, he surprised her with a sack of amaretti cookies he'd picked up from the baker's before heading home or a bouquet of yellow broom or pink pea flowers he'd thought to gather along his way. They both liked to brighten the rooms with the colors and beauty from the outdoors. Once, Allegra came home to find Johann had layered their bed in petals—white, pink, yellows.

When she arrived at the shore early the next morning, sleepy and rumpled, she shrugged, hiding a secret smile as her mother pulled a few stray petals from the tangle of her hair. "What have you gotten into?" she asked, letting the petals fall to the ground.

"I was in a hurry and didn't do a braid this morning," Allegra answered, avoiding the question. Her mother leaned into her and bumped her with her hip, teasing.

"Be sure to shut your windows at dusk," she mentioned as an afterthought. "The mosquitoes are thickening with the rain."

After their swim and morning harvest, when they were back at her mother's home sharing a midmorning meal, Allegra glanced at Lora. She'd been absent from the morning's gathering and was just now well enough to sit at the loom after two weeks of malarial fever. They'd all had the tiresome sickness this year. The island's boggy wetlands drew swarms of the infernal pests. Wearing their long-sleeved shirts, scarves, and hats helped some, but the weaver women couldn't swim in such attire, and everyone was vulnerable at night.

"I hate to wish for no rain, but wouldn't it be lovely if things dried up and all the mosquitoes went away forever?" Allegra mused.

"Perhaps," her mother agreed. "But it's not really for us to decide which creatures can live or die."

"We take care of the mollusks. We give *them* special treatment."

"But they don't rely on us. They would continue without us. It's about what they offer us." She gestured at the loom with her strong hands. "Such a delicate and unique sort of beauty for the world."

Lora perked up from her seat at the loom. "Signora Dona mentioned recently she'd heard of another remarkable material, one seen at a World's Fair in America."

Mamma nodded. "Yes, I know about that. The Spanish princess, Eulalia, saw a dress there and commissioned one for herself. It was a dress made of glass."

"Glass?" Allegra was astounded. The sea silk was delicate, but not so fragile it would shatter like glass.

Lora explained, "I know what you're thinking, but it was made like the Venetian glass. Its fibers are spun from a rod dipped in fire and then woven on a loom like we do."

"Not like the sea silk," Mamma corrected. "They mix in other fabrics with the glass fibers so the cloth won't shatter." She wrinkled her nose and waved a dismissive hand. "It may sparkle, but it's heavy and costly. Cloth made with byssus is so light it feels invisible, and its shine is like the sun, not a showy diamond. Don't be fooled, girls. There's nothing like our byssus in all the world."

"Which is why our family will always do this," Allegra said, pride in her voice. "Us and our daughters after us. With all that's going on in the world, isn't it lovely to have something beautiful to do?" It was the fall of 1911, and Etna had erupted in neighboring Sicily, leaving thousands homeless. Lately, if she went to meet the boats with their catches down at the main quay, all the talk in town was of Italy's brewing war with Libya. Allegra didn't want to think of politics and battles, of volcanoes creating chaos. She didn't want to imagine Johann doing anything but fashioning his bell-shaped fish traps and tugging off her headscarf to bury his face in her hair at the end of each day.

"Many things in life are beautiful, cara," Mamma reminded her. "A warm house, a mouthful of seada washed down with limoncello, and the love and comfort of family."

Lora chimed in. "I'm sure the pescatori think a school of sardo is beautiful," she said. "And the shepherds are smitten with their smelly sheep. People must think we're crazy for spending our time with the beards of mussels." She laughed at the absurdity, and soon all of them were giggling.

Allegra knew their profession—if you could call it that—was unusual. When she tried to picture herself baking cakes all day, sinking clay jars to trap octopuses, or standing behind a counter selling wares to blundering tourists like in the capital city, she simply couldn't conjure it. It *was* magical, like Johann had teased the first time they'd spoken. Weaving the golden fiber was an alchemy that drew her in, working its magic each time she wove the fine threads into some new geometry.

She wouldn't admit it to Lora and Mamma, but when she collected and worked the sea silk, Allegra felt the same sort of connection and satisfaction as when she and Johann were tangled together in their bed. It made her feel transcendent, part of something bigger and more important than anything that might happen on their tiny island. A participant in creation, making something beautiful from what most people considered ordinary.

Allegra rose and crossed the room to fetch some salted dried fish. She was hungry again, and she placed a hand on her stomach. Soon she would tell Mamma that she and Johann had begun a new work, a different sort of weaving that made her heart flutter with excitement. She imagined the tiny bean of life swimming inside her like a fish, submerged in the salty water of her womb, completely at home without breath, tossed to and fro by the waves of her own movements. The thought made her smile, and she had a sudden longing to wade into the shallows of the sea herself, to feel the tide's tug against her calves.

~

The next morning, Allegra rose before the first pink of dawn lit the panes in the window near her bed. Leaving Johann snoring under the blankets, she nibbled on a crust of bread and some sliced cheese as she walked to the shore. Humming to herself, she smiled at the scuttling crabs hurrying to dive into the sand before the hungry gulls came searching for breakfast. The sky's pink and soft lavender was beginning to mute the morning into a dreamy haze, and Allegra slipped off her shoes and stockings. The sand was still damp from dew and the recent high tide, cool between her toes.

A movement caught her eye up the beach, just below the dunes—a large brown shape near a scraggly hunk of driftwood. It was too far from shore to be a monk seal. Curious, she picked up her skirt and headed toward it. Ah, she'd come upon a nesting loggerhead. The turtle was intent on her task, her mottled flippers sweeping back and forth to dig a hole she judged deep enough to hold her eggs. Allegra crouched to watch.

When the turtle was satisfied, she positioned herself to face the ocean, her huge body covered in sand in the pit she'd dug. She grew still, her jaws slightly open. Utterly silent and her dark eyes dripping tears, the turtle focused on her life's task with Allegra as her sole witness. Allegra knelt in the sand nearby, her hand cupping her own abdomen. Already she mothered the baby she carried, imagined what it would be like holding her—she imagined it a girl—for the first time.

"Excellent, Mamma," she whispered. "Well done. Good for you."

When the turtle finished, she flung sand in all directions to hide the nest, burying the small, white eggs. Allegra estimated there must have been a hundred or more. Dawn had broken wide open, the sun rising orange above the horizon, and the turtle seemed to take her cue. Off toward the water she went, retracing the path she must have made hours earlier. Allegra walked beside her as she lumbered, awkward on land and crusted with damp sand. A sadness crept over her, although she knew this was nature's way. This turtle would never see her eggs hatch, would never know if her babies survived their dash toward their instinctual sea home.

Did turtles feel these things? Or did they do their duty and carry on? Allegra waded in with the turtle, then reached out a hand and brushed it along its ridged shell as the turtle ducked into the breaking waves, swimming into the deep. She stayed in the surf, unable to shake the melancholy, until she breathed a sigh and headed back to make breakfast for her sleeping husband.

Chapter 7

Allegra loved Sardegna in September, when the lacy petals of the jacaranda trees fell like rain, carpeting the ground with soft purple. Fields outside the small city buzzed with activity as farmers planted the crocus corms, which would bear the red stigmas of precious saffron in due time. The island was nearing the end of its "six-month summer," and the sun still warmed Allegra's face reliably on her walks by the sea.

The community of water women swam together less, focusing on tasks at home and readying for the next season. They managed to still see one another often enough as they roamed the hills and shorelines or shopped in the few negozios along the quay. Allegra spent the mornings gathering plants for dyeing, or if it rained, she sat by the studio window with Lora and Mamma, teasing and carding the sea silk until it was fine and uniform, ready for winter days of sitting at the loom.

Everyone knew she was expecting now. That sort of news didn't keep long. Allegra was young, only eighteen, and though she delighted in her body's new role and recognized some of the telltale changes pregnancy brought, it was still the early days. Which may have been why, when blood spotted her undergarment, she didn't worry, not at first. She didn't mention it because she assumed it meant nothing. There was no chance to try horsetail or sage because by the time the cramps came and the blood thickened, it was already done, and she'd failed at motherhood before she'd even begun.

Johann held her close and kissed her on the head. She could tell he was disappointed, but he had never felt the weight of this child, the certainty of the life she'd carried as she did—until she didn't anymore.

"We'll try again," he said, his words meant to console. He squeezed her. "What else is there to do this winter when I'm not on the boat?"

She managed a wan smile, trying her best not to give voice to her fears. What if she couldn't? Passing on this life here on the island, the legacy of weaving the sea silk, was Allegra's deepest desire.

"Of course," she told him. "I'm sure it'll be no time at all."

"I'll need some boys to help mend the nets and clear the barnacles off the boat's hull."

"I was hoping for a girl," she admitted.

"Some of those, too," Johann joked, patting his belly. "More hands to make pasta and bread are good for everyone."

"I meant for the byssus," she whispered. Her dark hair swung forward as she bowed her head.

"I know," Johann said, his voice low. He lifted her chin and tucked a strand of hair behind her ear. "Don't worry, Allegra. We have lots of time."

Time had other opinions about the matter. By the fall of 1914, Allegra was twenty-one and still childless. She had learned, again and again, that the hardest goodbye is the one before hello. She'd even grown quiet amid the camaraderie of the women as they swam together, harvesting the beards of the byssus. Their banter and companionship no longer lifted her spirits.

"Allegra," her mother coaxed, "this year you'll be Susana's mentor. She needs help with holding a breath, and you're able to dive longer than most anyone."

This was true, Allegra thought. She was strong and capable, at least as a diver. Susana was almost twelve and just starting to accompany the group on their dives. She was eager and sweet, the oldest daughter of Liza Bernetti. Ordinarily, Liza might have guided her own daughter, but she was—of course—in the late stage of pregnancy, when women typically abstained from diving.

While Johann ate supper that evening, she told him. "Mamma must have thought me the obvious choice," she said. "Who better to teach the younger divers than someone who is in no danger of being pregnant?" The dishes clattered in the washbasin as she spoke.

Johann leaned back in his chair and rubbed his dark beard. He'd grown it out this past year, and Allegra thought it made him look older. "Your mother wouldn't think that," he said.

"No? Ella's gone. Lora's still unmarried, and it's been four years now for me with nothing to show for it."

Johann caught her with his dark eyes. "Nothing?" He was hurt, and she softened.

"That's not what I meant." Allegra sighed. "I'm just frustrated. Why can't we have this blessing?" In her head, she heard her mother's soft voice, weary with its own hurt. *"We're stewards. Somehow, we must steward our pain so it's not wasted."* She straightened her shoulders. Tomorrow, she'd pay a visit to Signora Santos, who'd buried a child the week before. As a gift, she'd bring a little cornicello weaving she'd been working on, the twisted horn a symbol of hope, and they could share a cup of coffee and some time.

"It's not ours to know why," Johann said. He drew in a breath and stood. "I have to tell you something, cara."

At the sound of his voice, she stopped rinsing the saucers and wiped her hands on her apron. "What is it?"

He pulled a folded paper from his vest pocket. "I've been called to service. I'm to report in two weeks."

Allegra sank to the chair, her face drained of color. "No," she said, grasping his hands. "You can't."

"Several of us got notified today. The postal clerk delivered these to us personally. We'll stick together and keep our heads down."

"Where will you go?"

Johann shrugged. "I'm not sure yet, but there's talk of a growing front in the north, along Austria's border."

"This has nothing to do with us," she protested. "You're a pescatore, not a soldier."

"We're all soldiers, Allegra. Italy's going to be in the thick of it. After Ferdinand was shot, it's all war talk at the wharf."

Allegra rested her face in her palms. "It's too much," she said. "Without you—"

"You'll have your family and the water women," he said. "You must pray for me. Put all your strength into it. That will be the thing that brings me home."

~

The next two weeks seemed to slip through Allegra's fingers like sand. While Johann docked their small boat and tied up loose ends at the quay, Allegra's fingers were busy sewing and weaving. She fashioned a heavy vest lined with the warmest wool from their neighbor's flock. She took extra care rolling pairs of socks for her husband's feet, imagining him marching through unfamiliar alpine terrain, and she embroidered thin lines of prayers made of sea silk into the lining of his cap for protection and as a reminder of his beloved Sardegna.

When the days were spent and his bag was ready, stuffed with bread, dried meats, and amaretti for his journey, what else was there to do but say goodbye? The neighbor's white donkey stood in the street in town. He waited for the other three men who'd been called to service to climb into the wooden cart that would bear them to Cagliari, where they'd be picked up and transferred to their assignment.

After one final embrace to punctuate their separation, Johann hoisted himself backward into the cart, his legs dangling from the back like a child's. Allegra's hands held the ends of her apron in a tight knot that she twisted and untwisted uncontrollably. *Heaven protect him,* she prayed. *Have mercy on me and I'll protect the byssus forever.*

"Adiosu!" People cried and waved as the creaky wheels of the donkey cart began to turn. "Be safe! Be brave!" Allegra's voice failed. The stinging lump in her throat grew until she thought it would choke her. She locked eyes with Johann and said all she needed to say with that look. When the wind had blown away the dust stirred up by the cart, she turned to her mother and sister to walk back home.

Chapter 8

The affairs of government and nations had never concerned Allegra before. Sequestered on their beautiful island, focused on the sea and what the land yielded, such things had seemed remote and irrelevant. Now, whenever she could, Allegra visited the postal clerk near the quay. The office there had a radio, and if anything important happened, they were the first to hear it. She didn't understand much of it—the talk of socialism, labor strikes, and power struggles danced like drunken sailors in her head.

All through the long weeks of that first winter, she received only two letters from Johann. *I miss you,* he wrote. *How is the boat?* No real news about where they were or if he was hungry or cold. *Artillery training and weeks of waiting,* he said. *Weeks I could have spent bringing in catches to tide you over. The amaretti cookies are long gone.* Allegra read them over and over, the folds so deep the thin paper almost fell to pieces.

By spring, the news on the radio seemed charged with tension. It was official: Italy had entered a large-scale war, in league with Britain and France, against Austria-Hungary. Who knew how long this whole business would drag on? How many more battles might Johann have to face before it was over? It had been months since she'd had a word from him. She posted letters, but when or if they ever reached him, she couldn't know.

In May, the weavers went back to swimming regularly, but Allegra's nerves were so taut she nearly cut herself with the ivory-handled knife her mother had given her when she'd taken the water oath. When they swam, Lora managed to position herself nearby to keep an eye on her, Allegra knew. She remembered her prayer the last time she'd seen her husband: her end of the bargain was to be an excellent caretaker and weaver, and she tried to slow her breathing and be present in the world that usually brought her such peace and comfort.

She was still responsible for Susana Bernetti, the novice young diver. Allegra wished she could simply focus on her own tasks, which seemed hard enough these days, instead of having to check and monitor Susana. It wasn't the girl's fault, obviously. She was eager to learn and wanted to please. Allegra knew she could do nothing for Johann, but she couldn't shake the worry that tugged at her thoughts and jangled her nerves.

One morning in late May, Susana surfaced near her, and they placed the tangled threads they'd cut into a glass jar in the floating basket.

"There's an eel under the reef shelf right under us," Susana told her as she treaded water, her eyelashes dripping. "I'm going to see if I can spear it on this next dive."

Allegra nodded. "If you don't get it on the first try, it's not going to give you a second chance. You need to be quick."

Susana breathed deeply, readying herself for the dive. "Just getting a good breath. Come with me. I'll show you where I saw it." She dove in a quick motion, and Allegra followed her down to the reef. The others swam and dove in twos and threes some distance away. She watched them expertly clipping and stashing the byssus threads, signaling easily to one another in their underwater language.

A sudden motion next to her drew her attention. The spear had hit its mark, and Susana drew the eel out of its hole, its black body writhing in protest. She grinned and maneuvered the creature away from her, its mouthful of teeth out of range. Allegra pointed up, and they turned to ascend side by side, but when Allegra broke through the surface, Susana wasn't nearby. She waited a moment—the girl was a slower swimmer—but still nothing.

Allegra dove back under and quickly spotted the thrashing eel, still skewered on the spear, floating toward the sandy bottom. Susana sank in the crystal water, too, limp and motionless. Allegra shot toward the girl and reached her in seconds. She encircled her chest from behind and kicked toward the surface, dragging her upward. Lora appeared suddenly beside her, and with both of them kicking, they surfaced quickly.

"Sirvone!" they yelled. "Sirvone!"

At the call for help, the atmosphere in the water immediately changed. The others swam over as they surfaced, drawn by the commotion and noise. Using their floating baskets as a raft, they hoisted Susana out of the water as they made for the shore. Allegra tried not to panic at the sight of the girl's pale face, dark hair plastered to her skin, and her lips, a disturbing shade of purply blue. As soon as they had footing, they dragged her to the beach. Lora turned her on her side, and Allegra knelt in the sand, pounding Susana's back and slapping her face.

"Susana!" she yelled. "Wake up, wake up!" In a flash, she was back in the market with Ella in her arms. Every muscle in her body thrummed with adrenaline.

As others reached the shore, they crowded around, rubbing her feet, legs, and arms, sisters giving what they could to one of their own. Allegra couldn't shake the image of Susana's triumphant face as she held the squirming eel, lost now to the ocean's current. What had happened? What had she let happen? She knew everyone else must be asking the same question, but she had no answer.

A faint moan escaped Susana's sandy lips, and her eyelids fluttered.

Allegra fell back onto the sand, finally able to draw a breath of relief as the girl coughed, seawater spilling from her mouth and nose. Allegra found she was crying, holding a sandy hand to her own mouth to stifle the sobs. She heard a shout and looked up to see Susana's mother flying down the beach, stumbling through the soft sand with her long skirt. Someone must have run to their home. Liza had stayed with the family's new baby that morning. Allegra crawled a few feet away to give Liza and Susana space.

The girl sat up, coughing and disoriented. Liza knelt to hold her daughter, her face drained of color, as if she'd been the one floating beneath the waves. Allegra watched, trying to catch her own ragged breath, as Liza shook Susana, repeatedly touching her face, her hair, as if to reassure herself Susana was indeed safe, that the morning hadn't ended in tragedy after all.

"What happened?" she asked.

"I speared an eel," Susana said, and she searched the sand around her.

"You dropped it," Allegra said. "I couldn't—"

"It was just an eel," Lora said. "Never mind it." Her sister had moved to sit beside her and circled Allegra with her arms. Allegra was grateful. She suddenly felt cold and had begun to shiver, the adrenaline leaving her body in a rush.

"I don't remember," Susana said. "We'd been diving for the byssus, and I came up to get some extra breaths to make sure I could stay down long enough for the eel. I had it." Confusion furrowed her brow, and she shrugged. "Then, things went dark, and I don't remember."

"You took extra breaths?" Allegra asked.

"Yes. You were there. You saw me."

Allegra *had* been there, but she'd been distracted, diving from memory rather than being actively present. She'd been thinking of Johann and his last letter, wondering where he might be or if he knew how much she thought about him. She'd missed the signs. She witnessed the women exchanging glances. They were thinking the same thing, Allegra knew.

Liza helped Susana to stand. Her legs were shaky, but by some miracle of the sea, she seemed to have recovered. Some of the other women had gone back out to the byssus cove to retrieve the anchored baskets that had been left floating. There would be no more diving today.

As they walked home, dispersing in small groups, the normally boisterous and merry chatter was muted. Lora helped Allegra dress, and together they lugged their baskets toward their childhood home. Allegra had taken to spending much of her time there since Johann had been away. About halfway there, she finally spoke.

"She could have—"

"Don't." Lora cut her off. "She didn't. You saved her."

"I almost lost her," Allegra snapped. "She was my responsibility, my partner. If I'd been paying attention as I should've, I would've seen her overbreathing and stopped the dive."

"She's old enough to know better. Shallow water blackouts are a danger we all learn about." She shook her head. "She's naive and eager. She was excited about the eel and trying to prove she could get it. You should have been in a larger group with some backups. None of us was thinking."

"Thinking I'd be so negligent, you mean?"

"We all know you haven't been at your best, Allegra—and for good reason."

"Susana shouldn't have been a consequence of that."

"Perhaps not, but it could have happened to anyone. No one drowned today."

Allegra shrugged off her sister's arm and walked the rest of the way in silence, breathing quickly to keep her tears at bay. What had happened was just one more thing on the long list of sorrows she carried, and this one had been her own fault. She couldn't have forgiven herself if Susana had drowned. She could have been the cause of another mother's deepest grief, something she wouldn't wish on her worst enemy. Allegra had to get her focus back. Somewhere in the past few years, her joy and purpose had been scattered like broken shells left at low tide. All she could think of was what she'd lost—or almost lost. It clouded her heart like a gathering storm.

Chapter 9

One early morning the following week, Allegra walked to the beach alone. A cool wind blew in from the ocean, and the sky promised showers. She stripped to her short black suit and dove into the waves, her clothes in a heap on the sand. It was high tide, and without a midday sun overhead, the water was cool against her skin as her arms pulled her out past the usual reef. Her muscles relaxed into their customary routine, legs kicking in rhythm as she opened her arms in front and brought them to her sides, making a wide circle as she parted the water and distanced herself from the shore.

She opened her eyes, saltwater stinging as she watched the fish dart around the reef below. Urchins clung to the rock, their oxblood spines waving as she passed. She spotted a trio of lobsters creeping along the bottom, their segmented tails leaving curious tracks in the sand. A large, lone sunfish, its rounded disk body basking near the surface, looked at her with its funny, wide eyes. Every creature had its purpose, but Allegra felt adrift.

She pushed toward the seafloor, savoring the ocean's silence. Over the past week, all everyone had talked about was Susana, of course, and the averted tragedy. As much as she loved her people, especially the weavers, Allegra needed some quiet. The deeper she dove, the more the light changed, lapsing from dancing reflected rays to a dim glow. The world above was forgotten, and the water cooled further as she descended. Fine air bubbles lined her skin and each hair on her arms and legs. A crab scuttled across the bottom, dragging the remnants of a fish in one claw.

As much as Allegra loved this underwater world, she was an intruder here. *Other*. While the silver and blue schools of fish navigated around one another like dancers on a stage, they dodged the foreign currents she made, suspicious. She was meant for breath, and she rationed it as she floated, her long, dark hair fanning out like seaweed. The incident with Susana had been a stark reminder that they were interlopers under the Mediterranean Sea, hired help at best. Breath was everything, in the end. It was, according to their faith, the animation given by their Creator, Yahweh: *Yah*, that first intake of spirit at birth, and the faint *weh*, when spirit was released at death.

Allegra realized she'd been holding her breath much of the time lately, tense and worried about Johann, but it had begun before that, really. After her first miscarriage, and then the second and third, she'd held her breath every month before she bled, waiting and hoping for a miracle. With every breath she held came the certainty of more misfortune. Ironically, it was here, alone under the sea, where the attempt to draw in breath would mean the end of her, where the water worked its magic and the tension she'd been holding finally loosened and she let herself relax. With that faintest act of surrender, it dawned on her how much her whole being craved breathing freely as she once had. She'd had enough of clenching and grasping for control, of withholding trust in herself and God, as if such futility would ward off pain and misfortune. She realized how miserly she'd been, hoarding breath in anxiety and fear when she should have been breathing deeply with faith.

If tending the byssus had taught her anything, it was that simple, precious things were a gift meant to be lavished and freely given, not traded or bargained for. Her chest tightened, and Allegra kicked upward. When she broke the surface, instead of jealously gulping air, she paused for a moment to be sure she savored it, and then she breathed in deeply, filling her lungs and feeling her entire chest expand. *Yah.* Then she blew it out, long and slow. *Weh.* She let it flow through her body. Kicking backward, she floated on the surface, arms out wide, her body made buoyant by the breath she drew into her lungs. She drifted on the gentle waves.

She'd been trying to carry it all: her fear, grief, and anger, adding more and more to the load with each catastrophe. Had she thought it was some badge of strength? Some test? But perhaps she'd never been meant to carry those things after all, but to let them out like a breath, let them recede like the tide. Here in the water, she felt held by something bigger, an assurance that even if she never held her own child, even if she never touched her husband's handsome face again, she would continue to be held in this way, buoyed, carried. Allegra's heart opened, and its contents spilled out into the ocean. The tears that ran from the corners of her eyes dissolved into the sea, salt mixing with salt. She floated that way a long time, until she felt a lightness, emptied of the darkness and dread she'd been closeting inside herself.

The sorrows she carried remained, but their edges were no longer razors. The sun warmed her face and arms, and the salt tang of the breeze stung her nose. She allowed herself the pleasure of these things for the first time in a very long while, and the small glimmers of joy that pricked her heart brought a different sort of tears to her eyes. Yes, she had lost much. But what could she open her eyes to find?

The shadow of a cormorant passing overhead made her open her eyes. She watched as it glided low before folding its wings and needling expertly into the water. When it popped up, the flopping tail of a silver fish protruded from its beak. Allegra swore the bird winked at her as it tossed its head back to slide its catch down its gullet.

"Well done," she told the bird. Allegra turned and swam back toward the shore. She was supposed to meet her father at the quay as he came in with his day's catch, and the cormorant had reminded her of that. Her mother had asked her to be sure he saved some of the bluefin for dinner. Her older brother, Nicholas, had been called to soldier not long after Johann, and she knew it lifted her mother's spirits when the family shared a meal together. She was looking forward to eating with her family that night. For the first time in a long while, Allegra actually wanted company.

Chapter 10

September 1918

My dearest A,

I am well. Can it have been four years since we saw one another? Time here is different as one day bleeds into the next with dreaded sameness. It seems at once forever and nothing at all. I ramble. My mind drifts all the time to our beautiful island and its peaceful shores, rowing with you in the grottos for an afternoon and tasting the salt on your skin. You can't imagine how much I miss you. All I want is to go back to those simple times.

They say the tide is turning here. We know something about tides, don't we? Although some days, I admit, my hope is in tatters, like the flags we fly over the trenches, this letter is proof that I'm still here, still thinking of you. Morning and evening I run my fingers over your golden stitches, praying to whatever or whoever is still listening that I may make it back to you.

Think of me as you swim in our sea, Allegra. Think of me as you weave and dye and make lovely things. There is nothing at all lovely here, so you must do it to carry us both, to remind the world in some small way that something beautiful remains. Please give my regards to everyone. I treasure each letter you send. There is no accounting for when posts may reach us. Unless posts come by goat, it's not easy for them to arrive. Speaking of goats, you may think I resemble one when you finally see me: my beard is so grown, and I'm sure one hundred baths in the sea might not erase this smell. I will kiss you despite this, so brace yourself!

All my heart, Johann

~

Allegra had a small stack of such letters now. She kept them tied with a thin bracelet of byssus at the bottom of the oleander box that held her weaving sundries. She tried decoding: when Johann wrote of goats, she was sure he was referring to mountains or some sort of rough terrain. From this, she tried to ascertain where he might be and piece together bits of broadcasts that might tell her how bad it was where she imagined him to be. Did this help her state of mind? She wasn't sure, but she couldn't stop herself. Any information, even imagined, was something to cling to.

In most ways, life went on as usual in their little community. Boats still launched daily; sea silk still grew from the mollusks. After the terrible incident with Susana, Allegra had learned how to keep her worry shut away in a box when she was in the water. In fact, the water helped give her a purpose and reminded her who she was, with or without Johann. But outside the sea, truth be told, her heart grasped constantly for the thing it didn't have: her own small family.

Unfortunately, the war brought more than foreign soldiers and strange ships to the Sardegnan ports. In addition to the malaria they had to contend with regularly, a new sickness had taken hold. It gripped the lungs and swiftly left its victims so weakened that many didn't recover. A pall had been cast over their quaint community, and people slowly began staying at home, going out only when necessary to avoid catching this new plague that seemed to hang on like a barnacle.

In the past few months, the sickness had spread more quickly, but the government refused to close ports of entry because supplies and troop shipments were vital to the war. Allegra walked to the post office daily despite passing more and more homes where she knew families lay ill and suffering. She was determined to have news from Johann if he'd written, and this was where she'd been headed the day she met her brother and father coming home early from the quay.

"Papà?" she said, surprised at meeting them on the street. "Has something happened?"

Her younger brother, Tonio, walked beside her father, who had an unsteady gait, as if he'd been drinking. His hacking cough betrayed the real reason they'd anchored early, and Allegra felt ashamed as she stepped back, holding the edge of her apron to her face. Her father had the sickness, the influenza. Her post office errand forgotten, Allegra led the way home, running ahead to alert her mother and sister to prepare the back room and boil water for tea and honey.

All through the night, her mother nursed her father, wetting his fevered brow, trying to get him to sit up and drink a thin broth. It only made him cough harder. Allegra and Lora took care of everything else, brewing tea and airing out the linens. Nothing seemed to help this flu. The sole doctor from their small community had been called to service months ago, and the midwife offered only herbal remedies that they'd already tried.

In the morning, Allegra found her mother asleep in a chair beside his bed, her head tipped forward on her chest. She could hear her father's labored wheezing from the doorway. She'd brought a cool glass of water in hopes of easing his throat and fever. When she sat on the bed, the springs creaked and her mother jerked awake, but her father remained still, his eyes closed and his breath raspy. She leaned over and took her father's hand.

"Mamma," she said, lifting his hand to show her.

"Blue fingertips," she whispered. "God spare us." It was a sign the flu was strangling him. Allegra said nothing. She rose and opened the window, letting the autumn breeze waft across the quilt. She offered the water to her mother instead, her father too weak to sip.

Five days later, he was eating soup and able to take slow steps to the garden door, but now it was Lora and Tonio who lay in bed. Such was the randomness of the illness. Rumors from the quay were that the sickness had gained a foothold in the military, where men and animals were often packed in together. Some soldiers said that it was claiming more lives than the artillery. Allegra had no recent word from Johann, and she imagined him lying outdoors, shivering with fever, fighting for air, as she witnessed her sister and brother doing each day.

On an afternoon when she was forced to go to town for supplies, Allegra walked with her apron held against her face. The sun on her skin felt intoxicating, and at the same time, a guilty pleasure amid the worry at home. The byssus season was over, but ordinarily, she would have been swimming each afternoon, soaking in the last warmth of the sea before winter. She craved the quiet and peace of the waves.

Lora and Tonio weren't recovering like their father had. Though they were younger and stronger, they seemed weaker and more exhausted by the hour. Allegra had been dreading the moment when she'd feel the sudden fever and aches herself, but they hadn't come. As she selected salt, oranges, and a shank of lamb from the shop's limited shelves, snippets of conversation between the old men outside reached her.

"Roma and Venezia are filled with corpses, they say."

"They're keeping it quiet in the papers and on the radio. It's worse than we think."

"If we get through this winter with half the town, it'll be a miracle."

Allegra shook her head. She didn't want to hear such things. How much more could they all take? Would it ever end? She hastily paid for her items and pushed her way out the door, her head down. She didn't even offer a greeting to the men outside. Instead of going straight home, she headed inland, following the road to the rabbi's home and the church nearby. They'd been closed for weeks, congregants too nervous to gather in crowds, but each had its own cemetery on land that stretched behind the buildings, and Allegra wanted to see the situation for herself.

As she rounded the bend and the buildings came into view, she stopped in her tracks. The hillside that stretched for acres in the distance was dotted with mound after mound of freshly filled graves. Their neighbors and fellow islanders. At some, a person or two stood in mourning, heads bowed, but there had been no service, no gathering. These had been dug in haste. She turned and walked home, anxious about what she might find there.

In the end, Lora and Tonio joined those in the cemetery. The vicious thing about this flu was how it reaped the young and strong indiscriminately. They'd been reduced to a family of four. On a bright fall morning in October, they, too, stood beside the earthen mounds with bowed heads. As long as she lived, she would never forget her mother dropping to her knees in the dirt there, wailing like a wounded animal. That image often resurfaced, unbidden, in her mind, and Allegra's sorrow reverberated inside her like the aftershock of an earthquake. All she'd ever known was the boisterous clamor of her sisters and brothers, and the loss of them both at once felt like her heart withered in her chest. *Please let Nicholas come home,* she prayed. *Let him survive.* Though the news spoke of an armistice on the horizon and they'd heard of some units shipping home, the possibility of serious illnesses still remained. For the sake of her parents and their whole family, she needed him to be safe.

Allegra added two more locks of hair, bound with the thinnest strand of byssus, to the pouch that held her memory of Ella. Allegra couldn't help but notice that her father's gait seemed reduced to a shuffle, and her mother's hair showed more gray at her temples. Her mother, the maestra, had only Allegra to carry on in the line of their family's weavers. What, she wondered, was the gift in this? How could they steward this fresh sorrow? In a world where many died in childbirth and surviving childhood was not a guarantee, they'd beaten the odds for a time. They had so much more to do each day now, with fewer hands to do it, and their labor kept them moving forward, catching brief moments here and there to stop and let waves of sadness wash over them. Allegra determined to make her weaving even more beautiful, incorporating golden scenes of her sisters' favorite things—starfish and anemones, turtles and urchins—as a way to honor their having been here, once.

Allegra's father still took the boat out as he always had. Other pescatore families lent a hand at the quay so that he wouldn't have to single-handedly unload his catch at the docks. She knew he must be lonely on the boat all day without her brothers bantering and singing to pass the time because she felt that way at the loom. Probably, he grieved out on the water alone, she thought, because when he came home, he seemed steady and strong for her mother. As she'd done after Ella's death, her mother immersed herself in the byssus work and tried to be grateful for what remained. Meals were quieter. Fewer voices at the table meant less conversation and fewer opinions. Allegra missed Lora fiercely. She'd been a lifelong confidante and friend, even after Allegra had married. She constantly turned to tell her something or thought to ask her about a particular byssus pattern, then realized anew that Lora was gone.

Some weeks later, in mid-November, Allegra stopped by the postal office with a letter in hand. When the clerk saw her come through the door, he motioned her over to the counter.

"Signora, I have something for you." She'd been by the office almost daily since Johann had been called up, and he knew what she came for. Allegra was grateful for the man's compassion. When he had nothing for her, he'd simply meet her eyes at the door and give a slight shake of his head to spare her coming in and making small talk when her heart ached. Today, however, she had a letter, and she quickened her steps to the counter to take the thin missive he held out to her. The postcard bore the familiar Posta Militare stamp, and the additional Commissione Censura stamp from the Office of Censure obscured some of the handwriting beneath.

Ordinarily, Allegra would step outside to read it. Sometimes, she would force herself to wait until she'd reached home, savoring the anticipation along the way. She hadn't been expecting anything today. It had hardly been two months since Johann's last, so she stood against the wall as she examined his familiar tidy handwriting.

Dearest A, he wrote. *Expect me home to light the menorah. This fighting is finally over! Don't know for sure when I'll be on the train, but Lorenzo will soon need to meet me in Cagliari with his donkey. Tell him to feed some extra oats because we'll be going full speed all the way home. All my love, J.*

Allegra's hands shook. She read the words twice more before she allowed herself to believe it might actually be real. She clutched the postcard to her chest and tried to catch her breath. The news they got on Sardegna tended to be more word of mouth, brought from the mainland. Official newsprint could be days or weeks old. She looked again at the date and tried to figure how much time had passed.

"Good news, no?" asked the postal clerk. Of course he'd already read it. The man considered himself a sort of buffer between the letters he received and their possible effect on the recipients. If he knew he was about to hand over tragic news to a family member, he'd offer a chair or sometimes even a cup of coffee first.

"Very good news." Allegra beamed. "The best. Thank you." She turned and walked briskly out the door, on a mission to see Lorenzo, the owner of the strong white donkey with the wide cart. She needed to give him notice that he might soon need to be in the capital. When the time came, for his trouble, she'd send him with a hearty meal of fish and orzo and something sweet. She'd weave a fine pattern for his wife with the sea silk—perhaps a likeness of their donkey pulling his cart—as a gift. Allegra didn't care if she had to stay up all night for weeks to finish.

News from the train station arrived by telegraph just two days later. Johann would be home the following day, sooner than expected. From the moment she'd received the postcard, Allegra had thrown all her energy into readying the house. Her mother joined her to help. Allegra was touched by the way she shared her excitement and joy, even in the midst of missing the others. Her mother knew the toll Johann's absence had taken on her, and her happiness at his return was almost as great as her own. They washed and hung the linens, swept the tiled floor clean, and gathered purple crocus blooms to brighten the table and windowsills. Mamma helped her assemble a pot of his favorite seafood stew so that it would be ready to heat. When her mother had gone, Allegra soaked in a bath and drew a perfumed comb through her damp hair.

On the morning of Johann's arrival, before the pink ribbons of dawn unfurled across the sky, Allegra walked down to the shoreline. She remembered her promise from four years ago, the promise that if Johann made it home to her, she would tend to the byssus forever. As the cool water lapped at her toes, she stretched her arms wide to the sea and began the melodic song of the byssus, repeating the words generations of water women had sung. It was their anthem to the water, their craft, its gift, and their pledge, and this morning, it was particularly sweet to her. After so much time apart, she wanted nothing more than to see her husband again and sink into their beautifully ordinary life together.

She closed her eyes and breathed in the salt air, unbothered by the rush of a wave that soaked the bottom of her skirt. The endless war was done. As far as it was within her power, she would be available for her family and her craft and aspire to nothing more than that. For Allegra, there *was* nothing more. The distant clanging of a bell heralded the signal: Lorenzo's donkey cart had been spotted outside the town limits. Allegra ran home, her heels kicking up sand behind her. When she reached the stone avenue beside her home, her mother met her there, clean boots in hand.

"Well, you're a sight." She laughed, and it was wonderful to hear that sound. "Your cheeks all red and dress covered in sand." She brushed Allegra's skirts with a brisk hand as Allegra hopped into her black boots. "Hurry, cara. He's likely near town even now."

Allegra kissed her mother's cheek and flashed a bright smile. "Thank you, Mamma." She turned and trotted toward town, with her mother trailing behind. Her feet would not be reined in by decorum.

As she neared the quay, she saw the crowd that had gathered near the postal office. Johann had not come alone. Allegra saw two other men lifting their packs from the sides of the cart. One was surrounded by family, exclaiming and hailing him with kisses. Members of the town clapped the other on the back and shook hands.

Allegra stopped in her tracks, breathing hard. It hadn't occurred to her that Johann might have changed in the four years since he'd left. She imagined him as he'd been then, frozen in time, and she wondered if he'd see changes in her as well. But there he was, shouldering the pack he'd left with, long since empty of the amaretti she'd made, as if cookies would make a difference in a war. Her eyes traced his body desperately. He had both arms, both legs. His frame was thinner, his hair thick and unruly, and his skin had lost that sun-bronzed glow. Too much time in northern mountains where he didn't belong.

He was laughing and slapping the backs of neighbors and people he knew, but the whole time, his head swiveled over them, searching. It was the laugh she remembered. Allegra stood still and apart in the middle of the avenue. She could hear her mother coming up behind her, talking and laughing. Suddenly shy, she looked down to smooth her skirts and reached up to straighten the headscarf that had slipped as she'd run.

In that briefest moment, Johann closed the distance between them and stood before her, tears in those same topaz eyes she remembered so well. Allegra's hands trembled, and she reached out to touch his beard, speckled—impossibly—with gray. At her touch, Johann folded her in his arms and buried his face in her hair.

"I'm home, Allegra. It's really me. You're really you. You can't imagine how I've missed you."

"Oh, yes, I can," she whispered into his ear. "You're never leaving again. I may not even let you out of my sight on that boat of yours."

Allegra's reverie was interrupted by her mother's cry of surprise. She turned to see that she, too, had stopped short on the road and was staring in disbelief at the crowd around the wagon. Nicholas! Nicholas had come home!

"I brought a surprise with me," Johann said. "We met at the station, coming home at the same time. Lorenzo was more than happy to bring one more."

Allegra's mother fell upon Nicholas, weeping openly. Then, she held him at arm's length and looked him up and down as Allegra had Johann. Was he all in one piece? They would learn later he'd lost the hearing in one ear from a too-near artillery explosion, but otherwise, he was only thin and weary, and that they could fix. Given her chance, Allegra embraced her brother, burying her face in his chest. Pieces of their shattered family were settling back into place, and her heart swelled with gladness.

A spontaneous party broke out in the avenue, as neighbors and shopkeepers poured out to welcome them back, bearing bottles of wine. The baker dragged a table out into the street and laid out fresh bread and cheese, and others brought small sweets and sliced sausages. They suspended business for the day and brought out mandolins, organettos, and launeddas to play as people danced, black skirts twirling and flashing red and green above their stamping boots. Allegra and Johann laughed and danced along with them, the war and their recent losses suspended in the music and frivolity. There was a time for mourning and a time for dancing, and sometimes they overlapped in a surreal merging of currents.

Four men had left four years ago at that first calling-up departure, with many more to follow. Today, only two of those original four had returned, and the absence of the others wasn't lost on anyone. Later, there would be quieter visits to the families' homes with food and sober conversation.

As the afternoon wore on, the music wound down and the wine bottles emptied. The crowd dispersed. The pescatori would be coming in with their catches, and there were sheep to gather, meals to prepare, children to tend. Her father would walk in that night to see his son at his table. Although part of her would have loved to have seen their reunion, more than anything she wanted to go home, finally, with Johann. Allegra kissed her mother and brother as Johann pulled her toward their home. Allegra noticed he couldn't stop breathing deeply, filling his lungs with the island air. She skipped along beside him like a girl, her shyness gone. When they rounded the bend in the path and their little home came into view, Johann stopped short and took it in.

"There were so many times when I wasn't sure I'd see this again," he admitted. "Or you."

Allegra took his hand and squeezed, as if to reassure him it wasn't his imagination. Together, they walked toward home.

Chapter 11

If they'd been under some sort of curse, it broke with Johann's return. By the fall of 1919, Allegra held their first son, Lev, in her arms. Nineteen twenty gave them Avi, their second, and then in quick succession, two daughters—Marta and Dahlia—so that they'd grown to a family of six in a span of four years. Allegra's heart felt full.

Her life with Johann was in constant motion as she wrangled four children under five. With the help of her family and other women in their weaver community, Allegra managed to juggle home and the byssus. Johann took it all in stride, relishing the chance to be a father. His time in the Great War had imprinted on him gratitude for the simple pleasure of home and children, and he never failed to bounce his sons on his knees or rock his daughters to sleep. Many days, he brought the boat in a little early to allow them time to gather shells on the beach or venture inland to climb the strange rocky ruins and laugh at the antics of the wild ponies. In the first weeks of June, they'd walk to the wetlands that stretched behind the beaches to watch the crooked-neck flamingos alighting in clouds of pink.

Some weeks, depending on the weather and the season, Allegra had less time at home as she harvested the sea silk. When she could, she'd bring the children with her, strapped to her body or pulling them along in a wagon as she gathered plants or seaweed for processing. She taught them early to respect the water, never venturing out past their toes. By the time they were three, they could name many of the plants she collected and much of the sea life they found in tide pools.

As they grew, Lev and Avi naturally spent more time with Johann, and by the time the boys were seven and eight, they could quickly scrape the scales from a fish, cast a net, and haul in the clay jars that trapped octopuses. They adored their father and copied everything he did. Allegra marveled at the way they shared his confident walk and how they fell asleep with one arm flung above their heads, just like Johann.

Marta and Dahlia, younger but no less capable, spent many hours beneath Allegra's loom, playing with shells or stones or dolls made of carded wool. They were attuned to colors, and Allegra listened to them chattering to one another as she wove golden patterns.

"Yellow is glad," Marta said in her schoolteacher voice. "Red is exciting and warm, like fire."

"And blue is cold," Dahlia volunteered. "Sometimes sad, but not always, like the sea."

Allegra's fingers plucked at the threads on the loom, straightening and rearranging them until they lay how she wanted. "Did you know, girls, that blue is the rarest color in the world? Can you tell me some of its shades?"

"Indigo," shouted Dahlia.

"Turquoise," came Marta's answer.

"Cerulean," Dahlia said after a moment, getting the pronunciation wrong.

"That's a hard one," Allegra admitted. "All correct."

"Woad," said Marta. "That makes wool look like grass, and then, by magic, it goes to dark green and then blue."

"You've been paying attention," Allegra said, impressed that Marta's keen eyes had picked up on the dye process. It pleased her to no end that her daughters seemed to take so naturally to the skills she taught them. It was as much their joy as it was her own. There was never a day they weren't excited at the prospect of swimming together, gathering plants on long walks, and even the sometimes tedious process of rinsing and cleaning the byssus threads. They made it a game and laughed with their heads bent together over the pans. Their closeness reminded her of her own sisters, and watching them together, whispering and laughing, eased some of her ache for Ella and Lora.

~

It was the end of September 1927 when Allegra felt a familiar tenderness in her breasts that she hadn't expected to feel again. She was collecting the children from school when Dahlia hugged her tightly. A hint of a thought flashed through her mind, but she dismissed it as nonsense. Her youngest was six. She was thirty-five, and their family was complete. A few weeks later, when the smell of drying octopus tentacles set her stomach roiling, she knew better, and her heart rejoiced. A new baby! She couldn't wait to tell Johann and her mother.

The following summer, the baby came unexpectedly on an afternoon when they'd ventured inland for a rare day off together. This one, a daughter they named Zaneta, was bent on surprising her mother at every turn, it seemed. With four older siblings doting on their new baby sister, Allegra had no shortage of help as she managed their home and spent time at her mother's studio, sorting, dyeing, and weaving the byssus. Hopeful young women dropped by, shyly asking her for a blessing and braided rope of byssus, believing Zaneta, this surprise daughter after such a long time, to be a harbinger of fertility.

Allegra laughed, reminding them she'd been unable to carry a child herself for many years. She told them it was her oath to the sea, a promise she'd made when her husband had been called to war, that had finally brought them the blessing of children. True? Who could know? But she didn't want her little Zaneta, her unexpected joy, to carry others' burden of so much hope. She generously tied byssus bracelets on their wrists, knowing exactly how their hearts' yearning drove them to try anything if it might mean the promise of a child.

Zaneta sat splay-legged on the tiled floor, playing happily with spools and bits of fabric, oblivious to her mother's dealings. At the end of the afternoon, Allegra scooped her up and carried her on the short walk to the school, where her boisterous brothers and sisters spilled out into the lane, full of chatter and bounce. Sometimes, depending on the day, they'd walk to the quay to wait for their father's large blue skiff to appear from around the island's bend, and when they saw him, they jumped and waved as if he'd been gone for weeks. Allegra's eyes always stung a bit when she spotted Johann piloting his beloved lampara, its nets looped and piled high behind him. She whispered a quick word of thanks, remembering a time when the odds were against him returning.

Time on their island passed in much the same way as it had for generations before. Allegra and her mother worked together to weave a tapestry. An ambitious creation, it featured the sea at night, with a golden moon casting its shimmering path across the water and the creatures below. Jellyfish, schools of reef fish, and in one corner, sea-grasses nestling the *Pinna nobilis* and a passing sea turtle. Allegra wove the turtle herself. She'd never forgotten her encounter with the mother turtle that morning long ago. Since the harvesting and dyeing of enough thread to create even a few inches took almost two weeks, this particular tapestry was something the two of them had been working on steadily for nearly a decade. When it was finished, it would measure only two square feet.

Allegra let her daughters add stars to the night sky by embroidering byssus into the dyed fabric. Marta and Dahlia were so particular about it that they spent almost an entire week one summer lying on their backs on the beach after sunset, memorizing the positions of the constellations. Although Zaneta was too young to actually contribute anything to the work herself, she added her imagination readily enough.

"How about a falling star? Its tail streaked with gold?" she suggested. "Or shade the dark side of the moon with a deeper gold?"

Marta, unable to resist her little sister, stitched as she bid but drew the line at sea monsters lurking in a deep-sea trench.

"We're meant to show beautiful things with the byssus," Allegra reminded her daughter. "Its purpose is for lifting up and adding to the world, Zaneta. That's our job, too. There's enough sadness and darkness without us creating more. Whatever made you think of such a thing?"

"Yes, Mamma," her daughter replied. Allegra smoothed Zaneta's dark hair back from her face. Her heart held such hope for these children of hers, gladness that they hadn't had to live through the hard wartime as she had, gratitude that she'd lived through their entrance into the world and had been able to see them grow up. Hope that their days would be unencumbered by sorrow. They lived truly blessed lives here on the island. Simple pleasures of sand, sun, and a belly full of bread and fish, laughing around the table with the family and greeting their many friends in the streets in town. Allegra prayed then and there that this quotidian life might be all they'd know, and that the work they did with their hands—casting nets, weaving, baking bread, and making a meal—might always be enough.

Some of the islanders talked of leaving Sardegna and heading for America, where they wouldn't have to mine coal or scrape by for scraps, but Allegra couldn't imagine such an ambition. Although their family wouldn't leave much money or property to their children to inherit, the knowledge and experiences they'd imparted to their children were a more important inheritance than coins that could be quickly spent.

Chapter 12

Almost eight summers swept by in a beautiful blur of meals, bedtime stories, growing, and learning. The past few months, though, something had been niggling at Allegra, but she couldn't put the feeling into words. Her family was healthy and strong, the older girls had joined her as weavers, the boys worked with their father on the boat, and her youngest child would soon turn thirteen and was almost ready to take the water oath. She and Johann were aging, and her parents, too, but that wasn't it. Despite the reliable sunrise, the regular tides, and the lazy way the shepherds and merchants went about their days, she couldn't shake the uneasy urgency she felt.

Just the other day, Johann had let the door slam shut on his way out, and she'd nearly jumped out of her skin. It wasn't like her, and neither evening walks to visit with her family nor morning swims to release the tension in her shoulders seemed to assuage her anxiety. Maybe it was the change she was likely facing? It came sooner or later for every woman, but she didn't dread it like some of her friends. She'd raised her children and loved that stage of life, but she had plenty more ahead to do and was ready to get to it.

She'd had a disturbing encounter in town recently. She'd been shopping for a few items in the dry goods store and accidentally brushed up against someone in the shop. Although she'd whispered a quick "scusi," the woman had given her a brusque look and hurried away without speaking. She wondered later if she'd simply imagined it, but she knew she hadn't. Ari had also admitted to her that they weren't selling as much of their catch lately. People preferred to buy from others. When she'd asked who, what others, he'd said they'd sooner buy if you weren't Jewish. These sorts of sentiments didn't come from everyone, but enough to make Allegra wary, enough to make her want to gather her children beneath her roof, like a mother hen.

Whatever had her keyed up, Allegra found herself making odd decisions: writing her favorite recipes in a notebook and giving them to her Catholic friend, Donna; sketching crude drawings of the plants she gathered, cataloging them by the colors they'd produce when used as dyes; carding extra wool although they had plenty. She asked Johann to make her a new box from oleander, one that could be sealed tightly against moisture.

"Just a simple box, love," she said. "Not too large or heavy, but big enough to keep a spindle, a comb. Someplace to keep the byssus."

He'd gestured to the studio walls, hung with all these same sorts of items. "Looks like you have plenty of space for these things out in the open, where they're handy to use."

Allegra shrugged. "Yes, I know. I'd just like a different spot for some of my best things, just in case."

Johann frowned. "In case? Are you expecting Etna's next eruption will spill over onto Sant'Antioco? Sicily's arms don't reach that far."

"Can you make it or no?"

"You know I can, Allegra. I just wonder why you seem worried."

"Do I?" She sighed. "Honestly, I can't say. I'm just antsy."

"Consider it done, then. I'll trade you an oleander box for three kisses."

She softened and smirked at him. "Only three? You know where three kisses usually lead."

"I do, indeed." He pulled her close and nuzzled her neck, and for the rest of the evening, her box project was forgotten.

~

It was scarcely two weeks later when Johann took Allegra's hand and led her to the rear of their house. He'd burned extra kerosene to lengthen the end of his long days at sea, but he was a fine hand at woodworking, and the box he'd completed was finished. She'd watched him out their back window, his mouth and nose wrapped in a thick scarf and his hands covered by a pair of goatskin gloves. Oleander wood was strong and moisture resistant but also toxic if it wasn't handled properly. The air still smelled of the thick resin he'd used to coat its surfaces inside and out.

Allegra smiled when she saw it, and something in her relaxed, finally. The box was a lovely nutty brown, with a brass latch that fastened with the turn of a knob.

"Plenty of room inside for anything you want to ferret away," he pointed out. "The resin is still a bit sticky, but dry it in the sun for the next day or so, and it's good to last. It's the same stuff I use on the boat's hull, so no water's breaching that. Guaranteed."

"It's beautiful," she said. "A treasure to pass on someday."

Johann turned it upside down. "Here on the bottom, I added something extra."

Allegra leaned in to look. It was an etched drawing of Sardegna he must have copied from a map. In the lower left, he'd burned an outline of a house where their small village lay, and a distance from shore, there was a small sea turtle, near where the byssus cove would be.

"If I'd had more time, I could've added other things," he said.

"This is perfect, Johann. I had no idea you had an artist's hand."

"Maybe I've learned something watching you and the girls all these years, creating your stories and pictures on fabric. Wood can hold stories, too."

"It'll hold all our stories," Allegra said. "I'll make sure of it."

Give sorrow words. The grief that does not speak
Whispers the o'er fraught heart, and bids it break.
—William Shakespeare, *Macbeth*

Zaneta

1941

Chapter 13

Equal parts history, legend, and magic, stories flowed in their veins. Zaneta's own beginning, the tale her mother, Allegra, had relayed to her since she was old enough to hear it, was that Zaneta had been born as far from the sea as possible on their small island. Later, Zaneta often wondered if that had been some sort of portent or even a curse, a foreboding of the time when she would spend months away from the Sardegnan shore.

The family had been on a rare summer holiday on their home island, one where they'd packed up baskets of food and all four children, no small task. Despite her late pregnancy, her mother said, something urged her to make the trip to the Giara di Gesturi, though, except for the panoramic views of the coastline and towns below, the region was neither especially hospitable nor beautiful. Nevertheless, the story went, Allegra and Johann took their two daughters and two sons to the plateau, and there they spent an afternoon picnicking, feasting on cucumbers and melons, figs, and eggplant bruschetta. The boys, Lev and Avi, lobbed bigger and bigger rocks as they pretended to smash boulders.

The day had been warm and especially so on the high volcanic plain dotted with inclining cork trees and scrub olives, forced to grow at an angle by the strong mistral winds. Herds of hardy wild Giara horses foraged among the rocky soil, and the two sisters picked out their favorites: Marta liked the pretty mare with the white blaze covering her face, while Dahlia loved the solid black stallion standing sentry over his mares. Her mother hadn't gone to see the horses, nor was the picnic her chief concern. She told Zaneta she'd wanted to walk again among the nuragic ruins. It had been almost a year since she'd wandered among the stones, her ears straining to hear whispers of the ghosts there. So while Johann kept his eye on the children, Allegra drifted through the ancient sanctuaries, trailing her fingers along the basaltic rock walls, all that remained of the mysterious Nuragic people who'd disappeared centuries ago. Only pieces of their history had been discovered, but Allegra taught her daughters all that she herself had been taught, dutifully transferring the stories of their craft and its origins.

That day on the plain, she'd told Zaneta, time slipped away, and she'd let herself get too tired, too hot. She'd been caught up in imagining the people who must have lived in the towers and built the enormous graves and temples. She'd hunted, she admitted, poking among the stones for some overlooked treasure—an impossibly ancient spindle or shuttle, something that could never have survived the wind and weather of such a place.

"I know how it sounds." Zaneta remembered her mother's voice, clear as a bell. "Something demanded I be there that day. I felt such a connection to the stones, warm on my hand, and the ground beneath my feet. And you decided right then to make your entrance." Allegra never focused on the birth itself, although knowing what she knew now, Zaneta imagined it couldn't have been easy, even being her fifth child. Johann had fallen asleep in the shade of a cork tree, and the children, free and unburdened, had let him snore on, while up the slope his wife labored alone, her shouts carried away with the wind.

When he'd finally woken, with the sun slipped southward on the horizon and his wife not yet returned, Johann and the children had set off to find her. What a shock they must have had, finding her with a squalling baby girl wrapped in her head shawl, both of them smeared in sticky, dried blood and smudged black with volcanic soot. Lev and Avi had crossed their wrists and joined hands to hoist their mother off the plain and onto a seat of their own limbs, while Marta and Dahlia took turns carrying their baby sister. It was impossible, but Zaneta swore she remembered the melodies of the songs her mother and sisters sang on that trip back to the sea as they welcomed another into the line of water women. She still imagined the touch of her sisters' arms as their steps lulled her to sleep.

Chapter 14

That had been 1928, and by her thirteenth birthday, Zaneta Renda was well schooled in the secrets of the byssus, the sea silk they harvested, treated, and wove into artistry. She was an excellent swimmer, better than either Marta or Dahlia, and she'd developed a keen eye for plants and the colors they'd yield in a dye. No one could match her mother in weaving—she was a master—but Zaneta's fingers were nimble and her mind quick. She mirrored her mother's fingering at the loom, and although she sometimes had to stretch to reach across the warp, she'd completed several small tapestries on her own.

Marta and Dahlia had both taken their water oath already, and Zaneta was eager for her turn, but Mamma said she still had much to learn. Theirs was not the only family of water women on the island. At least six other households labored with the byssus, and they often came together for afternoons of singing and weaving. Zaneta loved these times, where she'd tuck herself into a corner, spinning thread, listening to the chatter of women's lives as they talked of babies, love, and hardship, laughing and sometimes crying with each other as they shared their lives. She longed to *really* be one of them with a seat at the table, not just a young apprentice.

From her mother, Zaneta learned what all weavers know—that the act, like all acts of creation, is sacred. The myths from their Greek neighbors were amusing: how Clotho, one of the three Greek Fates, spun the lives of mortals; how Athena transformed her master pupil into a spider when Arachne boasted about her weaving; that a weaver's distaff was a magic wand or divination tool. Why, Zaneta wondered, did people relegate so-called menial household tasks to women, and then, when women showed a keen ability to transform and create, plaster them with labels—witch, strega, pagan?

Her mother's tales were different from those of the Greeks, older. She reached back to the beginning, in Hebrew and Aramaic. *"Our bodies are an altar; to dress yourself can be a sacred act, weaving cloth a prayer. Those in the tribe of Dan were anointed with skill, ability, and knowledge, so they were able to craft with gold and weave sacred vestments and robes for the tribe of Levi. Our sister, Berenice, ensured the craft wouldn't be lost. This alchemy is our anointing, Zaneta, one we honor with our lives."*

For the women in the family, the craft wasn't simply a trade or mastery of a skill. In fact, it was prohibited to sell the thread, so they made no profit at all from their work, at least not profit in coins in the usual sense. The profit gained from byssus was something else entirely—a way to bestow blessing and a prosperity of the soul onto others. The way Allegra told it, it was a secret of the sea, their way of tying past to future, the same way God weaves time, experience, and lineage into a beautiful tapestry of connected threads. For their family and families like theirs, it was their calling, predestined for their line.

Zaneta learned to mark the years by the tides and the sea's production. Each season brought its own delights and duties. In winter, she enjoyed being in the cozy storehouse, cataloguing and tidying dyes; drying plants; and securing jars of dried insects that would, when crushed, produce the perfect tints and colors. In spring and summer, when the days grew longer and the Mediterranean sun rose hot and high, she loved being in the sea most of all, where for hours each day she swam and practiced holding her breath. She memorized the curves and contents of each reef and cove until the currents and creatures were as familiar as the rooms in her own home. The Renda women were planets orbiting their byssus sun. Her mother and older sisters were her playmates and teachers, always present and available for conversation and sharing work. They doted on her, their surprise little sister, delighting in her when she mastered a skill; pushing her to do her best; indulging her sweet tooth and requests for stories, ribbons, and treasures of shells or flowers. They were enough older that Zaneta looked up to them as examples of what it meant to be a friend and a woman. For Zaneta, it had always been so, and she couldn't imagine her life holding anything else besides this rhythm, this joy.

~

One afternoon in early autumn, when the water women had gathered at their home, Allegra beckoned Zaneta to her side and handed her a few lire.

"Run to the port for me," whispered her mother. "Ask Antonio for his best tray of baklava. I made some yesterday, but your sneaky brothers must have taken it with them on the boat, and we'll need something to nibble on later."

Zaneta nodded and scooted out the door. She was disappointed to miss Signora Franca's animated story about the wedding she'd attended in Genoa, but the promise of sweet baklava almost made up for it. When she arrived at the bakery, she couldn't even see Antonio, the baker, at the counter due to the number of people who crowded the bakery and stretched out the door. She spotted a familiar face.

"Luccio!" A few years older than Zaneta, he was a deckhand on one of the bigger fishing boats. She waved him over. "What's going on?" Her small nose wrinkled with confusion at the sight of the crowd.

He scooted next to her and, she noticed, turned his body so that his broad shoulders blocked her from being jostled. She was more than a head shorter than he, and her small, light frame was easily brushed aside by the larger men. "Is there a sale on bread? Everyone must have heard Antonio's giving it away."

Luccio laughed but shook his head. He had a broad smile and a kind face. A shock of dark hair flopped over one eye. It occurred to

Zaneta that his eyes were the green of the sea at first light. "No, it's the radio. They're making some kind of announcement."

She pushed and squeezed her way through the door, her thin frame granting her passage through the tightest spots. No one even seemed to notice, especially not with Luccio playing defense. Despite the crowd, everyone stayed strangely quiet, without the usual chatter and banter between neighbors. Sharp squeals and static filled the stuffy room as they all strained to hear the radio. Something important was being broadcast, but it meant little to Zaneta. She fingered the lire in her pocket and craned her neck to spot the baklava in the glass case.

It was something about the Italian conflict in Albania and the prime minister's ongoing efforts against their neighbor, Greece. She'd heard her father talking, of course, about Italy's biting off more than it could chew and PM Mussolini getting into bed with that German mouthpiece, Hitler. People wondered why the Italian king, Victor Emmanuel, let it continue. Zaneta wondered why everyone couldn't just mind their own business and let life go on as it always had, fishing and weaving and enjoying a good meal. Didn't everyone want those same things?

The radio mentioned an Axis that Mussolini was forming with Germany and Japan. Zaneta had heard this word batted around before but had no idea what it meant. She guessed it must have something to do with the grim-faced soldiers appearing more often at the port and the garish red flags marked with what she thought of as the black spider. She glanced around the bakery at the faces of her neighbors. Signora Olivetti, the wife of a shepherd who had goats and sheep just outside town, stood pressed against the counter, holding her small son's hand. He pulled and whined, no doubt flustered by the scene. When she caught Zaneta's eye, Signora Olivetti—Ruth was her name, Zaneta remembered—straightened the bright scarf covering her dark hair and pulled the boy away from her, hoisting her son up on her hip. She whispered in his ear and pointed to a cannolo, earning a wide grin. A bribe, for being quiet for the broadcast.

Zaneta cast a shy glance up at Luccio to see whether he'd witnessed the boy's victory, but she found his usual grin had faded to a somber frown, his brows knit together as he met her eyes. She didn't know why, but his expression made her want to press closer to him, to have him shield her from some unknown menace.

"What's wrong?" she asked him.

He shook his head slightly and cast a sideways look at Signora Olivetti. Zaneta glanced at her again and noticed her whispering to another woman, their heads together and both looking in her direction. Were they whispering about her? Had she done something wrong?

When the news announcer finished, the room erupted in voices. People gestured and shouted. Some seemed angry while others were plainly excited. She recognized an elderly man from their small synagogue and started to wave to him, but he seemed eager to slip outside unnoticed. Luccio witnessed the man's exit, too, and he stood even closer to Zaneta, placing his hand on her shoulder and guiding her to the counter. Zaneta remembered her task and waved her lire at Antonio.

"Baklava, Signor Listo? Your best tray, Mamma says."

The baker nodded, his usual broad smile faded to a thin line. He sliced and packaged the tray in brown paper and handed it to her across the counter. He seemed so distracted, he forgot to ask for payment, so Zaneta counted out the money and slid it across to him.

"Signore?"

"Ah, sì, sì. Grazie, Zaneta," he said, but it was mechanical, and he turned to the next customer in line as if she'd never been there. Zaneta tucked the package of baklava under her arm and edged her way out. Luccio tugged his hat down onto his head and pushed out of the bakery with her.

"What was that all about?" she asked. "People are acting so strangely." She almost laughed, eager to brush the experience off as a silly mistake, wishing that was all it was.

"People are saying things, Zaneta," Luccio said, his voice low. "Not very nice things about Jews. With Germany and Italy joining forces, people's opinions are changing with politics. They forget who they've been living next to their whole lives."

Her brow furrowed. That might be true on the mainland, where politics mattered more. Here on their island, what did they have to worry about but sheep and fish?

"Take care. You should tell your parents what happened here today."

"You're not Jewish, Luccio. It shouldn't matter to you."

He stared fixedly at her with his green eyes for a moment. "Yet it does. I don't like this new government," he said. She had the oddest feeling he'd been about to say something else. Then a thought occurred to her, and her stomach twisted.

"Wait. Do you think they'll start calling up soldiers from here? Would *you* go?"

"If it comes to that, they certainly will." Luccio shook his head. "But I'm out. Flat feet. I'm no good for marching long distances, and I don't think knowing how to throw a cast net would help much. My father was rejected from the last war for the same reason." They waved goodbye then, and she turned toward home.

Zaneta couldn't shake the palpable anxiety that had settled on her in the bakery. Seeing her neighbors and people from the village shouting and pushing their way out of the usually peaceful, friendly port set her teeth on edge. As she picked her way along the port road, she passed a black-hulled fishing boat that had been beached on the rocks. Zaneta looked around for the boat's owner but saw no one. Perhaps he'd been lured away by the broadcast? Oddly, the catch had been left partially processed, and pails of seawater sat half-full of fish, their crimson gills gasping for air. Opportunist gulls perched on the boat's sides and gathered nearby on the shore, their black eyes keen on an easy meal.

Zaneta forgot about the package of wrapped baklava she carried under her arm and quickened her steps, wanting only to reach home, where her father would explain everything. But Papà didn't sail into port until almost sunset that day. He and Zaneta's brothers seemed to take longer than usual to set out their catch, wash everything down, and secure the nets for the next day. Supper sat cold on the table when they finally arrived, smelling of fish, sweat, and brine. Papà kissed Mamma on the cheek and handed over a string of dripping white octopus tentacles, and Lev and Avi sank into their seats at the table, picking at the food that they normally would have set upon like wild animals.

"Tell me," said Allegra. Zaneta had relayed the scene at the bakery when she'd arrived home, and the women had broken up and headed back to their own homes soon after, the sticky baklava from her errand untouched.

Zaneta felt her father's gaze upon her and knew he weighed his words with care. "It's no good," he said finally. "Talk at the docks is nothing but enlisting or recruitment. I ran into a young man—Zaneta, you know Luccio, I believe. He said he'd seen you today. He told me about the announcement. Germany's helping with the embarrassment in Greece, but fronts will open up everywhere—Albania and Yugoslavia, and now we'll face England and France."

"We won't be able to keep out of it," Lev piped up. "I've heard of resistance groups in the south of Italy, and even in France, people are helping, finding ways to get us out of Europe."

"That doesn't mean *you* should be part of such an underground. It's dangerous." Allegra's voice held a sharp edge. "I don't know what you think war means, young man, but ask your father. It's not valor and glory. If you're caught—you know the things we've heard."

"Surely just propaganda," countered Avi.

"If not?" The waver in her father's voice betrayed his concern.

"Then it's better we sign on to fight with our fellow Italians and take our chances than wait to be caught in the Reich's nets like anchovies."

"The girls," Allegra cautioned. Zaneta and her sisters sat wide-eyed in the fading kitchen light. Electricity had been spotty recently, and no one had thought to light the candles or kerosene lamps.

"People acted strangely today at the bakery," Zaneta said. "Signora Olivetti. She pulled her son away from me and was whispering about me with another woman. I didn't hear what they said, but the way they looked at me . . ." She trailed off, unsettled all over again by the memory.

"You see?" her father said. "It's not just been your imagination, Allegra. Politics are reaching even here, even to people we've lived beside our whole lives."

Dahlia spoke up. She stood behind Avi, her hands gripping his chair. "We've all seen how people are acting strangely. You don't have to protect us, Mamma."

"Besides," added Marta, "we know more than you think. We have eyes and ears, too. Stefan's been worried. He talks with other students at the university in Cagliari." Her boyfriend, Stefan, was Marta's accepted authority on all matters these days.

"He shouldn't have troubled you with such things; I don't care how close the two of you are." Johann scratched his beard and ran a hand through his salt-and-pepper hair.

"We have some time."

"I'm not sure of that, Allegra," said her father. "Some families say we should take action now." He cast a meaningful look at them, and the hair rose on the back of Zaneta's neck.

"What?" she asked. "What action?"

Her mother drew a deep breath and sank into her seat at the table. "Some people are sending family away until all the sentiment against Jews blows over. Where they'll be safe. I didn't think anything would happen to us here, though. Our little island."

The statement caused almost as much of an uproar in the kitchen as Zaneta had witnessed at the bakery earlier. All the siblings spoke at once, protesting and arguing back and forth. Marta burst into tears, saying something about Stefan, but Zaneta couldn't see what *he* had to do with anything. It seemed silly to even think about such things when their family might be separated, when they might have to leave Sardegna and go . . . where?

"Your father and I will remain here," said Allegra. "We've already decided, back when whispers and rumors first reached the port. I can't leave the byssus."

"We protect the byssus, too. We took the vow." Red blotches marred Dahlia's pale face, like they always did whenever she grew angry or tearful.

"You are the future of the byssus," she said.

"But what about you and Papà?" asked Zaneta.

"Our responsibility is to you, not the other way around. We'll find a way. But it's not going to be tonight, so eat. Eat." She pushed the plates toward the boys and Johann. "Come on, girls, grab a light and a shawl and let's go down to the shore to sing."

Chapter 15

By the spring of 1942, their small fishing village had changed. No longer was Sardegna a sleepy obscure island no one had ever heard of. It seemed the world's powers had unfolded a great and terrible map and simply poked red pins in the portions they wished to seize or conquer. Germany's heavy black boot was intent on leaving its print wherever it pleased, and Mussolini, like an eager pup, trotted alongside, demanding more soldiers for Albania, Greece, and now places like Africa and Yugoslavia.

Johann still sailed his weathered, blue fishing vessel offshore to throw his nets, but now he was wary of being accosted, some new official demanding he produce papers or a new license or other such nonsense that somehow only applied to certain pescatori. He labored alone and anchored in the lonelier coves with fewer chances of running into other boats. Lev and Avi, helped by Signora Franca's relatives in Genoa, had obtained papers that changed their names, erasing the Jewish Renda surname from their records. Worse, they had left for the mainland, hoping to make it to France, where they might join a resistance group to help relocate Jewish refugees, despite their mother's protest. Instead, they'd been caught in a roundup and conscripted as Italian soldiers. Italy needed every able-bodied male to do his part. Now they were sheep in wolves' clothing, their falsified papers the only reason they'd been assigned to a military unit instead of shipped off to one of the horrible neighborhoods or ghettos rumors were flying about. The vise had tightened. Even with the mail and communication spottier and less reliable than usual, it began to be common knowledge that Germany was running not-so-secret work camps in Poland and elsewhere. A Jewish settlement camp had even been established near Salerno, a day's journey by ferry across the Tyrrhenian Sea from Sardegna, clarifying Italy's intentions toward its own Jewish citizens, had there been any remaining doubt.

When Papà stayed out late fishing, Mamma sent Zaneta into town to check for letters. Papà, having served in the first war and being too old now to serve, would likely not be conscripted. They still needed to eat, and although fewer people agreed to buy from him, her father continued to work to feed them. He'd already had to drop prices far below market value, but they could still purchase sugar and coffee if they were frugal enough. Zaneta could tell her mother was desperate for news from the boys, though she tried not to betray her worry. The family knew the brothers had become separated, Lev in Africa and Avi in the mess that was Greece, but they hadn't had a letter in weeks, and the bakery radio never broadcast anything encouraging. Her parents often spoke of the first war, when her father had soldiered for years and the flu had taken almost as many as the fighting. She knew her mother kept remembrances of her family in a byssus pouch that never left her apron pocket. The thought of any of her family being hurt or worse made her stomach twist.

Zaneta kept her head down when she walked alongside the port. You never knew what sort of people docked there anymore. Boats she'd never seen before anchored off the shore, and unfamiliar accents pricked her ears in the shops. The once friendly and busy village had sunk into a fog of suspicion. What did Signor Natale at the post office mean when he asked after the family? Did he really care, or was it something else? She hated the thin layer of fear that seemed to coat every interaction like a slimy film.

Her parents whispered late at night, when they thought Zaneta and her sisters slept. She knew they were keeping tabs as best they could on what was happening with the war and how long they might have to make contingency plans, weighing their shrinking options of staying or trying to send Zaneta and her sisters abroad. At daybreak, they still trekked to the rocky shore to greet the sun and offer their song to the sea. The *Pinna nobilis* thrived still, ignorant of the ships full of men that sank in a blaze of twisted metal and flesh off the coast, plumes of black smoke mixing with the clouds in the impossibly blue Mediterranean sky.

Zaneta harvested byssus alongside her mother and older sisters, diving with her short scalpel in hand to cut precise strands from the mollusk shells. There, beneath the water, where the only sound was the sea rushing in her ears, she could almost forget the world above that seemed bent on destruction. The grasses still danced with the waves, and schools of colorful fish still darted about, their silvery scales flashing with mirrored sunlight as, cued by some invisible signal, they switched direction all at once. Green turtles swept their fins forward and back among the grass as they swiveled their heads, searching for the choicest bites. She wished she could remain there among the ocean's creatures, breathing water instead of air, letting the tides carry her where they wished, away from war and worry—away.

All that long summer, Zaneta's mother picked up the pace of her lessons. As much as she wanted to hasten the time to when she could take the water oath, the added urgency made Zaneta's shoulders and head ache. It seemed they were racing toward something inevitable and catastrophic, and her mother's response was to stuff them with all the knowledge and secrets of the byssus she could before the time came when their lessons would end. Zaneta stumbled through the difficult process of making beautiful carmine dye with prickly pear beetles. Her mother scolded her for being distracted while they gathered the insects, so small they looked like seeds or grit. She squeezed too hard and crushed so many by accident, her fingers wore a bright-crimson stain. Making the cochineal required drying thousands of insects and combining them with alum to help the color adhere to cloth.

After many clumsy attempts before her mother was satisfied, Zaneta learned how to mix and apply the cochineal dye and moved on to producing vermilion and madder. Vermilion was her favorite because it was once almost as precious as the byssus itself, used with gold leaf for medieval manuscript capitals. She'd read of such illuminated books before, imagining their pages and thinking, *I could do that. Someday I'll make those colors and weave them into something beautiful, gilded with byssus.* Madder was easier, made from drying and crushing the unassuming root of a small yellowish flower, long ago used in paints in the lost city of Pompeii.

More than once, she'd noticed Luccio sailing near their cove after his workday on the big boat had finished. He owned a green dinghy with cheerful yellow sails that he used to travel to and from the docks. He lived farther up the coast, and Zaneta imagined their cove must take him a bit out of his way, but perhaps he enjoyed relaxing on the water once the fishing was finished. He always raised a hand to them as he passed, shouting, "Buongiorno, Rendas!" or "Ciao, Rendas!" Once, Zaneta had been out swimming when he'd happened by, and he'd idled in circles while she treaded water. He'd offered to take her aboard and ferry her back to the shore, but she'd waved him off, needing to complete the laps Mamma required for their swimming skills.

Late fall arrived, and still nothing from her brothers. They were fishermen, not soldiers, after all, and Zaneta imagined the worst. The night they'd left, the family had shared a simple meal and held hands to pray. Then the boys and their father had slipped into the family boat at sunset and sailed for Genoa with their prow lights doused. For two days, she and her mother and sisters had held their breath, waiting for Johann's return. When he'd finally come through the door in the middle of the night on the second day, his eyes were rimmed red, and his shoulders sagged. She'd never been so relieved to see anyone in her life. Zaneta tried to shake the memory from her head, tried to unsee her parents clenched to one another, rocking and weeping at letting their sons go.

In the interest of not drawing attention to themselves, the family had stopped meeting with the other water women, stopped gathering in their makeshift synagogue. Zaneta felt their lives shrinking as they tried to blend into the scenery. They were like the wily octopus she'd witnessed on a dive one morning. She'd come upon a shelf of rock when a movement caught the corner of her eye. Zaneta had paused to scan the rock and had seen a stone crab acting strangely, darting and retreating. When she'd moved closer, the camouflaged octopus had appeared from nowhere, crab in one of its tentacles, and she'd drawn back, startled. A master of disguise, the creature had all but become part of the rock, completely invisible. Unlike the octopus, Zaneta knew people weren't fooled by her family's withdrawal from the community. She knew they must stand out like the black jackdaws against a cerulean sky.

Mamma spoke about going up to the plains where the wild horses grazed, maybe disappearing for real for a time, so that loose-lipped people in the village might forget about the women who wove golden thread and knew Hebrew. She went so far as to pack a bag, filling it with enough to last awhile. As part of their apprenticeship, they were all able to withstand hunger and thirst, hunt for themselves, and find provisions from the land, but her mother left the bag by the back door, eyeing it like a talisman every so often, as if merely having it on hand might fend off the need to use it.

Chapter 16

Winter. Zaneta's mother gathered the best of their weavings, a collection of tools, and small vials of the most difficult dyes. These she placed in an oleander box lined with goatskins, one Zaneta's father had carved with his own hands. She tucked in other things as well: photos and heirlooms that had been handed down through the generations of water women, adding a few lire for good measure. One afternoon, when the slate-gray sky promised rain and few people bustled about outdoors, Zaneta and her sisters, along with their mother, carried the box to the shore, their hoods pulled close against the damp.

They stood for a long while on the rocks at low tide, letting the cold January wind whip their hair and sting their faces. Zaneta was glad for the wind. It made her eyes water and her nose run, disguising, she thought, the salty tears that wet her cheeks. After singing their ritual evening songs, the four of them followed the shoreline farther than usual. Dahlia and Mamma each gripped a handle of the box, and Marta and Zaneta walked behind, their boots sinking in the sand. After a half mile or so, they turned inland and headed for a jagged, black-rocked cliff. Behind the steep rock face visible from the water, the mouth of a sea cave yawned. At high tide, the cave would be inaccessible, and if you hadn't known it was there, it would remain invisible when the tide went out.

Wordlessly, the four of them climbed the rocks, balancing the box between them, and entered the maw of the cave. Pink anemones and orange starfish clung to the lower portion of the wet walls, waiting for the tide's return, and remnants of seagrass and algae littered the floor where the light still penetrated. Farther back, as they picked their way along the pitted floor, the plants and sea life diminished with the light. Zaneta lit a small lantern once they were well inside, and with its light flickering on the cave walls, they continued as far back as they dared, her mother craning her neck to search out a suitable spot.

"Here." She finally stopped. "Up there in that crag, it should remain dry enough."

Marta dropped Zaneta's hand and stepped forward. "Give it to me, Mamma. I'll lift it with Dahlia." The two girls heaved the wooden box as high as they could reach, shoving and pushing it into a crag in the wall.

"Zaneta, hold the light high," said her mother. "It can't come loose, can it?" She peered upward, her brows furrowed in the shadows.

"No, it's wedged in," said Dahlia. "The tide won't go that high, and unless you know it's here and can pry it out, it's stuck."

"Climb down, then," beckoned her mother, and she bid them all hold hands in a circle when they stood on solid ground. "Keeping this here doesn't mean we've given up," she told them, looking each of them in the eyes. "Dry your tears. This isn't the first time we've faced hard times, and it won't be the last. But do you remember? In the very beginning of creation, when the earth was still without form and empty and darkness covered all, even before light . . ."

"There was water," said Zaneta. "Above and below."

"That's right, my girl. The sea was first, and then it was filled, teeming with life, waiting to be used for further creation and in a service that connects and gives back to the divine. It won't come to an end because of a silly war between men."

"But Mamma." Zaneta started to give voice to her fear and worry, started to ask who would weave the byssus if none of them lived, but her mother placed one hand on her head and held her face with the other.

"Nothing can erase our spirits," she said. "Nothing can extinguish our love for each other. Let them try. We're stronger than that—*all* of us. The byssus remains. If, someday, it's someone else who comes to find our box, perhaps our line will be grafted in with theirs."

Zaneta nodded, wiping the tears that had somehow leaked out despite her best efforts. Hand squeezes all around, and the women hugged. "Tomorrow morning, Zaneta, you'll take the water oath. It's time."

Her mouth dropped open. "Tomorrow?" She was barely fifteen. She couldn't possibly know enough yet. Marta and Dahlia beamed at her and hugged her yet again. They had already known.

"You've worked so hard, faster than most, and given the circumstances, I think it best that we make it official." *In case I'm not here later to lead you through it,* she knew: words her mother didn't say.

It was full dark when they made their way home, and they walked without the lantern. They'd just surrendered their work to a cave, and despite what Mamma had said to lift their spirits, their hearts carried a heavy weight. They'd heard whispers, reports from Berlin about a final solution to the Jewish problem. Her father had received a letter from friends in Genoa warning them to flee while they could, but of course, it was too late. Where could they get papers now? Where would they go, an older man and four women? The stories of roundups, trains to nowhere, and families that'd been taken in for small infractions and never returned were all true. They'd certainly never been Orthodox and weren't even strictly kosher, but they did observe the religious holidays and could clearly trace their lineage to their Jewish roots. Outward appearances didn't matter to those who pounded their fists on the tables in Berlin and elsewhere. A few drops of Jewish blood were enough. Zaneta's father no longer sailed the boat from the port. He fished from the shore only enough for the family's food, making sure to go out before daylight in out-of-the-way inlets on the island. This spring—well, who could say?—but Zaneta didn't think they would be harvesting byssus like they'd done ever since she could remember.

Dawn broke the next morning, and Zaneta woke to rumbles of thunder that turned out not to be thunder at all but, they discovered later, air attacks in Cagliari and Alghero. Over the past months, fighting on Malta, their island neighbor south of Sicily, had been constant, and more recently, they'd heard Sicily had become a stronghold for the so-called Axis. Any spot of land that lay between the front in Africa and the coast of Europe was fair game. Apparently, that now included Sardegna. Mamma told her sisters to stay with Papà while they went to complete the water oath. Zaneta readied herself with shaking hands, dressing in a loose golden robe of byssus and wrapping herself in a warm coat to wear on the way. She stuffed her regular shawl and dress with its pullover sweater into a small bag so that she could change back into it afterward. She wasn't sure if her tremors were from nervousness at the impending oath or the air raids that were so close they rattled their windows. She could tell her father didn't relish the thought of them venturing out, but Mamma couldn't wait.

"Come, Zaneta, be quick now," she ordered. Dahlia and Marta gave her a kiss and smiles that told her how proud they were. Her mother squeezed her father's hands and told him they'd be there and back. All the plans they'd tried to make to send the girls abroad for safety had fallen through. They were on their own, their sole advantage being their location on the far side of a tiny island they hoped would escape the notice of the roving red eye of the German machine.

The oath was usually performed in the late spring or summer, when the sea was at its finest, warm and inviting and turned a crystal aquamarine by the ripe sun. Now, after they'd completed the recitations and the oath, after her mother had given her a slim gold ring and declared her not only a daughter but a sister in the line of women, the water was too frigid to swim in, the sun too low to make it sparkle like a jewel. The water was a deep violet, so dark it looked almost black. She was denied the ritual dive with her mother. Their hurry and anxiety prevented her from savoring the pride and gratitude she'd always imagined would come with such a moment.

Zaneta exchanged her byssus robe for her warmer clothes, folding it carefully into the bag she carried. They made their way back along the beachfront and had almost rounded the bend to reach the path to their house when Zaneta heard shouts. Her mother gripped her arm and drew her backward against the black rocks flanking the shore.

"What is it?" she asked. "What's happening?"

"Here." Her mother pulled a canvas bag from beneath her cloak and thrust it at her. Until that moment, Zaneta hadn't realized she'd been carrying anything. It was the packed bag that had sat by the back door all these weeks. Every time they ventured out, her mother hung it across her body. "Take this and go inland. Go as fast as you can and keep to the rocks and trees. Go to the nuragic ruins up on the plains and wait there. People not from here don't know about such places, and no one will be there this time of year anyway. I thought we'd have time to make a place up there for all of us." Tears spilled over onto her mother's cheeks.

Now, Zaneta could see soldiers leaving their house, the ugly black spider insignia on their armbands. Outside, they shoved terrified, weeping people into the back of a canvas-covered truck. Zaneta recognized members of all the other six families of weavers, not just the men. They must have come from the north and traveled the whole coastline, stopping at even the homes tucked up among the rocks before reaching their cottage. Frantic, she searched for Marta and Dahlia. Where were they? Her father? A gasp from her mother's lips told her she'd seen them. There. Marta and Dahlia appeared from the back of the truck, their hands reaching out for a man the soldiers pushed forward. She recognized her father's frame and cried out, but her mother took her face in both hands and forced her to look her in the eyes.

"Now, Zaneta. Do it now."

"I'm not leaving you, Mamma." Zaneta's eyes were wild, her throat so dry she could barely rasp out the words.

"Hush! Do as I say and go to the ruins. It's the only hope you'll be safe." Her mother shoved her roughly with both hands, and fear settled into Zaneta's gut. She'd never known her mother's hands to be anything but gentle. Almost as an afterthought, her mother pulled her back into a suffocating embrace, holding her so tight she couldn't draw breath. Zaneta was too frightened to cry. In a panic, her unreasonable thought was to memorize everything immediately—her mother's hair, face, eyes, the way she smelled, and the feel of that strangling embrace. She feared, even then, those flashes of memory would be all that remained to hold on to.

"Go, and remember who you are, figlia. My hope is with you." With that, her mother rounded the bend and ran toward the house, yelling and waving her arms. What was she thinking? Her father's head swiveled toward his wife's voice. His face was stricken, and he shook his head no. *No!* But it was too late. Already the soldiers approached her, shouting commands with their hands on their guns. A dog barked as the truck's engine revved. Every nerve in Zaneta's body screamed *run,* but her heart wanted only to be with her sisters and parents. *"What happens to one of us happens to all of us,"* she remembered Marta saying before her brothers left. When her mother climbed into the truck, her sisters' hands clutching her close, she turned her head briefly toward where she'd left Zaneta and nodded sharply, her hands pressed against her mouth.

Zaneta lifted the bag's strap over her head and committed the sin she would wrestle with the rest of her life. She ran.

Chapter 17

Zaneta spent most of that first terrible night afraid to move, pressed motionless against the stone wall on the plain, her mind replaying over and over the last moments: the truck loaded with her family, her father's face, her mother's nod. As the moon rose, Zaneta inched slowly along a stone wall on the scrubby plain, her pulse electric with fear. Sometime in the wee hours, shivering with cold and her eyes puffy from ceaseless tears, the stones behind her back disappeared, and she tipped backward into a pile of brush, lucky she didn't break her neck as she tumbled downward into the dark.

Zaneta sheltered in what she imagined must once have been a sort of temple. Built of heavy stones, the part that remained visible on the plain was circular, and toward one end, if you knew to clear away the brush and overgrown grasses, a steep stone staircase led beneath the earth to a room below. It was large enough for Zaneta to stand up in. If she hadn't had the lantern, and—after the kerosene ran out—candles, she would almost certainly have fallen in the well at the center of the room. Its source had long ago run dry, so it offered no water; this she figured out after tossing in a rock to gauge its depth. The space was a good place to hide, to crouch and cry in despair, and to toss in fitful sleep.

She spent the daytime hours after that first night in the shadows near the well, humming softly to dispel the panic that threatened to overtake her. She sorted through the bag her mother had packed, finding practical items like a blanket, candles, dried food and nuts, matches and medicines, but other things, too. Mamma had thought to include a handheld loom shaped like a lyre and pouches of folded cloth and spools of byssus, something pleasant to pass the time. Zaneta had plenty of that. When darkness fell and the temperature dropped a bit, Zaneta waited until the moon's milky glow lit the steps, and then she climbed up for a breath of fresh air and to search for food and water. The plains were sparse, but pools of fresh water dotted the area.

After that first day and then a second, she fell into a sort of routine. She hid by day, then ventured out by night. Often, she encountered the wild horses dipping their muzzles for a drink. At first, they'd bolted, fearing her a predator, but after several weeks, they grew used to each other, and they watched her from a respectable distance, their small ears swiveling and tails swishing. Besides the birds and red deer, the horses were her only companions. Zaneta talked softly to them as she poured out her heart in whispers, taking small comfort from the fact that another living being knew she existed at all.

Many thousands of years ago, when the ancient Nuragic people lived and died on the islands of Sardegna and Sant'Antioco, they could not have foreseen airplanes or bombs falling from the sky. Surely, they could not have known, long after their population had disappeared, that a slim, nominally Jewish weaver woman would use their once mighty edifice as a sanctuary. Zaneta actually thought of things like this as she settled among the nuragic remains, wondering if the half-standing buildings had been temples or fortresses. Neither would have offered much protection from the weather or the war as spring clawed its way forward in 1943.

She fretted endlessly about her family, praying they'd remained together, that they were being treated well, that her brothers had found a way to join the resistance. She flip-flopped between hope and despair, thinking one minute she'd never see them again and the next imagining them appearing at the top of the steps. It was maddening, and the only thing that kept her imagination in check was the feel of the thread between her fingers, weaving flowers and birds and fish on the lyre loom. When she finished one, she'd start another, and when the cloth ran out, she picked out all the work and started over. The terrible sounds of low-flying planes and air raids occurred so often she felt as if she were constantly covering her head, bracing for an impact that never came. Zaneta had no idea what she should do or how long she might stay there. She waffled, sometimes every few minutes, between whether to remain or whether there might be someplace better, more secret or secure. Her mother's only instruction had been to hide, so hide she did. When would she come find her? How would she know it was safe to go find them?

Desperate for news, Zaneta made up stories in her head. Her family had been taken to the mainland, probably, and maybe they were staying with friends there, with beds and plenty of food. They had a unique skill, so perhaps her mother had told them this and used it to bargain for their safety. They were being processed, detained in some building in the capital city, just for recordkeeping, and soon they would come. Soon, she might hear them call her name and tell her it was safe and time to come home. Was that her name she heard now, on the wind? Was it her mother's voice? Or perhaps Marta's? No, only the whistle of a jackdaw.

She rationed food from the bag. It had been meant to sustain their family; even so, after a few weeks of living in the ruins, the dried figs and fish dwindled, and Zaneta knew she'd have to venture farther to forage. She hoped the night would be enough to shield her if she could creep far enough to find someone's vegetable garden or an orchard of blood oranges and lemons. She didn't dare go as far as the coast, where the sea would offer her its plenty. She couldn't risk being seen, no matter how much she missed the water or how her muscles ached to swim. She pined for the dawns and dusks; she should be standing on the shore, offering her song and service. It had been over two months since she'd taken the water oath, and she hadn't been to the shore even once, already breaking the rituals and routines she'd been taught since birth.

Zaneta conjured her sisters' voices in her head, heard them singing the songs they'd all sung since childhood. She hummed the melodies in a whisper, hungry for company, if only in her imagination.

Once, she'd been out foraging in the moonlight and had lingered too long. Pink tinges started to streak the horizon, signaling dawn's arrival, and she hurried to make it back to the ruin. She passed an overlook and couldn't resist, not having glimpsed the village or people in so long. Zaneta allowed herself a moment to look down on the small hamlet but later she wished she hadn't. Two flags flew outside the post office now: Italy's familiar blocks of green, white, and red that always reminded her of Neapolitan ice cream, and the scarlet red with its black spider. Luccio had told her it was called a swastika, but she didn't care about its name; she yearned to tear it from the pole where it flapped smugly in the breeze. In the early light of dawn, Zaneta spotted soldiers walking the port, soldiers like the ones who had forced her family into the truck. The Germans were apparently permanent fixtures on the island now.

When she thought she might go mad with hopelessness and thoughts of her family, she thought of Luccio. Was he still sailing his green and yellow boat? Did fish still swim in the waters as if the world were normal? Did he sail by their cove where he once waved and laughed at them and wonder where the Rendas had gone? She was glad he was safe from the politics of the war, with his family and not in danger of them being plucked up like a snail in a gull's beak.

She lay on the stone floor and thought of Avi and Lev. If they could get away, could find their way to the resistance groups they'd wanted to join, maybe news would reach them about what had happened. They might come back searching for the family. Zaneta sat up abruptly. If they did, they'd find their home empty. They wouldn't know she was up here alone, wouldn't know to come find her. She went round and round in her mind about this. She couldn't leave a note, lest someone else find her. How could she go back there to leave a message, even a sly one, without risking being seen? They'd had no news of her brothers for so long now. They could be anywhere. They could already be killed, and no one would know.

Forced to sit in the dim light with bare walls, Zaneta catalogued each room in their home in her mind, wishing she could see even the simplest items again, imagining her family sitting around the table, enjoying a nice meal of fish flavored with lemon and saffron, bread. Flowers in the windowsill, shelves of dyes, the hook by the door where her father's vest hung and his boots on a woven rug beneath. Windows, with curtains fluttering in the ocean breeze. The loom, the bins of byssus. A plate of amaretti. She'd let this continue for only so long before she'd shake herself and think of something else. It was a nice escape, but it was also torture. When would she ever see their beloved home again?

Toward the end of March, Zaneta dug leeks from the ground one night near the edge of the plain. These had been her diet for a couple of weeks, and she was glad warmer weather would soon arrive. Each thought she had like this brought guilt bubbling up like a spring. How could she gripe about leeks when her family might not have even that? What an ungrateful, selfish person she was. She chewed the tough green stalks to fool her mouth into thinking it had plenty to eat. One small black horse, a young filly that had become comfortable with her, grazed nearby, blowing through her nose now and then. Zaneta rested on her heels to ease her back, and the filly raised her head and snorted.

"Take it easy. I'm not hurting you," she said, her voice soft and slow.

"I wasn't worried," came a voice in reply. A male voice. The horse bolted through the brush, and Zaneta felt the tremor of hooves pounding the ground as her companions joined the escape. She sat frozen in place, the leeks turning her stomach sour. She didn't know which direction the voice had come from, or how she'd missed the man's approach. *Careless, stupid girl,* she silently chastised.

"Stand up," the voice commanded in Italian. "Turn around where I can see your hands." He was to Zaneta's left, just past where the plain started to slope down toward the coast. She'd strayed too far. She obeyed, slowly rising to her knees and pulling her shawl close around her before standing all the way. Her eyes, accustomed to the darkness, found him immediately, and she registered all the pertinent facts. A soldier. German, though his Italian was passable. About as old as her brother Avi. He leveled a gun at her, its metal glinting in the moonlight.

When he saw the figure she made standing before him, he laughed and lowered the pistol a few centimeters. The laughter made Zaneta's knees wobble. She couldn't run and had nothing to defend herself, and he knew it.

"Not to worry, Fräulein. We're allies, after all, sharing the spoils, isn't that right? Il Duce and the Führer play for the same team. What are you doing up here in the middle of the night?" he asked.

Zaneta shrugged and held up a handful of leeks. She held them out to him, an offering, an impossible bribe. She imagined the truck leaving from her house, her family clutching each other inside.

"You're giving me onions?" He laughed again and swiped his brow with the inside of an elbow. "Where do you live?"

She opened her mouth but shrugged again, stared at her shoes. The fresh-dug earth beneath her feet gave off a rich, damp odor. He stepped nearer and glanced around, wary. It occurred to her to wonder what *he* was doing out here in the middle of the night. All this time and no one. There was nothing a soldier would want up here on the empty plain.

"You out here alone?" he asked. Zaneta wanted to lie, but a lie like that would be quickly discovered. She swallowed hard and bit her lip to keep from crying. She lifted her chin to portray confidence, bravery she didn't feel.

"Take me to your house," he demanded. "I'm looking for a place to—rest."

Zaneta's mind whirled. Should she lead him to a different ruin? Another tower somewhere? Nothing would look lived in; he wouldn't believe her. If she led him to her hiding place, her sanctuary wouldn't be safe anymore, but at this point, did it matter? He holstered his pistol and gestured at her to get going. She complied, still gripping the hard-won leeks in her hand. She decided to go to her ruin. Zaneta grasped at desperate possibilities. If he killed her, at least she'd be in a place where the spirits of her ancient Nuragic ancestors revered women and the water. Maybe their ghosts would rise up and save her.

When they arrived, she simply pointed, but the soldier appeared confused. "What, here? Fräulein, you expect me to believe you live in a stone circle with no roof?" Zaneta stooped and swept the piles of grass aside to reveal the staircase entrance. "Aha," he said appreciatively. "Aren't you the clever one?"

Her feet knew each stone step, and she navigated them perfectly, even in the dark, while the soldier had to steady himself with his hands against the walls as he descended. He held a small squeezer flashlight in one hand. Zaneta's heart sank further with each step, and she tried to focus on being strong for the rest of the family. She was their hope, Mamma had said, although hope was in short supply lately.

When they reached the floor of the small atrium, the soldier shone the beam of his flashlight over the mossy stone walls, lingering once on Zaneta's face while she squinted against the light. He seemed satisfied.

"What's your name?" he asked her.

"Zaneta," she answered, her first word.

"So you do speak." He nodded. "How long have you been hiding here? I assume that's what you're doing—hiding. This isn't a proper house."

She shrugged again. "Awhile."

"What do you eat? Besides onions, I mean." The soldier again wiped his brow with his arm. He wore no cap, and his sand-yellow hair was short and stood up in cowlicks. The uniform seemed a size too large, she noticed now, hanging on his frame.

"What I can find." Zaneta gestured up the stairs. "You'd be surprised." She held her hands out in front of her as a show of cooperation and knelt slowly behind a large stone in the center of the floor. She thought it might once have been an altar. Behind it, she'd stashed what she'd managed to collect—a few beets and potatoes, leeks, and blood oranges. She didn't reveal the last of the dried fish and figs her mother had packed.

The soldier crossed the small room in two broad steps, and Zaneta shrank against the wall. He ignored her and knelt beside the food, tearing into the oranges and potatoes until there was nothing left but scattered peels. "What else have you got? This is all?"

She spread her hands. "Of course, of course. You're hiding." He sat blocking the exit, his back braced by the bottom step and one leg straight out in front of him. He motioned for her to sit, too, so she did, directly opposite, as far across the room as she could be, and he regarded her, a wolf observing a lamb. "We'll get more later," he said, and Zaneta's stomach clenched. *We?* He meant to stay.

Chapter 18

So began what Zaneta came to think of as the time of her imprisonment. Not that she'd been free before; it wasn't as if she had been able to walk the shore or visit with neighbors or even go outside with the sun above, but now—now she shared her home, such as it was, and her food with the enemy. Now an intense wariness weighed on her. She was like one of the wild Giara horses, poised to bolt when the bushes rustled. He hadn't hurt her—not yet—but she suspected this was only because he needed her skills. His name was Jan; he'd told her that much. Having had no news for so long, Zaneta tried to pull what information she could from him.

"Won't they miss you at the port?" she probed. They sat in the flickering candlelight, although she hated to waste the wax.

"Not just yet, I think," Jan replied. With something in his stomach, he became more talkative. "My unit's on furlough. A well-earned break, let me tell you, Fräulein. It's been nothing but shit and shrapnel from Sicily all the way back home."

"Germany—I mean, we—are winning, though?"

He shook his head and spat against the wall. Zaneta winced. She still thought of this dark place as her sanctuary, and his casual defilement disgusted her. "Winning? That's what they said, at least before I landed here." He waved a hand airily. "In this luxury Italian apartment." He stared at her, his blue eyes empty of emotion. His features were pointed, his jaw angular and sharp, though its outline was hidden by the wiry beard that had grown in across his chin.

"Perhaps it will end soon, then?" She pulled her shawl tighter around her torso and tucked her knees up tight to her chest.

"Not likely. Now that Japan's got the United States' hackles up, they've been nonstop with the Brits. I'll tell you a secret." He leaned in. "More than one of us is sick to death of the whole business. Let's just divvy up the map and be done. I'm dying for a cigarette and a stout stein of beer. Not many left to drink it with now, though, are there?"

Zaneta pushed a handful of nuts over to the soldier. "Here," she said. "You need to keep up your strength for when you return to your unit."

He tossed back the handful in one mouthful and chewed noisily. Zaneta would have rationed them, allowing herself one every hour or so. Now she'd have to collect more. "Return? Ah, you're eager for that, are you? Save me from eating all your hard work."

"It's all right."

"You still haven't told me why you're here," he said. They'd been going on like this for a week so far. "What're you hiding from? Your parents Jewish sympathizers, is that it? Your brothers deserted?"

She'd considered her answer. "I don't like the shelling. My family was killed in an air raid in Cagliari, and I don't want to end up like them. It's quieter down here."

"Then why not invite your neighbors and share food? Why do you only go out at night?"

"It's quieter then. The war's been . . . hard."

He considered this. "What did your family do here? It's nothing like Berlin. Berlin's a big city, lots to do and see, always something stirring. Here—everything is slow. It's just the ocean and fish."

"But it's beautiful," she defended. "People sometimes come for holiday. And yes, fish. My father is—was—a fisherman."

"And your mother a fishmonger?" He snorted.

"No," she said proudly, before she could help herself. "A weaver."

"Is that what I've seen you working on at night?"

Zaneta's heart stopped. She'd been certain the soldier had been asleep before she dared pull out the precious lyre loom to occupy her fingers and calm her raw nerves. Again, she cursed herself for her carelessness. "The moon's up," she said, rising to her feet. "We should go out."

He followed her up the steps and out into the fresh air. Had she been alone, Zaneta would have stopped a moment and listened for the rush of the sea. Sometimes on clear, cold nights, she imagined she could hear its voice, even this far inland. With the soldier—she wouldn't call him Jan—she headed straight for a small grove of trees. She'd noticed the pink blossoms earlier and wanted to check on them. It had been a warmer and wet winter, and spring was coming early. Despite everything, the world kept turning, spinning its seasons in succession.

"I've been thinking," he whispered. He held the squeeze light, though Zaneta didn't need it. The moon had risen full and bright. "I'm going to go down to the port tomorrow."

Zaneta had found a dead tree among the grove and was inspecting it, but at his words, she stopped. The soldier knew the area now, where she looked for food, and of course, where the well room was. If he went back to town, he need only tell someone else, and they'd find her soon enough. Zaneta knew she probably lived on borrowed time.

She sweetened her voice as she replied. "What'll you do there?" A bright flower caught her eye, and she peered at the plant in the moonlight. Was it yellow? Clusters of the flowers spread on low bushes beneath the trees, and it sparked her mental catalog of plants, dyes, and their uses that her mother had insisted Zaneta know by heart.

"Military business." He sounded brisk, dismissive, as if she shouldn't worry her little head about such matters. "But I can try to pick up some rations, or maybe part of a catch at the docks." He meant to return. Zaneta felt ashamed: her mouth watered. It had been months since she'd tasted fresh fish. She still hadn't figured out why he hadn't returned to his unit, how he could spend such time away from the war.

When she remained quiet, he said, "Don't worry, I won't tell anyone about you. Your house can stay our little secret." Though the night was warm enough, Zaneta tightened her shawl and led the way to a puny abandoned vegetable garden she thought might yield some volunteer asparagus. A few bright green spears poked through the earth, but she decided to leave them to grow. She thought she could hold out for another day or so. If the soldier didn't return, she wouldn't have to share, and there would be more for her. Then again, she might be dead tomorrow. Sending every thought and decision through this sort of crucible put Zaneta on edge, and she sighed in frustration.

"No luck?" he asked, and she shook her head. He wouldn't know a spear of asparagus from an olive tree, she thought.

"No, we might as well go back."

Back in the atrium, the soldier settled against a wall once more. "You can weave if you like, if that's what you've been doing. If I can, I'll bring some candles, too."

"Why would you do that?" she asked all in a rush. "Why would you come back here when you can have all the food you want at the port? When you can be with your friends and walk about in the sun?"

The soldier stared at her, breathing steadily for a full minute before answering. "I'll tell you. My unit is gone. I was on a ship just off the coast of Sicily. A group of us had just boarded a landing craft when all hell broke loose. Must have been some dead-on torpedoes or maybe an air drop—there were those, too—but we lost the whole ship. Maybe about twenty men left on my rig, trying to stay low and out of the ship's pull." Zaneta listened without sympathy. Although the end of the story was sitting right in front of her, she irrationally hoped it would end with no survivors. Why was he telling her this? As if she cared anything about the loss of a German ship; it was less than they deserved.

"We were sitting ducks out there. Half of us jumped in the water to try to head to shore." He scratched the hairs on his chin, stared into space. "Something exploded on deck as the ship went down, and we were right in the path of that hailstorm. I figure I got knocked in the head because when I woke up, it was night, and I was floating somewhere in the middle of the Tyrrhenian. My life jacket saved me. You ever been in the water at night? Of course you have—you live on an island. It's more than a little spooky, thinking of all the things swimming below you." He shook his head to dislodge the thought.

"Next morning, of all things, a unit from North Africa happens by and I get picked up, so I guess it wasn't my time. They dropped me at the port here, figuring I could get back to base at Sicily, but I guess I wanted away from the water for a while, and I went for a walk." He glanced around the stone walls as if to say *voilà*.

"They probably think you're dead," she said.

He nodded his head slowly, and she understood. That's what he wanted. He was hiding out from the war, too. Not only was he a German but also a deserter.

"Still, I can probably get away with going down there. No one here knows me. Trouble is, I don't have any lire or marks. Nothing, really, to trade with. But you . . ."

Zaneta was incredulous. "What do I have? Spare onions?"

"You weave," he said. "I've seen it. It's some kind of gold?"

Her heart beat faster. "No, it isn't. It's just thread. You can't use it to buy things."

"Why not? It's unusual. I bet a lot of soldiers have never seen anything like it. I know I haven't. Just give me a few samples and I'll see what I can get for it."

Her mother's words echoed in Zaneta's head. It had been so long since she'd had such a clear memory of that voice that tears stung her eyes. *"Byssus can never be bought or sold. It's a gift from the sea that can only be given in return, never consumed. Any who break this covenant will meet a bad end."* She recalled the stories of greedy, powerful men who had used the byssus for their own gain, usurping the weavers' work. Their businesses had failed, fortunes crumbled, and worse. Zaneta's hands trembled.

The soldier frowned at her hesitation. "Look, it's the only thing we've got." Again, the *we*. "You must see that. How long can you last up here on oranges and half-rotted cabbages?"

She started to speak, but her throat was sand. Like a beached fish, her mouth opened and closed. She couldn't use the byssus to sell or barter, even for her life. Before she could think, the soldier had crossed the room and was on his knees in front of her. He'd snatched the canvas bag from its spot behind the altar and dumped it, roughly pawing through the photos and spools. Zaneta held her breath. She had sewn the lire and extra food into the lining, and in his haste and the dim light, he had overlooked it. She wasn't sure what he would do if he discovered she'd kept them secret.

"Here." He pulled out three weavings, small, frameable vignettes of seabirds by a cliff face, boats in the harbor, and a nuragic vessel under the moon. "This. And this. I'll take these. You'll still have some cloth left to weave more, right?"

She snatched up the photos and thread, reached to catch the vial of dye that rolled across the stone floor. "Don't," she said. The soldier stopped and handed her the bag. He breathed loudly through his nose and looked at her with his unblinking blue eyes. He said nothing, but he pocketed the three byssus weavings and let her pick up the mess. She was so thankful she'd thought to fold the robe she'd worn for her water oath and hide it beneath a crag in a dark corner. It represented her last good memory with her mother, and she didn't think she could bear it being sold by a German soldier.

In the morning, Zaneta woke with her hands aching from clutching the bag all night. She was exhausted after a tense, fitful sleep. A small shaft of sun shone down the steps, and she heard the faint chatter of birds up above. The soldier had gone.

Chapter 19

Zaneta bit her nails until she tasted the coppery tang of her bleeding cuticles. It was broad daylight, so she couldn't risk leaving the well and being seen. Her mind raced: Was he telling the Germans where she hid even now? How long would it be before their black boots stamped down the steps and they dragged her to her fate? What might he find out about her at the port if he asked? Despite her empty stomach, she vomited twice, the worry too great to keep down.

The sun had slid halfway to the sea by the time he returned. At the crunch of boots across the rocky terrain above, Zaneta froze against the wall, attempting to fade into the shadows. She held her breath and willed her heart to stop slamming against her chest.

"Zaneta?" It was the soldier. He was still alone, and the beam of his flashlight flickered as he descended the steps. He stopped when she stepped out of the shadows and he saw her face. "You were worried I wouldn't come back?"

She choked back her disgust at his arrogant presumption. No, she'd been worried he'd return with the Gestapo. If he hadn't returned at all, she could have continued as before. But she nodded.

"Good news." He held up a bulging cloth sack. Laying it on the stone altar, he opened the neck of it and pulled out each item, holding it aloft to show her. "Candles. Bread! Some early tomatoes, and may I present . . ." Here, he unwrapped a paper package. "Tuna fillets and a rind of pecorino! As I thought, the officers appreciated the weavings."

Zaneta's head jerked up. "This was from your trade of the byssus?"

"Whatever you call it," he said. "I brought more cloth for you to weave on. And some thread you could perhaps use?" She'd never seen him so animated. His eyes were shining. His foray into town, speaking his own language, had buoyed his spirits, apparently made him forget they were living caged inside an ancient well house. The soldier pulled out a bundle of fabric and some spools of thread that stopped the breath in Zaneta's throat. She knew those spools, that thread.

Measuring her tone, she asked, "Where did you find that?"

"I sold your weavings at a tavern by the port," he said. "That's where the off-duty officers sit and wait for orders to come in. The owner took an interest, helped me out quite a bit, actually, because he started telling the origins of the gold thread and the weavers who used to live on the island, called water women. When the officers heard the tale, it made the weavings all the more unique. They couldn't part with their money fast enough."

Zaneta fingered the cloth and the spools of thread—blue, scarlet, and a saffron orange. Memories flooded back: their home by the sea, constantly filled with the chatter of her sisters and brothers; distilled images of the family gathered around the table, a meal of fish, pasta, and artichokes; the giant loom in one corner; and the clack-clack-clack of the shuttle as her mother worked the warp.

He prattled on. "So many soldiers are coming in and out of the port now, no one even bothered asking about my unit. There's a lot of action in Sicily still. The bartender directed me to an old house, one of those abandoned places by the shore, told me I might find someone who could tell me more about the thread. So I poked around but didn't find anyone—they're all empty—and found those. No more of that pretty gold thread, though. I hope you have more because that's what they wanted most. If I sell enough of that, I can probably score a ticket back home—or anywhere else I want."

When she didn't speak, he stepped closer. "What?"

She clutched the spools to her chest and forced herself to meet his eyes, although she could no longer stop her tears from coming. She was furious that this soldier had pawed through her home, oblivious to the lives that had once occupied it and the sacred craft they'd fashioned from the sea's bounty.

"What did you think," said Zaneta through gritted teeth, "when you saw the way the family must have left, with dishes in the sink and clothes on the line? When the smell of ruined food hit your nose? Did you imagine their panic? Their sorrow when they knew they'd have to leave the only home they'd ever known?" Her eyes flashed, and she stood trembling.

The soldier's exuberant smile faded as understanding dawned. "That bartender, he hinted that some of the weavers might have been Jews." His mouth twisted in a sneer of disgust. *"You."*

"I'm a weaver," she said. "What some call a water woman. Turn me in if you wish, or I can, like you say, make enough for you to sell. The byssus is priceless."

His eyes narrowed, and for a long time, he didn't speak. Zaneta longed to ask what else he'd seen, if anyone had asked where he'd found the weavings, if there was news about the war, but she held her tongue. It was obvious he no longer saw her as any sort of partner or helper; she'd become a means to an end. An expendable one at that.

"Yes. Yes, you will weave, and I'll sell it. No telling how much time is left—the Allies are making mincemeat of the Italians—so you must work fast. They liked the boats—do more like that one. And for the officers . . ." He removed his uniform jacket and thrust the armband at her. "This. A byssus swastika could line the pockets, eh? Wouldn't the Wehrmacht appreciate that?"

Zaneta's stomach lurched. The ugly black spider symbol was the last thing the sacred byssus should be used to create. But what choice did she have? She had to stay alive—it was her mother's last hope—and now that the soldier knew she was nothing but a Jew, her chances of survival had just diminished greatly. She nodded. Bile rose in her throat, and she lifted her chin. She would not be the one to break the line of water women.

They made a fast meal of the food he'd brought, saving most of it for later, and Zaneta's weaving began that same afternoon. The handheld lyre loom seemed even more precious now that she could work thread that had come so recently from her home. It was a fragile connection, but one she imagined she could feel vibrating through her fingers. On a chalk-gray square of wool, Zaneta wove the swastika as the soldier watched. She cringed under his gaze, wishing he would at least move about the room. His fixed stare unnerved her, and she had to pick out and rework several lines of thread more than once. Achingly, when he was gone to town, she had carefully picked out rows of byssus from the robe she'd worn for her water oath. The supply her mother had stashed in their bag had run out. Zaneta couldn't afford not to use it. If she told the soldier she'd run out, that her usefulness was done, what would stop him from ending her?

Each night, once the moon rose, they ventured out as before, but now he kept a visual leash on her, questioning her direction and intention, as if she suddenly had somewhere to run and hide. Zaneta estimated the calendar had reached mid-May, judging by the limited produce the soldier purchased at the port and the types of blooms she noticed appearing on the plains. He went down to the town about once a week, whenever she could produce a finished weaving, and he returned from the port agitated and restless, always spurring her to weave faster, more. He'd let slip there had been Allied raids on Sardegna, and at night, if she stole close enough to the high cliffs to see the black sea merging with the dark sky, Zaneta could sometimes see lights twinkle offshore, which had to be from navy ships, though at that distance, she couldn't make out whose side they might be on. She was agitated and restless, too, from missing the year's byssus harvest, hoping the bombs and fighting hadn't harmed the mussels in the cove, and being under the soldier's constant surveillance and direction. Grief hung on her shoulders like a constant yoke, and she willed herself not to think of her family. If she let herself dwell on them, so close to the war's possible end, she thought she might break in two. Her shoulders ached with tension, and hungry and thin as she was, her stomach often roiled as though she'd had too much to eat. Exhaustion gripped her in its fist.

One night, Zaneta collected a handful of early almonds from a scraggly grove. She had just pocketed the nuts when her spine prickled, a primitive wariness. Zaneta whirled to find the soldier had come up behind her, his hand on his holstered gun. He stood so close she could smell the unwashed uniform and his musky sweat. When she turned, he didn't bother to step away but beheld her with hooded eyes, forcing her with his physical presence to move backward into the almond branches.

"I—I think I'm done here," she stammered, the bitter taste of one of the almonds acrid on her tongue.

He moved swiftly, grabbed the back of her head, and tangled his hand in her hair. Zaneta didn't scream. If someone heard, it would only bring more trouble. He seemed to consider her a moment, and she wondered what he might read in her eyes—contempt, defiance? Could he fathom the hatred that simmered there?

His eyes raked over her face, the dirty smudges that surely streaked her cheeks, the shape of her chin and nose that betrayed her ancestry. Zaneta tried not to wince as her neck twisted. She met his gaze and slowed her breathing. She would not be afraid of this deserter, not when her family faced worse. A collective of voices vibrated inside her with a rising chorus: the song of the sea, reaching from the past to lend its strength to her. Something in him seemed to shift, and he jerked his hand away as if he'd received a jolt. He shook his head at her, and she imagined he almost laughed. She was a pawn, nothing more, useful for now, but once her usefulness was done?

They walked silently back to the well room, but his actions had quickened something in Zaneta, a renewed resolve to see the end of this war, to swim in her sea and embrace her family again. The helplessness and despair she'd felt for so many months in hiding had shifted. A palpable rage had been slowly climbing its way from the depths of her, a rage built from pointless loss, deprivation, and destruction. What could this one soldier do to her that hadn't already been done? As she felt the rising of this new emotion, Zaneta somehow knew it was preparing her for something, a resolve to act, to save herself and thereby preserve her family and its legacy.

As she picked her way through the scrubby plain, she let her thoughts drift. She imagined the day—she'd been no more than six or seven—she'd swum to the cove with her sisters and her mother. Dark clouds had drifted overhead after they'd arrived, and her mother had hurried them along, not wanting to be caught out in lightning. At first, Zaneta dove and surfaced with the others, but when the first fat raindrops plinked divots into the water's surface, she'd let herself sink to the sandy bottom, where she could observe the rainstorm from below. Schools of silver-scaled fish swirled as usual—water was nothing unusual to them; it came from above, below, and everywhere. But for Zaneta, the sound changed from simple current and waves to a kind of static hiss like trying to find a station on an old radio. The zigzag pattern of sunlight across the rocks disappeared as the water darkened, and from where she sat, the upside-down surface of the sea looked like hammered pewter, gray and pockmarked where the raindrops left their imprints.

The soldier couldn't follow her there, when she sank or drifted in the sea in her mind. There, the water enfolded Zaneta like a blanket, her memory of her life before safe in its embrace. It became a useful exercise, especially when the soldier toyed with her, demanding favors besides food or weavings. She couldn't run, so she floated in her imaginary sea. Zaneta spent more and more time letting her mind wander to the waves, recalling the path to the cove, the cry of the gulls, and the darting schools of fish that moved as one. She reminded herself that the knowledge she held, the skill her hands knew, was as secret to this man as her father's box filled with their family treasures wedged in the cave wall. Holding that knowledge close gave Zaneta some small comfort.

One afternoon, two months since the incident in the almond trees, as he watched her weave, stretched lazily against a wall, Zaneta noticed idly that since he'd been able to go out in the day, to linger at the shore and lift his face to the sky, his pale face had become bronzed. She looked forward to his trips to the port for obvious reasons but also because, maybe perversely, she knew that when he returned, he would bring with him the salt smell of the sea, tiny shells and sand still plugging the treads of his boots.

"I'm thinking of a story from when I was a child," he told her. "Watching you weave on that little loom reminded me. In German we call it *Rumpelstilzchen*—do you know it?"

"Tremotino," said Zaneta. "I think it's the same. In Italian, it means 'little earthquake.'"

He shrugged. "No matter. There's a girl spinning straw into gold for the king, right? It's a strange tale. Rumpelstilzchen was a goblin, I think, some wretched creature." He laughed. "You'd probably say that's my role in the story. He gets rich in the end from all the gold, if I remember."

Zaneta didn't respond. The last time the soldier returned from the port, he'd been in a state, pacing and muttering. The island's port was emptying of soldiers, he said, and she detected traces of worry in his face. Slivers and hints of information were all she could pry from him, and even that was grudgingly given. But she gathered that by July 1943, the Allies had taken the neighbor island of Sicily. The soldier spat in the dust every time he mentioned the treachery of Italy and its so-called partnership with Germany. He told her Prime Minister Mussolini had been arrested, and Germany now fought against its former ally, which, it turned out, hadn't been truly all-in from the start. The soldier tortured her with the news he'd gathered. Despite the weak stomach of some Italians and the pathetic pockets of resistance groups that persisted in working against it, Italy's Jews, especially in the north, continued to be deported. He thought surely Italy would be rid of all of them soon. The Germans were gathering quite a population of Italian POWs as they retreated back north. He dangled that before her, amused by the anguish in her response. Zaneta thought she'd cracked a tooth, biting back her emotions and the words she wanted to hurl at him when he happily delivered news he expected would hurt her. Round and round her thoughts tumbled. Did the emptying port mean the war's end? Could she return to her home in a month? A week? Would that mean the return of those who'd been taken away?

All of that would have been enough to deal with, but Zaneta reasoned that her island of Sardegna floated far south of Germany, and now that the port was empty of his comrades, the soldier was alone, and he needed a way home. He couldn't hide his accent. He'd told her the officers so keen on relieving him of his byssus wares had gone. Every day, Zaneta would catch him counting the lire he'd collected, assuring himself he had enough for transportation off the island. He could hire a boat, he said, but the tricky part would be finding false papers. Why he told her all this, she didn't know.

It was true, the soldier was the imp in the Rumpelstilzchen story, gaining riches from her weaving of the golden thread, making bargains, and pretending to help her out of being a prisoner. She remembered the story well. She had a mind for oral history and, like all water women, was a keeper of stories. In the story, the girl discovered the imp's weakness—his name—and was able to slip out of the impossible bargains she'd struck. She knew he was a deserter. That small bit of damning information alone would certainly be enough for him to get rid of her. He still had his gun. It would be easy enough.

The soldier's growing desperation made him more dangerous. Zaneta was under no illusions about what awaited her once he no longer had use for her—her fate now lay in her own hands.

Seek and you shall find. Sant'Antioco had provided. From Zaneta's first taste of early almonds back in the spring—auspicious, considering the timing—a seed had germinated. She recalled the bright-yellow blossoms of honeysuckle azaleas she'd seen near the almond trees and the dead one, its trunk shriveled and hollow.

"I noticed something by the almond trees," Zaneta said. "Tonight, if we bring that empty jar from the pickles you found, I may have something to fill it."

"A surprise? Have you been keeping a secret, Fräulein?" he asked.

In the moonlight, it was hard to find the tree she remembered, but finally Zaneta found it and picked her way through the low underbrush until she was close enough to give it a sharp shake. Sure enough, a low hum rose and fell inside.

"It's a bee tree," she told him. "There'll be honey inside."

"No joke?" He held his light aloft and, striking a match, lit the stout bundle of sticks and dead leaves she'd given him to carry.

"Problem is, it's dark, so they'll all be inside instead of out foraging. If you wave that around the entrance, it'll help."

The soldier took a step back. "You're going to stick your hand in there? Ha! Be my guest, but I'll just stand over here." He handed her the smoking bundle and retreated.

Zaneta set her mouth in a line. Was she really surprised at his cowardice? For the first time in a long time, she sang, slowly at first, the familiar mix of Nuragic, Hebrew, and Italian, and then, as her courage rose, a little louder to soothe the bees. She thrust the end of the smoldering bundle into the opening in the tree trunk and held it there a few seconds. The buzz increased inside, but only a few bees flew out to investigate. The rest, she knew, were head-deep in open honeycomb, the smoke signaling them to eat their fill and be ready to flee.

"Have the jar ready," she called back to the soldier.

Slow and steady, Zaneta eased her hand inside the entrance, angled downward, until her fingers hit the soft and pliable wax comb. Bees covered her hand and crawled up her arm. The only thing she knew to do was hum, the melody of the sea songs comforting her even if these landlocked insects knew nothing of the sea and its mysteries. Her fingers poked into something moist, and she knew she'd hit some honey stores. She thrust her fingers through the comb. It was only about an inch thick; she broke through and tore off a piece small enough to pull back out the entrance. Slowly, slowly. More smoke, ignoring the ones crawling up her shoulder, buzzing furiously as they stuck in her hair.

"Jar. Jar," she whispered, her voice hoarse from the acrid smoke. The soldier pushed it to her across the ground using a broken branch, his arm stretched as far as it would reach. Zaneta couldn't help her exasperation at his timidity as she stood elbow-deep in the hive itself. She gave the piece of comb a sharp shake to get the bees off and jammed it into the jar. He covered the jar with a sack, and she went back for more, repeating the process. After she'd removed a third piece of comb, the hum in the hive had intensified. Zaneta kept humming, kept breathing steadily. She dropped the smoking bundle on the ground outside the hive entrance and backed away.

"They're all over you!" he barked, and he moved to brush them off.

"Don't," she ordered. Zaneta stood still as a stone, waiting, humming. The bees were not happy, but neither were they suited for flying at night, and the sound of the workers in the hive, already busy repairing the torn comb, lured most of them off her until she was able to shake the others free. She started to lick her fingers but stopped.

"Amazing!" the soldier exclaimed. "Bravo." He waited while she washed in one of the freshwater pools nearby, and they walked back to the well house. He couldn't stop opening the jar, running his fingers around the edges where the honey had dripped, smacking his lips as he licked the sticky gold stuff from his hands.

"I can't believe you didn't get stung," he said. "Don't you want some?" He held the jar out to her, but Zaneta shook her head.

"Too sweet. It hurts my teeth," she lied. "And I did get stung. Four or five times at least, but no matter. It's a special treat. Since you might be leaving soon." She cut her eyes at him as they walked, thinking he was just arrogant enough to believe that she could have developed some affection for him, might actually miss him when he was gone.

"Wild honey straight from the hive," he raved. "It's delicious and still warm."

"Glad you like it. Eat all you want. You can chew the comb, too. Get every last drop."

And that's what the soldier did when they reached the well house. It had been a long time since they'd tasted sweetness, and he licked the jar clean like a bear fresh from hibernation, savoring the honey until he was sated. Zaneta laid several handfuls of almonds on a sack between them, and these he ate, too, until they were gone. He didn't seem to notice she ate nothing, busy with her weaving, occupied by the byssus.

Toward daylight, in the early hours, the soldier woke with a start. Zaneta sat in the same position, the lyre loom in her hand. She'd watched as he dozed and was not surprised when his eyes sought her out in the dim light.

"Wrong?" he choked. "Wha-what happened?"

"What do you mean, Jan?" Zaneta's voice was low and measured, just above a whisper. If he noticed she'd used his given name, he didn't say so.

"Can't . . . what's wrong with me?" He was groggy, his speech slurred.

"It was probably too much honey," she said. "You ate so much of it. Greedy, if you want me to be honest."

He strained to look at his hands and legs, blinking his eyes slowly in confusion.

"Hexe! Strega." She laughed when he used the words. No matter which language, it was plain he meant *witch*, a common accusation in her line of ancestors. He managed to inch away from the wall, his limbs flapping and twitching.

"Bees are funny creatures. They only forage on one source of nectar at a time, and this time of year, they cover those particular yellow flowers. It's fine for the bees, but that nectar is poisonous to people."

He groaned and fumbled forward, his eyes on the steps, as if he thought he might climb out and get help, but Zaneta ignored him. She stood and leaned over him, slid his gun from its holster while his eyes widened in outrage. "I'll tell you a story. Do you know," she told him, "in ancient Turkey, Roman soldiers overran the city of Ephesus? If you've never met them, let me tell you the Turks are a notably hospitable people, and they offered those soldiers honey with their supper—the same kind of mad honey you ate, actually. It didn't take long for the natural toxin to paralyze the soldiers. As the story goes, the Turks took their revenge and got their city back.

"The sweetness of that honey masks the taste of the almonds. I don't know about Germany." Zaneta wrinkled her nose. "We Italians love to make amaretti and lots of dishes with almonds, but you must be careful, you see. The bitter ones, like those you ate, are filled with cyanide. Even a little can be bad for you." Beads of sweat formed on the soldier's brow as he grimaced with what must have been terrible contractions of his bowels. "I wish you'd never come here," she said, blinking back tears. "I wish none of this had happened." Her voice broke, finally. "I know I'm just a Jew to you, less than nothing, but that's no excuse. I told you that byssus cannot be sold. It's against the sacred way of things."

The soldier growled, his contempt clear even now. His breath came in wheezes and gasps as he used the last of his energy to push himself toward her. With a weak swipe of his arm, he managed to send her lyre loom skittering across the floor, and Zaneta yelped. It clattered against stone somewhere in the darkness. The loom! As she turned to leap after it, the soldier's hand closed around her ankle, and she fell on one knee, wincing as it smashed against the stone floor. Zaneta jerked away from the touch of his clammy fingers. He was weak now, too weak to hold her. Still, she recoiled, instinctively kicking at him with her other foot.

He half scooted, half rolled away from the blows. Zaneta didn't pity him; she pictured her mother's face nodding from the back of that truck, intent on her daughter's escape. At first, Zaneta was confused when her foot suddenly kicked at nothing. Then she saw his dim form disappearing into the darkness. An odd thump echoed in the room, then a terrible silence. Zaneta scrambled up, her eyes straining to search the ashy shadows. The well. She dropped to all fours and felt her way along the stone until the well's maw opened before her. As her hand waved over the black void, she thought she heard a faint exhale of breath from below.

Zaneta sat back against the wall, a safe distance away from the well's edge, and pulled her knees up to her chin. It wouldn't be long. She estimated he would be dead before dawn.

Chapter 20

By September, Zaneta had contracted malaria from being forced to be outside during prime mosquito hours, still scavenging what she could find from the land. The memory of that last meal of cooked fish with the soldier could still make her mouth water. She was amazed she could even think of food, given her overused gag reflex over the past weeks while the soldier's body moldered at the bottom of the well. When she could see that next morning, she'd tossed the evil black gun in after him. She'd kept the flashlight.

Though she scoured every inch of the stone floor, she couldn't find the lyre loom. The soldier must have knocked it over the edge just before he'd fallen in. Its loss hit Zaneta like a fist. It was her last connection to her mother and their work together. It had kept her sane, occupying her hands during the hours of idle time she'd been cloistered here. Perhaps it was her price to pay for what she'd done. Hands of the water women should deliver peace and grace through the sea's gifts, and she'd sullied them. She would bear the loss of the loom as a penance.

Zaneta hadn't thought far enough ahead about having to share the space with the soldier's smelly corpse, but by then it was too late; she spent as much time as possible outside or sitting on the highest steps where she could breathe the fresh air. She took to singing again like she had before the soldier had appeared. The songs of her mother and sisters soothed her fevered brain and led her to dream of the sea, still rolling and obeying the moon's pull even if she couldn't see it.

One night, in a haze of delirium, Zaneta leaned against an outcrop of rock and tried to make sense of what she was seeing. The violet sky above erupted in colors, bursts of white and red falling in streams like anemones stretching in a tide pool. At first, she thought the explosions must be a new kind of bomb, part of the never-ending Allied air raids, but the wind that night—she thought it was a dream—carried less familiar sounds, laughter and singing. Zaneta discerned the traditional Italian melodies that had once been a staple in her childhood. *Fireworks.* The word came to her, finally, as she idly observed the strange sight playing out beneath the lemon slice of a moon.

It had to be a good sign. No one would risk such a thing if there was danger of inciting a raid. A weary heaviness weighed upon Zaneta like wet sand. She pulled herself upright and shook off the dizziness that made her vision swim. Was it over? Had the war ended? Zaneta stumbled as her leaden feet, of their own accord, followed the path down the hillside for the first time since she'd fled. She tried to recall how long ago that had been. Ten months? Twelve? She'd lost count.

She wanted—she wasn't sure what she wanted exactly—to swim in the sea with her sisters; to eat with her family, laughing and teasing; and to see her friends again. Most of all, she wanted to hug her mother and tell her she was sorry for running, for leaving them as she had. She imagined walking through her front door and seeing them all sitting at the table. Zaneta's heart leaped like a porpoise, spurred by the spark of hope that had flared inside her. Her feet scuffled forward. She didn't know to what end. She was vaguely aware she wasn't thinking clearly, but she couldn't remain in the nuragic well house for another minute with the ghost of the soldier moaning in a voice only she could hear.

A miracle. Her home stood intact by the shore, its windows glowing bright green and yellow from the light show over the water. Zaneta's hand closed over the cold knob, and she pushed the door open. It was mostly how she remembered. Sand had been tracked in over the floor, of course, and the cabinets pillaged for food. The loom stood in the corner, the shadows of its structure stretching across the wall and onto the ceiling, almost as if it were spreading wide its arms to welcome her back. For a moment, her stomach lurched, and Zaneta shuddered. She imagined the greedy soldier here, his hands casually rummaging through the tidy bins of thread, his eyes falling on their photos, the clothes that hung in the closet, their shoes abandoned by the front door.

She'd never been so tired in her life. With her last bit of energy, she moved toward the bedroom she'd shared with her sisters. In front of the window hung a whimsical mobile Dahlia had made—stars, moon, and sun that would sparkle with light when the sun hit the byssus edges just right. The sight of it caused hot tears to sting Zaneta's nose. She reached a finger out to touch one of the stars, and the mobile danced and circled, sending shadows spinning across the ceiling. She collapsed on the bed nearest the door and pulled the quilt up to her nose, scooting until her back pressed against the wall. Her eyes followed the dancing moon and stars until she drifted into an exhausted sleep.

The brisk songs of greenfinches and warblers outside the window woke her. Zaneta's eyes opened slowly as her brain registered that she lay in a bed instead of on the cold stone floor next to the well.

"It *is* you," a voice whispered. Zaneta froze. "Zaneta? Don't be afraid. It's me."

The fog in her brain receded, and her eyes focused on the man who sat on the bed opposite hers, Marta's bed. Zaneta scrambled to her feet, weak and dizzy.

She recognized the dark curls and tanned face, kind eyes, and upturned mouth. "Luccio?" Seeing someone she knew—who knew *her*—took her breath. She'd lost count of the months she'd been denied such a gift. She must have looked a mess. How long since she'd had a proper washing?

"I saw the door open on my way home and came in to make sure everything was secure. I've been keeping an eye on the place since—well, since your family left. I can't believe it's you."

It was too much. Zaneta threw herself against him, this boy—man—she hardly knew, really, and buried her face in his chest, the sobs welling up from a place so deep inside she'd hardly known it had existed. Luccio held just as tight, letting her go on until she'd cried herself out, his arms the first safe place she'd known in too long.

When she'd finished, composing herself finally as she wiped her eyes and sniffled, she stepped away and looked up at him, full of questions she didn't know how to ask.

"Sit," he said. "I'll get you something to eat and we'll talk." She did as she was told, sitting at the kitchen table and running her palms over its surface while he opened a sack and set out fruit and smoked fish, a jug of water, and a loaf of bread. Zaneta tried to remember manners, willed herself not to tear apart the meal like a wild animal. Luccio held back, gestured for her to eat all she wanted.

"Go ahead. I snacked while you slept. I'm not hungry." In spite of this, Zaneta heard his stomach grumble while she devoured every crumb.

"Thank you," she said between bites. "This tastes like heaven."

"You've been sick." It wasn't a question. "You're very pale." His brow creased with concern.

Zaneta nodded. "Malaria, I think. I've been taking doses of wormwood. But it's been a while since I've sat in the sun." She waved away the subject. "Tell me. What news?"

"We surrendered to the Allies. Sardegna is done with the war, I hope. It's been hell. I'm sorry, Zeta." He used his nickname for her. In spite of herself, Zaneta smiled. "Over in Kefalonia, Italy resisted the Germans, but it was no good. They outright killed all the POWs as some kind of punishment."

"The Greek island?" Zaneta swallowed a swig of water to wash down the lump of bread that stuck in her throat. "What do you know?"

Luccio shook his head. "I've been watching the postings for families from the village. There've been so many losses. Every family. Between the fighting and the air raids, hardly anyone lives in the houses along the shore anymore."

"And the deportations," she said. "Don't forget those."

"Yes." His shoulders sagged. "I thought you'd been taken when the trucks came. Where have you been, Zeta? How did you get back here?"

She shrugged. "I found a place. It doesn't matter."

Luccio drew in a deep breath, like he was fortifying himself to tell her something. "I saw a soldier here, at your house. A German." She stopped chewing. "Not long after, I heard talk at the port about a weaver able to spin gold. They passed around the byssus pieces in the tavern like it was an auction block. I hoped . . ."

"Anyone else?" Zaneta hardly dared ask it.

Luccio hung his head. "No one's heard from any of them since they were taken," he admitted. "The other families—weavers like yours—are gone. The only reason this house wasn't looted more was that I kept watch and claimed it belonged to a relative of ours."

Zaneta swallowed hard. No one? None of them were left? Perhaps they might still return. Perhaps they hadn't been allowed to send letters back home from wherever they'd gone. "Well. I'm grateful." Already, the seed of resentment sprouted, that she should be grateful for what was rightfully hers and her family's.

"I don't expect gratitude, Zeta. I wish I could've done more. I wish I'd known where you were."

"No, it wouldn't have been safe. It was best I was alone." She realized the lie as she spoke it; she had hardly been alone.

Luccio reached across the table and held her hands. "I have to tell you: Avi and Lev were on the list of POWs executed at Kefalonia. More than that, I don't know. But I'll help you. We'll find the others."

Zaneta let the tears stream and hung her head. Her brothers dead. She said nothing.

"The war's not over yet, but I think here the noose is loosening. I've still got the boat, and the fish haven't gone anywhere. The byssus is still there." At that, Zaneta lifted her head. "I sailed near there just a day or so ago. I kept a watch on it, in case." He stopped, held her gaze. His earnestness made her want to weep. "I'll take you to the cove when you're feeling better. I'm going to go to the clinic today. I'll get something for the malaria."

"The wormwood will work," she said. "I've collected enough and know how to fix it. Thank you, Luccio. I'm so glad you were here. It—hasn't been easy."

He squeezed her hands again. "Let me help you. I can't tell you how happy I was to find you here, sleeping, like an angel had visited, appearing out of nowhere. It may take a while. We've all been through a lot. But I believe everyone longs for things to go back to how they were. The things that have been in the news . . ." He trailed off. "People are trying to face what's happened. I think you're safe here. It's your home."

Zaneta smiled at him. Besides her animal hunger, she still wore her wariness like a cloak. True, it was a comfort to have Luccio here, his familiar voice and face, a reminder of better days. She could use the help—she had only the house and didn't know when or if she'd see her parents and sisters again. Already, she realized, she'd relegated her brothers to memory. She'd wondered how her neighbors would receive her, but Luccio had been reassuring. Luccio, with his dark beard and merry smile, had always been kind to her and her family, a good friend.

"Your family, Luccio? How are they?"

"They left for Assisi. There were rumors it was safer. The air raids here were constant, German Krauts everywhere, and you know Mamma can't see well. So I stayed. This place—Sant'Antioco—I couldn't live anywhere else, and I wanted to do what I could so there might be something to return to." Zaneta remembered that about him: how he loved the island and its waters, much like she did, but for different reasons.

"A church there helped them out. Friend of a friend, everyone's pulling all their strings these days. Leo, my younger brother, got involved in a group there, helping shelter Jewish families." Luccio swallowed hard, took a breath. "He was caught. Shot in the street, and the rest were arrested and sent north." His mouth set in a firm line.

"I'm sorry," she whispered. A ridiculous response. Words that solved nothing.

"Yes," he said. "And here I am. And here you are."

Zaneta nodded. It was what they had left, tatters of the life they'd each lived before the war. Though she was barely sixteen and Luccio not much more than that, they'd aged beyond their years. She rose from the table and moved toward him, touched his shoulder. He stood with her, only hesitating a moment before he drew her to him, the top of her head tucked neatly beneath his chin. Whether for shared solace or in memoriam of some long-past flirtation, the embrace signified some new, unspoken agreement.

Zaneta mentally tallied what they shared in common: loss, loneliness, survival, guilt. In the positive column, there were memories of each other's families, happier times, and a love of the island and its gifts. Between them, perhaps it was enough to make a whole person, live a whole life. Alone, she wasn't sure she had the strength for it.

Chapter 21

They married quickly and soon became Luccio and Zaneta Mazza, a young Italian family with a baby in tow. She came early, Zaneta still recovering from malaria in her half-starved and weakened state. They celebrated their daughter Mira's first birthday the same week Italian airwaves carried news of Mussolini's execution and, two days later, Hitler's suicide. Photos of the work camps had already begun surfacing, and Zaneta sank into a distant and dark pool, where breath seemed casually optional. She hardly noticed when Luccio came home from throwing his nets to find the curtains drawn and the baby wailing, her frightened eyes wide on her little, tearstained face. It wasn't the baby's fault, of course, but Zaneta, though she knew it was unreasonable, even cruel, heard the baby's cries as confirmation that the weight of her sorrow made her incapable of mothering. It seemed pointless to even try when she felt so empty. How could she provide or nurture anything from her endless well of nothing? Sometimes the thought of caregiving made her so ill she'd pull the baby from her breast as she nursed, unable to bear even the touch of her small, needy fingers.

Luccio, the voice of reason, learned to take over when the clouds of Zaneta's moods gathered. He paced the floor with Mira over his shoulder, shushing and bouncing her until she quieted. He took her for walks by the sea to get her out of the house, out of her mother's earshot, and Zaneta winced, seeing them from the window as they sang, splashed on the shore, and spotted the birds dipping and gliding above the water.

She wanted to be good—to be a good mother, do good in the world. She did love Mira in her way, protected her and taught her words and songs, but whenever a ray of that light trickled into her heart, it would just as suddenly snuff out, driven back by the shadow memories of that dark time hiding in the ruins. If she happened to let a moment of happiness in, or find her lips curving in a smile at the sight of Luccio and Mira together, her broken heart whispered her disloyalty to the memory of her family. In this way, her love for Mira was fractured, never quite solid and sure, the fissure too deep to heal.

In time, Zaneta told Luccio about the soldier, as much as he needed to know. He'd guessed, actually, remembering the one he'd witnessed selling her woven byssus creations for profit at the port. What she didn't say, among other things: *I poisoned him and left him in a well to rot.* Not because she feared Luccio's response—had he been there, he would've done the same, or worse, on her behalf—but because of her terrifying lack of remorse. It was the same dead absence of feeling that sometimes crashed upon her like a wave when she watched Mira play or eat. Survival was one thing, but what kind of person responded that way to a baby? Zaneta cowered from the inky shadows that wavered inside of her. No water woman should harbor such things. She was a disgrace to her line.

"No one needs to know about the deserter or that you had anything to do with him," Luccio assured her. "And we have Mira to live for now, and each other."

"*I'll* know," Zaneta had replied. "How can she be here while they're not?"

"She's a baby," he pointed out, as if she hadn't pushed the child out of her own body. "Hope that life goes on. Wouldn't your mother be grateful for that?"

Zaneta snapped, "She's not here. It's not so simple. Not for me. I'm trying."

Slowly, their community restored itself. The homes of the weaver families remained empty. Zaneta and Luccio, after a long while, hesitantly entered them one by one. Zaneta had decided, as part of carrying on their tradition, that she would gather what byssus and tools she could from them. It would honor them to put it to use. They also collected photos and other items and kept them in a small trunk, a labeled collection of history that would preserve their memory and work. Zaneta, on Luccio's arm at first, ventured back into town to the post office and the market. She held her head high, defiant and brusque, so different from the shy girl she'd been. When someone met her gaze, they would inevitably be the one to look away, and Zaneta felt some satisfaction in seeing their shame, even if it went unspoken and unacknowledged. They couldn't deny what had happened here. Yes, they'd all lost family members in the war, but some of them had been eliminated outright. For a solid year, the town seemed a shell of itself, the once vibrant and lively port making a careful and tentative return to the way it once was. People were weary. More than a few families struggled after the war, having lost their main wage earners.

But gradually the cafés opened and people ventured out to visit one another with cautious smiles and offers of condolences—*"Mi dispiace. Mi dispiace"*—until Zaneta was sick of hearing the phrase, sick of saying it. It didn't fix anything, didn't call any water women back to the island, had there been any left. Zaneta was the only one.

Since the war's official end, it seemed the lists were endless. Lists of casualties, name after name on the dreaded rosters printed in the papers or posted near the port: soldiers, civilians, prisoners, wounded. Separate lists came out tallying those liberated from the so-called work camps and seeking family members, so many lost or displaced. Zaneta's trembling finger ran down the lists as often as they appeared, searching for the Renda name, stockpiling grains of hope each time she failed to find it. Those grains vanished the day Luccio came home clutching a page he'd torn from the paper. Zaneta took one look at his face, gone pale, and snatched it from his hand.

Johann Renda, Allegra Renda, Marta Renda. The names of her parents and sister leaped off the paper. Three more statistics from the war, but Zaneta's entire life. She had proof now, certainty she would never see them again. Except for Dahlia. Her remaining sister's name was missing, and Zaneta clung to that fact like a jealous miser, vaulting it in her heart.

Slowly, slowly, Sant'Antioco recovered. The colorful fishing boats came back, taking their rightful places where the ugly gray naval vessels had previously crowded the docks. The empty bakery case filled once more as rations lifted and staples like sugar and salt became available again. Signor Sanna, the dry goods shop owner, beckoned to Zaneta when she passed in the street on one of her visits to town.

She stepped inside the familiar store, its shelves still sparse. "Signora Mazza," he said. "Once these windows had a display of the island's byssus."

Zaneta looked at him pointedly. "Yes, I know."

He had the grace to cast his eyes to the floor and squirm uncomfortably. "The Germans had never seen anything like them. I should have thought to take down the display when the soldiers started to arrive, but they'd always hung there, a testament to our island." He was stammering. "I didn't think."

Zaneta sighed. No one ever did. "I had heard they were buying byssus weavings in the port," she said. Let him wonder how she could've heard that, where she might have been all this time. She didn't have a numbered tattoo on her arm, but she'd suffered in her own way. "I was sorry to hear it." She wouldn't let him off the hook so easily.

He spread his hands. "What could we do? With a gun in your face, you handed them what they asked for."

"Mmm." They certainly did. She placed her hands on the counter to steady herself.

"Could you," he began. "I mean to say, would you, Signora, honor us again with something to hang in the window?" He met her eyes, and this time he didn't look away.

Zaneta thought of her mother then. She would have gladly agreed. It was about the byssus, not them. "I would." She nodded. "I may have some things already at home I can bring in next week. It might show people that perhaps the war didn't take everything."

~

As part of the war recovery, the island hosted hundreds of workers who claimed to be on a mission to get rid of the rampant malaria. It was the worst region in all of Italy, they said. Since the Germans had flooded so many inland areas to hamper Allied soldiers, it seemed everyone they knew had battled malaria in the past year. It rattled Zaneta's nerves when they repeatedly knocked on their door and came in to dust every inch of their home, dousing them each in clouds of the marvel they called DDT. It had halted the typhus epidemic in Naples, they said, a lifesaving miracle. *Lifesaving,* Zaneta scoffed. *Suddenly they're concerned about lives?*

When the sun warmed the sea and stretched its yellow fingers to the rocks and sand on the shoreline, Zaneta swam. Whenever she could, she left Mira with Luccio and lingered in the cove of *Pinna nobilis*, letting the water carry her weight and absorb her tears until she could no longer tell the difference between the salt water that held her and that which leaked from her eyes. Often, she swam and harvested with ghosts. Her memory conjured the songs and chatter of their lively group, bantering and laughing away an afternoon. Underwater, her eye would catch the shadow of a cloud passing above, and she'd turn swiftly, thinking her sister had appeared at her elbow, offering to hold the basket. She hummed to herself as she walked back home along the sand, but it was her mother's voice that echoed in the melody. Alone, Zaneta felt the pull of the byssus more than ever. Luccio, a child of the island himself, understood the heritage and her passion for it, but he could never feel it the way she did, bound to the line of those who'd gone before.

"I'm so happy your harvest is going well, Zeta," he said to her. "You should have enough to make bracelets for every bride and baby in the area soon!"

She nodded. "There's lots to do. It'll take me a while to prepare all the dyes by myself." People had begun to visit the house again. Word of the weaver had spread. Now that they knew one of the water women had returned, they were eager for blessings from the byssus, hungry for any sort of salve for their hearts and good fortune for a happier future. No one spoke of what might have become of the once vibrant group of the byssus artists.

"Maybe the three of us can take some time for a walk? Maybe something different, like a picnic on the plains?"

Zaneta stiffened. "You can take the baby if you want. I probably won't have time."

"Surely the byssus can rest for a day?" Luccio nudged. "It's survived pretty well, wouldn't you say?"

She regarded her husband. "Yes, I suppose it has, despite everything. But now that I'm here, instead of leaving it for a vacation, I'd rather do what I can to protect it. It's hardly enough."

"To honor them, you mean."

Zaneta bowed her head and kept rinsing the tangled strands she'd harvested that morning. Luccio pulled the wicker picnic basket from the cabinet by the back door. "We'll miss you, then," he said.

At the window above the sink, she watched them go, Luccio bouncing Mira in his arms with each step. He was probably singing to her or telling her a story. The child patted her father's whiskers and gazed up at him. Some part of Zaneta wished she could join them, a happy family on a sunny day, but the cloak of sadness she wore was too heavy to throw off. She watched until they disappeared around the corner and, with a sigh, bent her head to continue her work alone.

Theirs wasn't a marriage of overt physical passion, though there were moments when they turned to one another. Two more children joined their family—both boys, Johann and Isaac, to Luccio's delight. The youngest was a difficult delivery; there had been a close call and a flurry of decisions before a last-minute surgery that meant no more children. No more daughters. Zaneta's penance, it would seem, continued. She girded her loins to teach Mira the craft.

For the most part, she had to admit, the child was bright and applied herself well, eager to please. Zaneta was as exacting and as careful as possible with her lessons. They were beginning again, braiding the tenuous thread of water women in the hope that it would strengthen enough to continue. Mira had to know the importance of this task; she couldn't be allowed to take it lightly. So, of course, Zaneta showed little leniency, gave little praise. Mira needed to learn to work the byssus right. Everything depended on it.

Life wasn't always sunshine and roses; Mira had to understand that so that she could prepare for hardship and be able to persevere, although the girl seemed oblivious much of the time. Zaneta worked through the days despite—or perhaps because of—the grief that sometimes descended upon her like a thick flock of black crows, cawing and beating their wings so loudly that it drowned out all else.

As the years passed, she and Luccio never stopped trying to find her sister Dahlia. New data banks and organizations helped families trace individuals they'd lost in the war. After years of corresponding with such places, Zaneta finally received the news she'd dreaded. There was proof, an eyewitness statement of Dahlia Renda being part of a group execution in a forest in Poland. Nothing more. No explanation of how she'd arrived, why she'd been separated from the rest of the family, nothing.

It was in that moment, when Zaneta had just learned her sister's fate through a few sparse sentences on a single thin page, that young, school-aged Mira had burst into the kitchen, blathering about a dance. *A dance.* How could the world go on dancing when Dahlia lay in an unmarked forest grave? An image of the soldier's face swam before Zaneta's eyes. She imagined him laughing, mocking her, calling her Fräulein. His face blurred into Mira's, the daughter who stood before her in her own kitchen, and Zaneta had lashed out.

Luccio, she knew, tried to keep the peace and mend the rifts between them, but what could he do? He couldn't pass on the craft or teach the thousands of things Mira needed to learn. She would have to make the best of it and hope the girl would toughen up. Someday, when Mira took the water oath, the yoke that had pinched and bruised Zaneta's neck for years would ease a little. Still, just the two of them remained in the line of water women. Zaneta had stopped believing any of the other families might return.

Mira was capable of weaving beautiful pieces, she could complete the process in her sleep, and she was probably one of the strongest swimmers on Sant'Antioco. Some of the weavings that hung in Signor Sanna's dry goods window had come from Mira's trained hands, the designs all her own. Zaneta dared hope that when Mira grew old enough to marry and have children of her own, what she'd worked for all along would come to pass: the line would continue despite everything. She had tried her best to ensure Mira knew this responsibility and would step into the role as she herself had. Zaneta had made a silk purse from a sow's ear.

In Zaneta's later years, some afternoons, when the honeyed light fell through the studio's windows just so and the sound of the clacking loom and their humming in unison made a sweet rhythm, Zaneta almost—fleetingly—let herself forget. She could almost imagine she was back in her childhood home, surrounded by the songs of her sisters and mother. Then, a part of Zaneta mourned the missed opportunities with Mira, her sole daughter, the connection she'd shared with her own mother that she might have shared in turn. Back then, she couldn't allow herself the indulgence.

"When will you stop punishing yourself, Zeta?" Luccio asked her once. "It wasn't a crime to survive the war."

"Am I punishing myself?" she'd asked.

"Yourself and Mira," he'd said. And then, "All of us a little, I think."

"You're a good man, Luccio," Zaneta said, the corners of her mouth drawn into a sad, resigned smile.

"I still see my vibrant Zaneta Renda in there from before the war. Only glimpses, though. It makes me sad you keep her locked inside." He poked a gentle finger at her heart and stroked her graying hair, his fingers firm and strong. Zaneta blinked back tears.

"I can't forget."

"Of course not," he replied. "But we can make better things to remember." A row of white teeth shone bright as the ends of his mustache curved in a smile. "We can do things differently."

"You mean *I* can," she said.

"Maybe I carried things okay, but that doesn't mean they weren't heavy."

Zaneta laid her head on Luccio's chest, and he tucked his chin over the top of it. She remembered the day she'd come back to this house, when she'd stumbled in and fallen asleep in her sister's bed, exhausted and sick. Luccio had been there then, and he was here still. A weariness had settled deep into Zaneta's bones, weighing down her heart like an undertow, much like how she'd felt that day she'd ventured back from the well. Maybe Luccio was right. She didn't know if she could keep dragging the past and its load through the wet sand anymore.

"Zeta." It was a question. Would she let him help her learn how to live? She tilted her chin up at Luccio, where a wellspring of hope shone in his eyes. "You only drown if you stay in the water. I'm giving you my hand. Take it." She laid her head back against his chest, and his heartbeat, steady and even, thudded against her cheek. She thought of Mira. She thought of Dahlia, alone at the end, and knew her sister would be furious with her for following her to that same end. And Luccio, still here despite everything, still pleading with her to look up and see him. She owed him that much.

Zaneta nodded her head ever so slightly beneath Luccio's beard. She was ready to try. She was ready to open the prison door.

Nature's first green is gold,
Her hardest hue to hold.
Her early leaf's a flower;
But only so an hour.
Then leaf subsides to leaf.
So Eden sank to grief,
So dawn goes down to day.
Nothing gold can stay.
—Robert Frost

Mira

Sardegna 1951

Chapter 22

Those who study such things say the youngest babies, when their eyes grow strong and adapt to the light and dark around them, are first able to see the color red. Mira imagined her first discernible color must have been gold. Not the brassy metal of dirty coins or shiny trinkets, but gold in its purest form, like the sun poured out liquid into a vessel of light. Her earliest memory was sitting beneath her mother's loom, streaks of sun filtering through the windows in the late afternoon. She remembered the room filling with light as her mother's fingers worked the loom, its huge rods moving up and down high above where Mira played on the juniper-planked floor. She wasn't old enough even to know what a loom was, of course, nor the bobbin that her mother passed back and forth in a rhythm that matched the beautiful song her voice and hands seemed to sing together. And certainly, this was long before she knew anything about byssus and the threads that knotted one generation to the next.

Mira stared at the dust motes sparkling like fairies in the shafts of sun, rapt with wonder at the glow that reflected back from the cloth beneath her mother's hands. She reached up and tried to catch the color as it spun and twisted in the air. Her mother's hands stopped their constant motion for a moment, and she laughed. Perhaps it was that rare and magical sound that cemented the scene so firmly in Mira's memory, the briefest slice of time, like a photograph capturing the moment a bird rises from a branch in flight, the sense of her mother delighting in her.

Mira knew there was no photograph of that moment—how could there have been? But she remembered it in sharp focus all the same, as if it had been framed in a gallery exhibit she'd visited many times.

Later, when she was a little older, Zaneta showed Mira a kaleidoscope of gold, subtle variations in the shade that few but Master painters might recognize. Mira studied the painters, memorized their hues with names like Rubens's lead-tin yellow, Cézanne's Naples yellow, and Van Gogh's sunflower-inspired chrome yellow. She became familiar with gamboge, the Cambodian substance that produced such a luminous yellow it was almost fluorescent, and the canary-yellow orpiment so special it had been chosen to illuminate the Book of Kells and other medieval texts. Mira learned, too, the value of such a palette on an apothecary's shelf, gamboge being a powerful purgative and orpiment containing a deadly measure of arsenic.

Once, when Mira was seven, the whole family took the twelve-hour ferry ride to Roma, a sort of Italian pilgrimage every native-born child must make at some point. Her brothers loved the Colosseum, the grand piazzas, and the Pantheon, anything larger than life and with plenty of space to run and tussle with each other. Zaneta had led them, tight-lipped, through the Vatican and twenty or more Roman Catholic churches that began to blur together in an endless display of saints, paintings, tombs, and, of course gold. So much gold and gilding that Mira became impervious to it, the lire scattered on the marbled floors in tribute to long-dead saints, the candelabras and crucifixes, the tiny crowns adorning statues in rows along the nave of every cathedral. An odd outing for a coastal Jewish family.

On the return trip, Zaneta quietly quizzed Mira about what they'd seen. "What were the paintings framed with?"

"Gold," Mira replied.

"And the crucifix in the nave?"

"Gold."

"The candlesticks and inlay in the marble?"

"Gold."

"Why do you think this is?" Zaneta asked.

"It's beautiful?"

"Money," Johann interjected, kicking his legs beneath the seat. "How many lire is all that worth?"

"Hush. I'm not asking you," Zaneta admonished him. "Mira?"

"Money, too," she guessed. "It shows the church is wealthy."

"Don't just parrot your brother's answer, Mira. Think for yourself." Johann smirked at her from the ferry's window seat, and not for the first time, Mira resented her gender. Her mother only questioned *her*, peppered her with endless quizzes and history lessons. Her brothers were free to mostly do as they pleased. Was it because she was somehow deficient? Needing more than what was taught at school?

Zaneta examined her hands, her nails rough and short. "Gold has always been scarce." Mira watched as the sun set over the sea, the seabirds silhouetted as they dipped and dove. The water sparkled with the final rays of pink and white, and the glass-like waters darkened from turquoise to violet. "The gold we saw on display in Roma was mined from the ground. Someone, somewhere, likely slaves or poor laborers, had to pry it from the earth's clutches. Because it's rare—and because it glitters—it's prized."

The rocking of the ferry and drone of its engine made Mira sleepy. "People are like ravens," Mira mused, stifling a yawn. "Wanting shiny objects."

"All that glitters is not gold, Mira." Zaneta hummed to herself. "The earth is the Lord's and everything in it; the world and all who live in it." Her mother recited the psalm almost like a chant. "Gold is in the earth for a reason. It's rare. It reflects light. It points people to what's special, divine. That's why the churches use so much of it.

"It can also reveal our darker side: greed, envy, theft. I've told you the story of King Midas? When his wish was granted and all he touched turned to gold, it meant he couldn't eat or touch anyone he loved. Gold shouldn't be easy to grasp. It's a gift we must labor for and one we shouldn't covet or profit from."

"I wouldn't want all that gold anyway," Mira sniffed.

"Indeed." Mira felt her mother's gaze upon her like an eagle, appraising her. "When we get home," she said. "We'll begin your lessons."

"More history?" Mira sighed, her eyes heavy.

"Much more than that," Zaneta replied.

Before sunrise, Zaneta shook Mira awake while the rest of the household still slept. She rubbed her eyes in confusion but didn't protest as she slipped into her dress and shoes, following her mother outside into the cool, still night.

"Where are we going?" she finally asked as she placed her feet in her mother's footsteps, trying to see by the light of the moon.

"You'll find out."

Every few steps, her short legs had to trot to keep up with her mother's brisk stride. Zaneta didn't look back to see if she was following or if she'd fallen behind. Mira wasn't afraid, even when a stray dog slunk behind them for a few yards, eyeing them for a scrap of food. The small neighborhood and all the people in it were her home; nothing sinister lurked there, and even at her young age, she'd wandered with her brothers and sometimes alone by the shore and rocky inlets.

They passed a couple of sleepy fishing boats that bobbed and danced, tugging against their anchors like restless horses, their nets folded and traps stacked on their decks. In the moonlight, their wooden sides and masts appeared gray, the color of dark slate, but Mira knew the sun would reveal the hulls' bright hues of yellow, green, and blue. Ropes slapped against the masts with a clank of metal like the clapper of a bell. The tide whispered against the rocks as the sea crept inland, irresistibly drawn by the moon's pull. Mira, trotting to keep up, caught the haunting melody of the song her mother sang, carried on the salty breeze.

Finally, Zaneta slowed and glanced behind her, as if remembering for the first time she'd asked Mira to follow. Together they rounded the inlet's curve and came into a small cove, the rocks giving way to coarse sand that made walking more difficult. When Zaneta removed her shoes, Mira copied her, and they continued on until they reached a natural quay, where Zaneta stopped and waded out into the sea. The water was calm here, where they were sheltered from the wind. The current gently tugged at the hem of her mother's dress. Was Mira supposed to wade in, too, or wait on the shore? She chewed her thumbnail as she hesitated.

The light grew less dim. It was almost morning, and Mira would need to get ready for school soon. She didn't want to get in trouble with her teacher. Worry twisted in her stomach. The barest beam of orange yellow haloed the tips of the islets that stood like sentries against the horizon. Zaneta turned to Mira then and beckoned to her.

"Come out in the water," she said, extending her hand.

Mira dropped her shoes and waded in. The water was cold at this early hour, and while her mother stood knee-deep, on Mira's small frame it reached much higher. She drew in a sharp breath when it slapped against her warm stomach, and she held her arms high, trying to stay dry. Zaneta put one hand on Mira's shoulder, and as the colors on the horizon brightened from amber to saffron, Zaneta began to sing. It was more of a chant, really, and Mira tipped her chin up to look at her mother, strands of her dark hair lifted on the breeze, her eyes closed, and her right hand lifted to the rising sun. This was so different from her usual brusque and dismissive manner that Mira wondered what had come over her, what magic had transformed her.

"I give my life to
"Being and weaving," she sang.
"Gifts from the sea,
"Blown by the winds—
"Ponente, Levante, Mistral, and Grecale.
"As an offering to those
"Before and after."

The first time through, Mira followed the Italian words easily, although the meaning and purpose of the song were unclear. She recognized the second repetition in Hebrew as well, but the third language, although the melody was unchanged, she'd never heard before. By the time Zaneta had sung it three times, the sun had risen, and she dropped her hands. Mira blinked her eyes against the dazzling Mediterranean sun as it shone across the water. The spell was broken. Mira wasn't sure if she was supposed to say something, so she kept quiet. They returned to the shore, where Mira shivered slightly and stole glances at her mother as she wrung seawater from her dress.

"So," Zaneta spoke. It was a decree. "That's how we will begin each day. Every day from the time I was seven, this is what I've done, and my mother and grandmother before me. And it's what you will do, too. When the season is good, we'll swim."

"I've never seen you do . . . this before."

"Because you were still sleeping, silly. And when you were a baby, your father looked after you until I returned."

"But . . . but, *why*?"

"This is who we *are*, Mira. It's what we *do*. It's what your life will be about. Put your shoes on and I'll tell you on the way home. I have to get breakfast, and you have school."

Mira slipped her wet, sandy feet into her shoes, not even minding the way the grit rubbed between her toes. Something about sharing this moment, this task, with her mother made her brush the annoyance aside.

"Do Johann and Isaac know?" she puzzled. "But they're still asleep."

"This is only for women, figlia. It's not a path for your brothers. We are water women."

Mira brightened. "Like mermaids?"

"Hardly." Zaneta had come back to herself again. There was the scornful glance Mira was used to. "Mermaids are fairy tales. The water women are as ancient as time. You and I will carry on the secrets of our craft as a sacred duty."

Mira nodded, trying to sort all this into something that made sense as she picked her way among the rocks. Ancient women? She was a schoolgirl of seven, just mastering addition and making her way through chapter books. What kind of sacred duty could she have?

"You won't understand it all at once. For now, each day starts this way. We wake before sunrise, go to the westernmost point, and offer our prayer just as dawn breaks. We greet the sea as it wakes, promising to protect and guard it and the treasures it offers. We harvest the gift of its golden thread, and we weave it into beauty to offer back in return."

"The work you do on the loom? This is part of being a water woman?"

"Yes. And now you'll learn as well. It's more than simple weaving, though that's hard enough. You'll have to work hard, memorize many things, and practice, practice, practice. Even then, you may not master it. I'll do what I can to show you, but in the end, it's up to you." Zaneta sighed and brushed off a bit of sand that clung to Mira's cheek. Mira's eyes shone up at her. Was she to be chosen, then, somehow, to carry on some important task? Was she special after all? "Heaven help us," Zaneta said. "Given what we have to work with."

Chapter 23

True to her word, from then on, each day Zaneta roused Mira in the dark, and they trekked together to the inlet, but that was the easiest task. Between the ages of seven and twelve, Mira's fall and spring were a balance of school, chores, and lessons from Zaneta. Summers, she swam.

Born on an island, of course she could swim. Before she could walk, Mira's father dangled her legs in the sea, letting her splash and kick at the waves as they rose and fell. Like her brothers, she could throw a net, cast a line, and dig an oyster by the time she was five. They all swam for fun or to cool off when the sun beat down in the cloudless sky. This was different. Zaneta took Mira to the cove, and some afternoons they swam for hours, until Mira's muscles ached and her lips were pickled in salt brine. She swam laps like she was trying out for a swim team or a channel crossing. No floats, no fins, no aids.

"You can do more than you think you can, Mira. Do it underwater this time, and I don't want to see your head pop up until you've made it across the cove."

Zaneta set timers around the house. Sometimes, while Mira did her homework or took a bath, Zaneta would shout "Time!"—her cue to begin holding her breath while continuing her task.

"Breath is God, Mira: spirit. God is forever. Your breath will last longer than you think if you let Him hold it for you. Trust. Quit being afraid." One minute. Two minutes. Gradually, she increased her time. The practice she did while out of the sea lessened the panic once her head was underwater. Zaneta pushed and insisted. Once, when Mira was getting over a head cold, they ventured out to the shallows, and Mira quickly grew tired of the laps she swam.

"Too lazy to swim? We'll dive, then. Get ready." They both breathed deeply for a count of five, then slowly exhaled, signaling their bodies that air would not come quickly. After the fifth repetition, Zaneta nodded and they went under, face to face, until they sat, cross-legged, on the sand, swaying like seaweed in the rocking of the water. Mira watched her mother's face. It was impassive, calm, a mere observer. For the first minute, Mira was calm, too. She noted the silver arrows of a school of barracuda as they flashed in the sunlight, a crab scuttling along a section of rock. After the second minute, she began to squirm under her mother's scrutiny and felt an itch in her lungs, too early, too early.

Mira needed to cough, and her sinuses started to throb. She unfolded her legs so that she could push off the bottom and ascend, but Zaneta shook her head and pointed to the sand. *Stay*. Mira's concentration had broken. The sea pressed in around her like a cloak, and air bubbles released and rose from her nose, her mouth. She shook her head at Zaneta and pointed toward the surface, her eyes wide. Zaneta frowned and patted the seafloor, sending up a cloud of sand. She tapped at her left wrist, signaling time. It wasn't yet time. She grabbed Mira's ankle to anchor her.

Every cell in Mira's body now begged for air. She knew it wasn't time. She'd been under far longer than this before and knew she could do it if she could only concentrate and calm her thoughts. She tried not to look at Zaneta's face, where she knew she'd find disappointment and impatience. The tickle in her throat was insistent, demanding, impossible to resist. Finally, she coughed out a burst of air in response, not thinking that her weakened lungs would reflexively respond with a natural intake of breath. Except there was no breath; there was only water, and despite her hours in their world, Mira wasn't a fish. The intake of water where air should be sent her feet into action. She kicked off her mother's hand and dug her toes into the sand, vaulting the short distance to the surface, where she sputtered and gasped, her hair plastered to her face and salt water streaming in her eyes. She coughed repeatedly, belching and trying to calm the spasms by breathing through her nose. Zaneta stayed underwater. Mira could see her there, still cross-legged on the sand, waiting out the clock, or perhaps avoiding her daughter's display of weakness. They didn't speak on the walk back to the house. She heard her parents' raised voices that evening as she fell asleep, heard her father mention the word *pneumonia* and her mother's derisive hiss.

"There are much worse things than that. She has to overcome."

Mira practiced even harder afterward, using the clock on her classroom wall in school to hold her breath during quizzes or while someone read aloud from a book. When she no longer worried about when her next breath would be, Mira started to relax during her swimming. She took time to notice the way the sunlight shimmied on the seabed, and her eyes picked up the movements of other creatures below the waves—eels, urchins, and once, an octopus that had camouflaged itself against a rock. When she swam past, it flashed from dark brown to mottled green and thrust its tentacles in a jet of ink to escape. It surprised her, but she wasn't afraid. She was spending so much time in the water that it was becoming her second home, and like her neighborhood above with its quaint fishing boats and nonnas minding their grandchildren, the sea brought Mira a measure of comfort.

"Mamma, you've told me the history of byssus. I know the ancient stories, back to Berenice, but where are all the others now?" Mira once asked. She was seventeen. It had been ten years since she'd begun walking the byssus path. She'd learned to parse out her questions carefully, not too many at once, making sure she'd tried to reach an answer herself before bothering her mother with something she should already know. They were kneading dough for dinner, and her mother's hands had stilled a moment, knuckles buried in the yeasty mass.

"It's just us. Your grandmother and aunts are gone; you know that," Zaneta snapped.

"Aren't there others? Other families who weave?"

In a rare moment of openness, Zaneta mused. "It's 1961. There's been a man in space, now." She shook her head in wonder. "The world's changing quickly. America's President Kennedy is seeing to that. Maybe it's too busy for such a thing as weaving. People think they're too advanced to bother with such things, but look, Mira, at the wall going up in Berlin, the hate dividing people in America. Despite all they know and how fast they know it, we still need what the byssus represents, beauty, peace, proof that the world still has gifts to offer, and it's up to us not to let it be lost to the past. What are you doing to prevent that?"

"I'm up to three minutes underwater," she offered. "And I know the life cycle of the *Pinna* and when to harvest. I can rinse and clean the threads, and I spin the cotton, linen, and wool well." Mira cast her eyes down. "I know I need to improve spinning the hemp."

"You're still clumsy with those," agreed her mother. "And you have yet to learn to handle the cloth from the prickly pear and palm. Next low moon, we will spin those as well."

"How much more is there?"

"Before what?"

"Before I am . . . like you?"

Zaneta smiled sadly. "You shouldn't wish to be like me, figlia."

"I mean, until I can do all that you can."

"Oh, that." Zaneta waved a doughy hand. "Many years yet. There is spinning, weaving, dyeing, and much more about plants and their secrets. It takes a lifetime to become a master."

Mira sighed and pinched under the ends of her braided challah bread. For the first time, it occurred to her that this meant she must always learn from—and stay with—her mother, for as long as it took. Already, some of her friends at school talked about their futures, what they might study, where they might go. None of them had to hurry home after school to spin or swim.

Families didn't stay in Sardegna for generations anymore. Several of her friends' older siblings had gone to the mainland or even farther instead of staying to work in mining or farming like their fathers and grandfathers. What would it feel like to have many futures as a possibility? What would it feel like not to carry the family's expectations? For the briefest moment, Mira wondered whether she actually *wanted* to be a water woman. As soon as the thought occurred to her, she glanced, stricken, at her mother, as if she might've uttered it aloud.

Mira took it back as soon as she'd thought it. It was beyond her. This was her calling in life, the singular way she mattered. She held the end of the thread; she was the only one who could keep the sacred tradition alive. Doing so meant that, thanks to her, something beautiful would remain in the world. Mira glanced at her mother as she turned to slide the tray of bread into the oven. Someday, Mira thought, being a water woman might actually make her beautiful, too.

Seeing the byssus in its raw form in the shell before it came to life filled her with both reverence and a measure of fear. Her mother had instilled both. Her voice echoed so clearly in Mira's head, sometimes she couldn't tell whether it was her mother's voice or her own that automatically scolded her.

"Careful, Mira, no clumsy fingers. Pay attention so you don't strip off more than necessary. No, no, no! You've ruined that piece. Don't you know how precious that is? How long it takes to collect just this small amount?" Mira had lost count of the admonishments, corrections, hours of practice and study. How many times had she come to Zaneta as a child of eight, ten, twelve, a piece of the flock in her small hands, offering it shyly for her scrutiny? Her mother's dark eyes would pierce like an eagle's as she'd snatch the byssus from Mira's hands and hold it up to the light.

"Do you know what I see?" she'd ask, and Mira's heart would plummet at the question. Mira would shake her head, certain she'd cleaned and rinsed the byssus the full twenty-five days, leaving not a single speck of impurity.

"Carelessness," Zaneta would reply, her mouth twisting in a frown. "Hurry. Rush. Not good enough," she'd say, handing back the flock with her head turned, Mira already dismissed without excuse. Johann and Isaac, her younger brothers, would watch from where they played in the yard or where they sat near the hearth playing chess or checkers, free from the chores Mira was required to complete. They had their own household tasks, to be sure—everyone did their part in those days—but none as fraught with criticism and reproval as tending the sea silk.

Only once had Mira dared to complain. It had been winter, the year she'd turned twelve. She'd received good marks at school, studying hard and putting in extra time with math, her weakest area, and her teacher had praised her efforts. On the way home from school, eager to present her grades to her parents, she'd been approached by a boy named Tomas who pulled her away from her friends. He was tall and shy with warm brown eyes and a rakish smile. There was a winter dance, he'd stammered. Would she like to go?

The rest of the way home, Mira's best friend, Carmina, had laughed and teased her about it. She'd been the first to be asked, and she'd walked with her shoulders back and a skip in her step, feeling like a sleek cat strutting in the sunshine. When she'd arrived home, a smile playing on her lips, she'd seen the curtains drawn against the bright day, and she'd known Zaneta would be in one of her dark moods. Lingering at the doorstep, she'd waffled about entering as she overheard snippets of her parents' conversation as they sat at the kitchen table.

"It never ends," her mother had snapped, her voice carrying a waver that betrayed her.

"Zeta, you already knew." Her father, Luccio's, low voice, gentle and sad.

"There are different kinds of knowing. This makes it final somehow. What a brilliance wasted."

Mira had chosen that moment to enter the kitchen and greet her mother, her teacher's signed paper in hand, just as Zaneta had hurled a teacup into the sink, shards of porcelain flying everywhere. Her mother had whirled around, startled.

"What is it?" she'd sniped, her hands waving in the air like shooing a housefly. "What could possibly be so important?" Her mother's dark eyes were wet, her cheeks flushed.

Mira had weighed her two pieces of news and chosen her words carefully. She'd folded her grades and slid them behind her back. "There's a dance," she'd said, the words halting and cautious, the question implied. "I've been asked to go."

Zaneta had laughed, a brittle sound in the small, airless kitchen. "Dancing? *That's* what most concerns you?" She'd run her long fingers through her black curls and lifted her chin. "Impossible." Her final pronouncement. "We have work to do. Everything rests on us now."

Mira had looked to her father, her eyes silently pleading. "It's just one evening," she'd dared to argue. "Surely you can spare—"

Her mother's temper had flashed. "So. You presume to know what I can spare?" She'd barked that bitter laugh again. Mira's father spread his hands, trying to soften the blow for his daughter. "I have nothing to *spare*, Mira. Maybe if I had a spare daughter, you could waste time at a dance that means nothing, but I have only you." The way she'd said that last word had pierced Mira's heart like a saber. Her mother had sighed, folding a paper of her own that Mira finally noticed on the table. She'd fixed Mira with one of her stares, pinning her to the spot, a butterfly on display. "You will have to do." She'd shaken her head. "No time for a dance."

Mira couldn't help the quiver in her chin, the sting of tears that sprang to her eyes. "Come now, Mira," her mother snapped, rolling her eyes. "It's not a death sentence." Mira had dropped her head, letting her long hair slide forward to cover her face.

Her father had coughed and tried to salvage the situation. "Did you bring something from school?" he'd asked, his voice bright with false cheer. He scratched his dark beard, and wrinkles deepened in the corners of his green eyes as he smiled.

She'd already forgotten about the grades and the warm hand her teacher had placed on her shoulder. She'd shrugged and passed the crumpled paper to her father on her way out to do her chores. "It's nothing," she'd said. "Nothing important."

Chapter 24

Mira accompanied Zaneta to the lagoon in the spring, a pouch belted to her waist. She dove alongside her mother, flanking her like a dolphin calf, watching and learning as she pointed and signed underwater, indicating which shells were healthy, which needed more time to produce. Mira watched her mother's scalpel nick the ends of the keratin threads floating from the *Pinna nobilis*, and she tucked them safely in her pouch to carry home.

The shells of the creatures were ugly, really. Rough and covered in algae, small corals, and opportunist barnacles, the mollusks attached themselves to rocks and rested, unassumingly, in small colonies. Filter feeders, their only interaction with other sea life was playing host to a small species of marine shrimp that acted as a sentinel for danger, causing the bivalve to clamp shut—or clam up, as it were—for protection. Inside was a different story. Inside the shell grew a coat of luxurious mother-of-pearl.

Their homely nature was a good thing, her mother said. "If you saw a field of bright green emeralds lying on the seabed, you'd pluck them up until they were all gone. The sea silk hides here in raw form in the seagrass where the turtles swim, the soul of the sea right under your nose."

Once the threads had been harvested, they worked night and day for almost a month, rinsing and cleaning it, washing it with a mixture of eight different seaweeds to purify it. Someone had to watch it like a baby, lest its fiber crumble, tending it every three hours and then bathing it in lemon juice and a tannic juice made from cedar. They hung it in bundles to dry in the shade and the wind until it became elastic and ready for dyeing. After memorizing all the necessary plants and how to extract dye from them, Mira had to demonstrate her skill. Her mother might present her with a linen cloth or wool and ask her to make it a particular shade of purple or brown. Her eyes had to know the difference between violet, magenta, plum, and archil; whether to use blackberry, safflower, nettle, alder, or lichen; and how much of each. Mira had learned some chemistry at school, but her lessons at home taught her how mixtures, compounds, and reactions truly worked together.

Only once the dyeing process was finished and the byssus had been carded and spun on a spindle made of oleander could they use it to weave or embroider. It was years before Mira could even touch the byssus for this purpose. When the day's work was done, or if her mother was out at the market or busy in the yard, Mira sometimes sat alone in the small workshop where the loom and all the tools were stored. She grew to love the smell of the various dyes in their containers, the way some burned her nose with their acid and tannin and some smelled almost sweet. As she had when she was a baby, she studied the loom and its great arms. She imagined it as a sleeping bird when it was still, the upper crossbeam and bottom like stretched skeletal wings, the threads strung between the two its sinews.

Her mother described it to Mira like this: "The upper beam is the beam of heaven, and the bottom represents earth. In between"—she ran her hand across the warp and weft of the weave in process—"is the world of creation, where beauty is made."

Mira longed to make beauty like that. She yearned for her clumsy fingers, stained with dye, to create something lovely that others would weep for when they received it. Every week, someone came to the workshop seeking such favor, and Mira worked silently in the background, rinsing or dyeing or cleaning, while her mother met with the visitor. Sometimes it was a young woman, murmuring about a fiancé, an approaching wedding. Sometimes it was a weathered old nonna, come to ask about a christening gown or perhaps a few stitches along a bonnet's trim for a granddaughter's arrival.

Mira wished she had something special to ask for, some occasion dear enough for her mother to lean in close and place a hand on her head or shoulder and offer kind words of counsel or congratulations. She marveled as the young women, some not much older than herself, smiled and hugged her mother through their tears as they received her gifts, lovingly and perfectly stitched handkerchiefs, braided bracelets and garters, or baby clothes with embroidered edges of byssus. In those moments, her mother became someone foreign, so different from the woman Mira lived with that had she bumped into that version of her on the street, Mira doubted she would even know her. She wondered how many separate people it was possible for one woman to be. Were there other parts of her mother it had never dawned on her to wonder about?

Always, the visitors offered payment, and always, her mother refused. "Byssus is the soul of the sea. Would you sell the arc of a rainbow? The wind across the cliffs?" When they had no answer, she'd spread her hands. So obvious. It was settled. No payment. All the harvesting, tending, rinsing, dyeing, spinning, and weaving was a sacrificial labor of love and service. It was its own reward.

"Ah," the nonnas would say, understanding. "*La madre.* Like being a mother." If Mira happened to be nearby, they'd wink at her, certain she must feast on the fruits of such love. How full she must be, how lucky.

~

When Mira graduated from school, she secured a part-time job near the port at Books by the Sea, a tiny bookshop owned by Carmina's family. She was elated to have a job of her own, where she earned actual lire instead of giving away all her hard work. Mira already imagined what she might buy: chocolate, a silver clip for her long hair. Her heart was full. Although the pocket money would be appreciated, mostly she craved a change of scenery. Not that her familiar town port was especially exotic, but it wasn't the same four walls she'd stared at her whole life.

Two of her friends from school had gone on to university. It was the early '60s, and most girls in the area, if they didn't get married straight off, settled for secretarial posts or, if they left their families and moved inland, selling perfume or clothing in bigger stores. There was no chance of Mira going abroad or even to Roma or Firenze. There was no money for that on her father's laborer salary, even if she'd been given the option. Mira's course had been charted from her birth and even earlier, and she didn't question it—why should she? It was a fine path. As her mother said, it was who she *was*. Mira was happy to settle for a few days a week at the quiet, tidy bookstore, tucked between the bakery and the fish market along what passed for a boardwalk.

Signora Petrolus soon grew to appreciate the help, and on slow days, she sometimes left the shop entirely in Mira's care while she ran errands or chatted with friends over limoncello or espresso. On a quiet afternoon in early March, Mira stood on a short ladder in the back of the store, cleaning the tops of the sturdy wooden shelves. It would be several weeks before the byssus harvest began.

The brass bell clanked against the shop's door, and she didn't even turn. Carmina had promised to bring her some leftovers from the bakery. "What is it today, amaretti or torrone?"

A man's low voice startled her with an answer. "I didn't know you bartered cookies for books." Mira jumped and turned on the ladder. "I can go next door if you tell me which you prefer," he teased.

Mira put a finger to her lips and considered. "Definitely amaretti." She stepped down and walked the few steps to the front of the shop. The man removed his hat, and Mira took in his sandy hair and dancing blue eyes. His cheeks were red from the wind, and he blew on his hands.

"Looking for something in particular?" she asked.

"Just dashed in to get out of the wind for a minute," he said, gesturing to the door. "Starting to rain out there." He paused, and Mira grew strangely warm as he glanced around the shop, his eyes landing on her. He stuck out a hand. "Dante Barone."

"Mira Mazza." The hand he offered was cool and soft, definitely not a laborer or angler.

"Perdonami, but you've got—" He reached a tentative hand toward Mira's hair and plucked off a tuft of dust.

She laughed and smoothed her unruly curls. "Thank you. Where are you from, Signor Barone?"

"Call me Dante. Sicily, originally, but I'm thinking of taking a teaching position at the school here. Math."

Mira wrinkled her nose. "I always struggled with numbers."

"I'm sure you've got plenty of other talents." His teeth were straight and even beneath his trim mustache and scruff of beard. "So, is this what you do here on the island? Sell books?"

Mira opened her mouth reflexively and almost told him how she worked with the byssus and was in the line of water women, but she stopped herself, imagining how that might sound. She might as well say she was a traveling magician or some sort of fortune teller. A twinge of guilt stirred in her chest as her thoughts betrayed her lineage.

Instead, she swatted away her conscience with words. "I just work here a few days a week. It's not my shop, but it's nice to be out by the port where people come and go. You meet some interesting tourists once in a while. Once, a whole family of Orthodox all the way from the United States. So many children, in and out of the shelves. It made my head spin! The shop cat—Turnip—was skittish all day." As if in response, the white tom raised his head and licked a paw in the window, where he sat trying to soak up what little sun peeked through the low gray clouds. "I always wonder what brings people to want to visit such an out-of-the-way place as this."

"I like it here. Life runs at a slower pace; there's nowhere near the traffic. Some days I can walk three miles along the shore and never come across another soul. Not to mention the beauty everywhere." Dante's eyes unmistakably fixed on Mira's, and a current ran through her. She couldn't help the blush that rose to color her face. A deep rumble of thunder shook the windowpanes, and the loud patter of raindrops echoed off the tiled roof above them.

"Looks like you're stuck here for a bit." Mira shrugged. "How about I get the Moka pot going for some espresso and you can tell me about being a teacher?"

Dante took off his jacket and accepted the stool she scooted out for him. The rain had set in, and there was no chance anyone else would stop by for the rest of the afternoon. Mira's ladder stood abandoned in the back of the store. They whiled away the day like they were old friends, laughing and talking about their favorite parts of the island, books, music, food, family. Dante told her his father was a university professor and his mother taught languages in the local school in their Sicilian town. He was, in fact, from a long line of teachers, so wanting to teach came naturally, he supposed.

"Maybe it's kind of old-fashioned to have a profession in your family line, like being shoemakers or—" He searched for another example and breathed deeply as the aroma of fresh bread from next door filled the room. "Bakers. But I think it's a treasure. People don't pass things down like that anymore."

That was when Mira's heart cracked open the faintest bit, letting in a sliver of hope along with the tingle of something else she'd never tasted before, something more delicious than Signor Donetti's pastries and sourdough.

~

The rest of that spring, in the late afternoons when Mira was scheduled at the bookshop, Dante stopped by most days after school had let out if he didn't have students to tutor. He brought amaretti from the bakery or a sack of fresh-baked cookies stashed in his satchel, and they'd share the treats with espresso. Signora Petrolus busied herself in the back, poring over ledgers that were already perfect or peering in Mira's direction over the tops of her glasses "to see if customers are coming." Carmina joined the pair sometimes, when she had time off from the bakery, and the three of them played cards or checkers when Mira finished her tasks.

Toward the end of April, Carmina sat at the front counter, munching crackers spread with artichoke paste, while Mira finished putting away a new order of gialli, the so-called yellow books of suspense and crime. Carmina licked her fingers and came out with it.

"Has he kissed you yet?" she asked.

"We sit in the front of the shop, between your mamma and a plate-glass window. When would he have done that?"

"Plenty of shelves to duck behind," Carmina observed, waving her sticky fingers.

Mira tucked her hair behind an ear. "No, he hasn't."

"What's he waiting for? In another week or so, we'll be lucky if we see you at all." When Mira stayed quiet, her friend's eyes widened and her mouth opened in midchew. "You haven't told him yet?"

"I don't know how to explain it." She'd been agonizing over this very thing. Mira rushed on. "What am I going to say: well, you see, Dante, I can't see you anymore because I have to dive for these clams every day and practically live as a hermit while I turn their threads into gold."

"When you say it like *that*," Carmina admitted.

Mira chewed her fingernail. "I don't want him to think I'm odd. It *is* odd. Do you know anyone else who does what I—what *we*—do?"

"Well, no, Mira. What you do is unique, obviously. But it's beautiful and special."

"I hope Dante sees it that way."

"Well, *I* hope he kisses you and whatever spell you're under with him is never broken."

"You live a constant fairy tale in that head of yours, Carmina," Mira said with a laugh.

Carmina counted on her fingers. "We have the handsome prince and the pretty maid who's secretly a witch."

"Carmina!"

"I'm joking." She paused a moment to consider what she'd said. "You're the one who said you spin thread into gold, not me."

The bell jangled loudly as the shop door swung open. "Mira." Zaneta's voice was a reprimand. "You need to give notice to Signora Petrolus," she said. "You'll be working at home for the summer."

"I think I can do both, Mamma," started Mira.

"We'll be much too busy for that. Besides, you'll have more to learn now that you've turned eighteen. Be home by dinner." The bell protested once more as the door banged shut behind her, and Mira sighed.

"How am I going to see Dante *now*?" she whined.

"Every fairy tale has a dragon," Carmina said, frowning at the shop's closed door. "We'll figure something out."

Chapter 25

"It's time to decide, Mira. Are you going to take the water oath and uphold this tradition, or do I return the knowledge of thousands of years to the water?" Zaneta fixed Mira with an unflinching gaze. Despite the pressure, Mira felt powerful; it all rested with her, and Zaneta knew it. All the years of initiation and apprenticing, the hours of memorizing, diving, and developing in her hands the muscle memory of weaving patterns were meant to converge here.

"Tell me again what I must give up." She was stalling.

Zaneta took a deep breath. Mira was trying her mother's patience, but she couldn't afford to show it. "It's not so much about the sacrifice as what will be gained. *You* are the thread that connects over thirty generations of women. All the names we recite and give thanks for at each dawn and evening prayer—*you're* the continuation of that. Someday, your name will be added to those names as your granddaughters and great-granddaughters honor you and your place in the line of water women."

"Yes, but—"

"Don't be so quick to dismiss that. You don't see it now because you're young, but someday that legacy will mean everything."

"I understand."

Zaneta tried again. "What will you give up? You'll give up traveling the world to remain close to the *Pinna nobilis*, to stay on this beautiful island that's been a good home to you. You'll give up material things because the byssus is the heritage of all people and can't be sold or bartered. Time, I suppose." Zaneta shrugged. "You know how long it takes to harvest, process, and weave. That takes time, but what would you do with it otherwise? Waste it with entertainment and leisure?"

"I think I'm ready." Zaneta visibly relaxed. Mira continued. "But there's one other thing I need to consider." Her mother's dark brows arched high on her forehead: a question. "I'm going to marry Dante, so he must be part of this."

~

It had been a long summer. Absent from the bookshop, Mira had to find other ways to see Dante, and the two arranged stolen spare hours whenever they could, meeting for gelato or a walk along the shore whenever she was in town and he could get away. He knew she was kept busy at home, that her mother needed her help. That wasn't uncommon. Many families still worked in traditional ways, the next generations learning from and helping the previous one. More than once, her mother had scolded her for being drowsy during lessons, but Mira had been careful to complete all her tasks with extra care. She was devoted to the work of the byssus, even if her heart was distracted.

It was hard to stay focused when all she could think about was Dante's gentle voice, the persistent way he pried and poked until he got her to divulge her dreams and hopes, something no one but Carmina had ever been the least bit curious about. Mira had let a few details slip—she and her mother worked on a loom, the materials they used were available seasonally, which explained her busyness in the summer months. She wanted to tell him more, wanted to share everything, and several times almost started to, but she worried it would seem strange to him. What if he expected a more traditional life? What if one day he changed his mind and wanted to go teach on the mainland? She and her mother were the only two women doing this work, and it was important she continue it. It was so much to explain, and she realized how odd it seemed when compared to everyone else. Sometimes she just wanted to be like any other girl.

She loved how he made her laugh when his beard tickled her face, how he genuinely listened when she talked about the sea or wondered about the stars. Captivating, he called her, bewitching. Mira, a girl used to the scorch of the sun above the water, had never felt such a heat as when Dante sat close to her on the rocky shore, their thighs touching and her head resting on his shoulder. When he brushed her hair off her neck with his fingers and his lips found hers, the world spun, and Mira didn't want it to stop.

Toward the end of June, when Dante had a break from teaching full time, they walked together on some of the shepherds' paths in the fields a mile or so from town.

"Don't you think it's about time I meet your parents?" he asked.

Mira stiffened. This wasn't the first time he'd asked. "They're very busy." A weak excuse, but what else could she say? It had been a miracle that Dante hadn't ferreted out her father at the quay to introduce himself, but as luck would have it, her father had been docking at a small town down the road from theirs to help another pescatore who'd been injured.

"It's not right, Mira. Why should I be a big secret?"

"I told you," she said, "that my mother can be difficult, demanding."

He stood tall and straight. "I can take it if it means we're together. Are you ashamed of me?"

Mira couldn't put it off any longer. The salt sting of tears burned her eyes, but when he lifted her chin and brushed them from her cheeks, the love and concern on his face firmed her resolve. "I have something to tell you," she began, and from there, the spool unraveled. She spilled the story of the water women, the words coming in waves like the tide, and he listened, holding her hand, his eyes never wavering. When she told it like that, all at once, it sounded strange and wonderful, full of mystery, beauty, and reverence, and it came to her that she really was one of them, her life part of a priceless golden tapestry.

"My whole life has been dedicated to learning this and preparing to take the water oath, which will mean that it's my lifelong vow to continue the service." Mira finally stopped and took a breath, waiting for the part when Dante decided he'd fallen into some sort of quicksand he wanted out of.

Instead, he said, "Why in the world didn't you tell me before?" In the alluring way he had of framing ideas, he elaborated. "Think of it this way. I work with the language of numbers; you make a language from fabric and thread. *Text*, meaning 'words,' and *textile*, meaning 'fabric,' come from the same origin, meaning 'to weave.' Words create a language; threads create fabric. Both of us are linguists, creating beautiful things with our languages. We make perfect partners!"

Mira stood there with her mouth agape like a beached fish, bewildered to find itself in a world of sun and sand.

"I can't leave the island. My first loyalty would be here, to the sea."

He nodded as it sunk in. "Of course. That first day we met, I told you I liked it here. My home doesn't have to be a particular place, Mira. I could live on the polar icecaps if it was with you."

"I don't think they have amaretti at the North Pole."

"A serious drawback. I'd love to see what you do. Will you show me?"

She brought him home for dinner soon afterward. Mira's father peppered Dante with questions. He was so different from Luccio, his head full of numbers and his clean hands a clear indication of the chasm spread between them. Zaneta's eyes squinted with suspicion as she doled out heaping plates of seafood linguini. "What about your family?" she probed. "What ties lie back in Sicily?" Johann and Isaac elbowed each other at the table and cast smirking glances at Mira and her "friend." They knew him from school and, before he arrived, complained about having the math teacher join them at their home. They shouldn't have to socialize with their teacher. Mira glared at them to hush and threatened to pour honey in their hair while they slept if they didn't behave.

After their meal, Mira took Dante to the small studio and showed him the loom and its great birdlike arms. She told him to close his eyes and hold out his hand.

"Now you can touch a piece of cloth. Feel it?" she asked, placing a square of woven byssus in his palm.

"No. You haven't given me anything yet."

"I have." She laughed. "That's how light it is."

"It's like holding a cloud." He marveled. "Or trying to grasp breath."

She held threads of it up to the shafts of sunlight streaming through the windows and showed him how the stuff seemed to drink up the light, absorbing it like a parched sponge until it shone golden and impossibly clear all at once, a sunbeam in his hand. He walked slowly between the framed pieces on the walls, examining the detail and symmetry of the weave that formed pictures of lions, menorahs, lyres, and lambs.

"Incredible. You wove these?"

"Some. My mother is much more skilled, but I'm getting better. I don't know if I'll ever be as good as she is."

"Why do you do that?"

"What?"

"Sell yourself short. Talk that way. This work, these are masterpieces. They belong in a museum."

Mira ducked her head, unaccustomed to such praise. "You don't see all the flaws like I do."

"Fine. Strive for improvement, but give yourself some credit for what you've already done. It's stunning. That's what *I* see. You're an inspiration."

~

With Dante's full support, Mira fulfilled her promise and took the water oath. One day that July, just as the sun pinked the horizon, Mira waded into the water at the byssus cove. She wore a loose, flowing robe of pure byssus, one she'd never seen before, that Zaneta had had locked away for the occasion. It had been worn by generations of water women on their Morning of Vowing. As was their custom, she and her mother recited and thanked in unison the generations of women before them. Then, her mother led her in a solemn affirmation.

"I swear upon the life given to me by our Father and the gifts offered up by the sea that I will never profit from weaving the byssus; that I will, each morning and evening, offer my song to the waves to spread my words of peace and love all over the world; that I will keep sacred and secret the art of weaving and working the byssus, keeping it in memory only until it's passed to my daughters or her daughters. If this thread cannot be woven, I vow to return my knowledge to the water from where it originated. I vow, as a woman of the water, to dedicate my life to this work and this service as I have been called."

Her mother waded into the sea and held out a hand to Mira, who placed her right hand in her mother's. "Upon this oath, I give you this ring, its likeness worn only by true water women." Her mother slid a thin gold band on Mira's ring finger. It had been forged of gold but incorporated a strand of byssus inside, gold within gold, sea within earth. The oath was complete. Together, they sang an ancient weaver's song, one mixing Aramaic and Hebrew, Italian and Nuragic, a language as old as the island's beginnings, one that reached back to Queen Berenice herself. When the last strains ended, she and Zaneta waded out farther, where the shore ended at a sudden rocky drop-off. Here, with an unspoken signal, they dove deep, spinning and twirling underwater like porpoises. Mira brimmed with happiness, buoyed by her joy and the salt of the sea. Her golden robe swirled around her white legs as she kicked, sending schools of silver fish zigzagging around her.

How was it possible to feel such pride and such deep humility at the same time? Dante's words returned to her, and for once, Mira allowed herself a sense of accomplishment and confidence, knowing how hard she'd worked and how much she'd learned. She turned toward her mother as they swam, and Zaneta reached out and grasped Mira's wrist. Reflexively, Mira grasped back, and they remained that way, mother and daughter, bound and breathless, before rising to the surface for air.

Chapter 26

After that, Mira began receiving her own visitors to the workshop. On days when Zaneta was at the market or on some errand, she no longer had to turn people away, telling them to come back later when her mother had returned. Now, Mira sat in the light of the window, holding a woman's hands as she poured out her heart, the way she'd witnessed her mother doing. She wove tiny byssus rings and bracelets for the children brought by their mothers, coaxing a promise they'd return when it came their turn to be wed.

"If you come back when you're engaged to your sweetheart," she told the young girls, "you can trade that ring for a pretty pillowcase for your bed."

For the women who ducked through the workshop doorway, their bellies heavy with a baby, Mira gave them bracelets for good fortune, a gift from the fruitful sea that provided them with food in all seasons. She prayed with them in a mixture of Hebrew and Italian, lifting up blessings on their behalf, a kind of priestess of the sea and its Maker.

Mira and Dante waited a year to be married, until he was established at the school and she had settled into her new role. Mira's father wasn't against the union but said a year of commitment wouldn't hurt anyone. Her mother, rather than being happy with the news, seemed to grow snappish and aloof, helping only reluctantly with planning the wedding. Mira was disappointed but honestly not surprised. Perhaps her mother worried marriage and a family would distract Mira from the byssus? But Mira sensed it was something else, something she wouldn't or couldn't talk about from the past. Her mother never discussed that time, no matter how many questions Mira asked, a refusal that once used to fuel Mira's curiosity but now simply exasperated her.

"One wedding is like any other," her mother said. "The rabbi will perform the ceremony, and that's that."

"Didn't you have more than that when you got married to Papà?"

"That was different. There wasn't money for finery and fuss."

"I don't want or expect either," Mira said, "but Carmina at least has to be there, and Dante's family will come."

"We're Italian. We'll be hospitable and have a respectable meal and wine. No one will expect more, given our means."

"I wish we had more family who could attend," Mira lamented.

Zaneta's hands stopped their rhythmic motions at the loom. "If wishes were horses, beggars would ride," she snapped. "Papà's parents will come, though they're so old they won't want to stay long. Everyone else is gone."

"Maybe I could carry a piece of your dress? Or wear your veil?"

"I told you, Mira, there wasn't any of that. We had to marry quickly." Zaneta seemed to check herself, then added, "Because of the times. It's not about the wedding anyway. It's about the marriage. You'd better be sure about it."

"Of course I am. Dante's perfect."

Zaneta shook her head. "You have stars in your eyes. Life isn't a fairy tale."

Mira smothered a laugh under her hand, tucking that comment away to share with Carmina later. What would her mother know? She'd never so much as seen her parents kiss goodbye. They were civil to each other, and her father was certainly tolerant of Zaneta's dark moods. She and her brothers were proof that her parents had shared at least some passionate moments, but there was no magical spark, no giggles or sly kisses like she and Dante shared. She supposed that could be some sort of love, but it wasn't the sort she was after. Dante did more than tolerate her. He encouraged and celebrated her talent; thought up new compliments every day; and made her swoon when he held her close, smelling of chalk and ink and coffee. Mira couldn't wait to get married.

~

The night before her wedding, she tossed and turned in bed, unable to quiet her mind enough to sleep, and she overheard her parents talking outside.

"Can't you be happy for one day, Zeta? Not just for Mira but for you? For us?"

"I'm as glad for Mira as I can be. You should know by now happy isn't something I'm very good at. I suppose this has all been stirring up memories I've tried to lock away, ghosts long buried, and it makes me think of how it could have been different, how it *should* have been different. I wish my family were here to give a blessing. How much of a heart do you need to be happy?"

"I'll give you some of mine," her father said, his voice so low Mira had to strain to hear it. "It's always been available."

"You're a good man, Luccio." Zaneta sighed. The locks on the door clicked, and Mira heard them pattering about the house, shutting it up for the night. A piece of her iced into place in the empty pit inside of her, as she wished for the millionth time that her mother would be excited and happy for her. Carmina's mother, Signora Petrolus, had been over the moon for months, full of questions and wedding chatter. Mira would give anything if her own mother would act like that. She swallowed the lump in her throat and willed away the heaviness that settled upon her chest. Tomorrow, she would marry Dante, and life would have more happiness than she could hold.

When the day came, on a late afternoon in April, the year Mira turned twenty, she and Dante stood under the chuppah in front of a small gathering of friends and family—their parents and many of Dante's relatives she'd only just met—on a sandy stretch of the

Sardegnan Mediterranean shore. The sun cast its shimmering golden light on the sea while tawny speckled kestrels and white gulls drifted on the fading mistral winds. Mira had never looked lovelier. Pieces of her hair hung loose and curled, while the rest had been braided lavishly around her head. The effect of her simple white dress was stunning against the turquoise backdrop of water and sky, its sole adornment an embroidered trim of byssus thread that reflected the light and sparkled like diamonds.

Dante's dark suit complemented his tanned skin and beard, and a smile played on his lips during the entire ceremony, though his hands shook slightly as they held hers. Because he wasn't Jewish, Mira had had to coach Dante through certain aspects of the ceremony—the ketubah, hakafot, and logistics of the processional—because he'd been concerned about doing everything correctly, still determined to prove himself to her parents. Mira's left hand received a slightly larger ring than the one she'd received for taking the water oath. While it contained no byssus threads, it was dear to her heart because of the new vows she took, those that anchored her to a lifetime with Dante Barone.

Despite her mother's reservations about fuss and finery, Mira's father relented, and they held a joyous and festive party after the ceremony, with her mother playing the gracious hostess. Mira laughed until she was breathless at the face Dante made when his chair tipped during the dizzying hora dance, and she drank too much wine, sipping after each "Mazel tov!" offered. Even Johann and Isaac wished her well, saying they would miss her not being at home as much. Mira had always acted like a second mother to the two of them, especially when her mother sank into one of her moods and did nothing but shush and scold. They'd gradually gotten over having a teacher at school date their sister. Sacks of amaretti cookies went a long way to sway young boys' affections.

Mira and Dante planned to spend a week together in Sicily, part honeymoon, part introduction to the larger Barone clan and the places where Dante had grown up. After the third day, a restless tug pulled at

Mira, and she stared out the window at the sliver of yellow moon while Dante slept. She surprised her new husband early in the morning by pulling him out of bed and toward the water outside the cozy beach cottage they'd shared. It was so early, the crickets still chirped in the wet grass as they walked.

"What are you up to?" he teased her, pulling on her long braid.

In reply, she shed her thin nightdress and spun around on the sand in the chill air while Dante stared openly at her nakedness. Mira laughed at his expression and, delighted she could have such an effect, ran splashing into the waves until they knocked her off her feet. Dante gave a darting glance in either direction and then left a trail of discarded clothes and followed his bride, shaking water from his hair when he surfaced, sputtering. She was a nymph, a siren, and she urged him farther out until neither of them could touch the rocks beneath their feet. Despite all the lessons and treasures it had offered her before, the sea showed Mira yet another as it cradled her and Dante in their union.

"You've been quiet," he commented later, once they'd dried off and eaten, stuffing themselves with cheese and bread. "You've drifted off; where'd you go?" Mira shrugged and curled on her side against him with her eyes closed. "You want to go back—is that it?"

She looked up at him, surprised he knew. "It's wonderful here, Dante. That's not it."

"It has been wonderful," he agreed, "but it's time we return. I no longer have your undivided attention." Before she could protest, he held up a hand. "No apologies, Mira. It's getting close to harvest time. I understand."

"I'll make it up to you when we get back," she said, already bouncing off the bed and snatching up stray items of clothing from the backs of chairs and the floor.

"I'm counting on it," he said.

Chapter 27

With help from his family, Dante and Mira Barone set up a modest home about a half mile from Mira's family. His teacher's salary provided all they needed. Mira was accustomed to living frugally, and as she explained to Dante, part of her initiation into the life of a water woman had included proving she could hunt and fish with her hands and that she could tolerate hunger and thirst.

"I hope it won't come down to hunger and thirst," he joked. All the same, as part of her daily routine of swimming and visiting the sea twice a day, Mira often gathered olives, pomegranates, and greens on her walks. She dug for oysters, and they regularly ate fish, urchins, or crabs she caught for dinner. She always took a net or short spear with her when she swam, and because she could hold her breath for so long, it was easy to catch supper. The sea eagerly provided. The moon waxed and waned, and she and Dante settled into their cozy married routine.

Aside from the fishing and the evenings she spent at her own home, Mira's life went on much the same at her mother's byssus workshop. She'd held out a small measure of hope that once she was married and out of the Mazza house, the two of them might grow closer, leaving their old roles behind, but it had been several years, and still her mother's walls refused to crumble. Since she'd taken the water oath, Zaneta had shown her the respect of a colleague, veiling her criticism when it came to working the byssus, but it was unhampered when it came to Mira's personal life.

If Mira showed up in a good mood, humming or with a lightness to her steps from an evening well spent, her mother focused on her fingers while she wove, exhaling pointed, heavy sighs.

"Do you mind, Mira? This is a difficult pattern, and I need to concentrate. Quiet would be helpful. Or you can sing the weaving song."

"Of course. Sorry, I didn't realize I was doing it."

"To be in such a fine temper, maybe you have some news?" she pressed.

"No news." Mira shook her head, her voice bright. Always the same topic.

"The sooner the better." Zaneta wagged a finger. "Daughters aren't a guarantee. One of our line bore seven sons before a daughter came. Seven!"

"We'll just have to give it time."

"Don't you want to start a family?" carped Zaneta.

It was Mira's turn to sigh. "We *have* started a family. Dante and I are a family of two." She couldn't have this conversation again, not now. "I'll be outside rinsing the thread."

Mira's tears fell into the acid wash, and she hoped the tiny bit of extra salt wouldn't affect the mixture. Two days prior came the unmistakable signs she was miscarrying—again. It was the third, and with each one, she knew Dante grew more concerned, not that they might not have a child, though that would carry its own grief, but that she fell into such a deep and punishing sorrow each time. No matter what he said, she wouldn't believe it wasn't her fault, that he was happy—more than happy—with their family of two.

On this island, in their culture, children were expected. On summer evenings, families gathered around the supper table and lingered over the meal, and if you walked down the street, you could hear them through their open windows, talking, laughing, and drinking. Mira loved that about Sant'Antioco—the boisterous chatter and the nonnas serving dish after dish of steaming seafood or pasta while children ran underfoot in the kitchen. Her friend Carmina had married a boat captain a year after Mira and Dante had wed, and she already had a son in her nursery and was talking about having another soon. Mira hadn't told her about her own difficulty. She hadn't wanted to dampen Carmina's happiness, and truthfully, they didn't see each other as much as they used to anyway. The bustle of her friend's motherhood left little time for the leisurely talks over espresso they used to have.

Though Mira had gone out of her way to embroider beautiful pieces of byssus for Carmina's baby and stop by with helpful meals after he was born, she was jealous; of course she was. Seeing Carmina hold her small son stirred up such a longing in her that she could hardly stand to be in the same room with her friend. Her arms ached to hold a child knit from parts of her and Dante, and she knew he would make such a kind and encouraging father.

She'd heard stories from the war times from farmers on the island. Some said that after the house-to-house mosquito dustings, their livestock suffered. Beehives emptied, and sheep failed to lamb. Fish, they said, floated in some of the wetlands and were not as plentiful for several years after. Mira was intimately familiar with nature, bound as she was to the sea. More than once, she remembered her parents talking of the men pumping dust in their home, on their children—her. Could that have anything to do with her difficulties? The DDT had wiped out mosquito larvae. What had it done to the eggs she carried in her own body?

Mira wiped her tears and placed a wet hand on her abdomen, which throbbed with the familiar dull ache of emptiness and failure. Dante had brought her hot tea in bed that morning and urged her to stay home, but Mira had refused, pretending she had bounced back, that she wasn't shattered into pieces by a third loss. How many more would there be? Was this a sign she would never conceive? As her mother never stopped reminding her, the continuation of the line of water women demanded that she have a daughter. If she couldn't, the thread of master byssus weavers would break, and the disappointment of generations would fall solely on Mira's shoulders. The strain of such added pressure showed in the shadows that darkened under Mira's eyes. Zaneta acted like she was refusing to conceive on purpose, as if she wished for nothing but to be free to live a carefree, indulgent life. Truthfully, Mira couldn't bear to tell her mother the difficulty they'd been having. She was sure it would be confirmation that she was the disappointment her mother had believed her to be all along. She couldn't withstand the added sting of her mother's judgment on top of her own disappointment and sadness.

Mira had lost count of the number of women who had knocked on the workshop door over the years, worry etched into their faces. So many came for a blessing, a prayer, a token of byssus to wear for fertility and good fortune; for healthy pregnancies and deliveries; for sons, twins, daughters. Some, like her, must have also struggled. Sometimes, as she or her mother wrapped their wrist with a byssus bracelet and offered a blessing, their lips would tremble and tears would brim. She wasn't the only one who'd miscarried, who longed to carry a child but couldn't, but she thought she must be the only one who couldn't share it. Who would want to come to a water woman for such a gift if she wasn't able to help herself?

Mira had been surrounded by such golden tokens her whole life, yet they seemed to bear no luck for her, no blessings. Still, she dutifully walked to the shore twice a day to offer her life and her prayers in service and peace. She tried to mask her want, to pretend it hadn't crept in like a fog and fanned out inside her to fill every hidden corner, as if she could perhaps fool the universe into believing that if a child didn't mean so much, it would be merely a small shower of blessing to grant her heart's desire, easily done.

It occurred to Mira that, besides the ring from the water oath, she'd never actually received a gift of byssus, not in the way those had who had come to their door. The water oath forbade her to use byssus for personal gain, and since it could only be given or received, she couldn't very well give it to herself. While she easily granted the priceless treasure to others, only one person alive could present it to Mira, and apparently, she had not thought to do so. Mira couldn't bring herself to ask Zaneta for such a thing. If there was anything she possibly wanted more than a child, it was her mother's understanding, the sort Mira had watched her give freely to others all her life. Why was it so hard for Zaneta to love her? Mira couldn't bear facing her mother's refusal, not for this, not when it proved she was unreliable for continuing their line.

~

Byssus saved her. After the fourth and then the fifth miscarriage, Mira's sorrow threatened to pull her under like an anchor. Her limbs felt weighted with sand, and even simple conversations required too much effort. She went robotically through the motions of each day—rinsing, dyeing, spinning, carding, weaving—but it was an empty exercise; she might as well have been moving pebbles uselessly from one box to the next. Mira's mind could only focus on its singular goal. The world had shifted. Her vision became like the strips of photograph negatives she'd seen once in the post office, when a man, a foreign journalist visiting the island, had emptied an envelope and held them up to the light to examine the images. She'd asked about them, and he'd handed her one. Those curious images seemed to highlight everything that wasn't, and that was exactly how the string of losses had shaped Mira's perspective. Each sunrise began a new day she wasn't carrying a child; each meal she ate nourished an empty womb. The peaks and valleys of hope and despair, telling and untelling rose and fell with such sudden drops, Mira remained braced for impact, jumpy, teeth on edge.

"This can't go on." Dante finally said it one morning as he watched Mira dully pick over a cheese pie at breakfast. "It's time to stop trying."

Mira's head jerked up at him. "What are you saying?"

"I'm worried, cara. It can't be good to keep doing this to yourself, your body. Not to mention what it's doing to your heart."

Mira dropped her fork, and it clattered on the plate. "Dante, we can't just quit. What about our family?"

"You're the one who always said we already are a family. I actually believe that. Don't you?"

Tears leaked down her face, and Dante knelt beside her to take her hands in his. "We've already lost so much. I feel like I'm losing you, too, like it's all sweeping you away. You're living inside it, this cave of grief. Please, for us, come out."

Dante's dark eyes pooled with tears, and Mira's face crumpled as her last shreds of hope dissolved. She knew he was right, had known it for some time, but hadn't been able to let go of the possibility. Although she desperately wanted a child of their own, she knew that in letting go of this, she would also be letting go of her lineage, leaving no legacy to continue the craft.

"Can't our life still be good? You're enough for me, Mira." She nodded, her words strangled on the stinging lump lodged in her throat. She was grateful for him. He was enough for her, too. He would have to be.

Together, they boxed the few items they had allowed themselves to collect for a nursery, and Dante climbed the attic stairs to place it in a corner where they wouldn't run across it easily. He drove them to the synagogue in Cagliari, where they prayed for gratitude and joy. They placed five smooth stones on a single piece of granite they'd brought to the Jewish cemetery, a symbol of past remembrance and trust for what lay ahead. Slowly, patiently, Dante coaxed her out of the clutches of grief with small, quiet advances. He brought her bunches of wild laurel and bright-pink oleander he'd gathered on his way home from school to brighten up the kitchen. He convinced her to venture out on walks along the shore on warm afternoons when the sun was sinking and the tide was out, Mira's favorite time of day. Sometimes, when Dante wasn't teaching, they'd drive inland to explore the trails among the mysterious nuragic ruins or sit by waterfalls to talk and remember how to laugh.

Eventually, Mira reached out to Carmina and began spending time with her friend again. Seeing Carmina with her young children still stung, but it was no longer a dagger to Mira's heart. A small measure of peace settled on her as Mira created a space for grief to live inside of her instead of her crawling up in its lap to take refuge. Dante assured her they weren't moving on—because they would never get over this part of their life—as much as they were moving *forward.*

Dante's tenderness and gentle prodding gave Mira something else as well—a sense of worth and gratefulness for all she *did* have. Seeing herself reflected back in his eyes instilled her with strength. If he looked at her like that, Mira thought, maybe she was more capable than she believed, more able and strong and lovely. Dante was her weight-bearing wall, and Mira's heart nearly burst from her fierce love of him.

It was Dante who helped Mira see her byssus work in a new light. One evening, Mira came home and laid aside several pieces of weaving she'd done that day. Dante had set the table and poured the wine while she finished sautéing the onion and mushroom sauce for their simple pasta meal. Mira looked up from the stove to see Dante standing by the window, admiring first one piece, then another, as he held them up to the fading light.

"What?" she asked. "What are you thinking?"

"What it means to create something," he mused. "How you do this strange kind of alchemy, spinning gold into patterns so beautiful they take your breath."

Mira cocked her head. "High praise. You're sweet." She poured the steaming sauce on their plates and walked them to the table.

"I think these are some of your most striking pieces, Mira. Better than your mother's work." At that, Dante ducked his head and glanced out the window, making a show of being sure his words hadn't been overheard.

"You really think so?" She joined him at the window, examining the intricate scene she'd created with the golden threads lighter than a strand of hair. It was a flock of sheep lying in an idyllic pasture, sleeping and grazing near a towering golden lion. Each hair of his gilded mane was so lifelike it appeared to shift and move in the light.

He laid the cloth down and turned to her. "Byssus is your child, Mira. It's your creative work, the deepest part of you that you tend and nurture and allow to grow. It's your legacy that lives on."

"Come eat," was all she said, but Mira tossed the thought around and let it settle over the next few days as she sat at the loom. She realized, in a sense, of course, Dante was right. She gave her life to the byssus, her time, energy, talents. When she sent a piece out into the world, she hoped it blessed someone and brought joy. Art like this endured.

~

Zaneta continued to needle Mira despite her trying to steer clear of the subject. One morning, while Mira worked at the loom, its bars and spindle clacking with its hypnotizing rhythm, a young woman knocked, seeking her mother's blessing and a token of byssus for good fortune.

"Teresa, mia cara, come in and let me look at you." Zaneta beamed as she held her arms out, exclaiming over the young woman's round pregnant belly. Mira dropped her eyes, tried to concentrate on her fingers' task.

"You must be near term. You're blossoming. Come, come sit." Zaneta gestured to a chair by the window and started combing through the top drawer of an olive-wood chest that stood in the corner.

"Here, I have just the thing." Zaneta sat across from Teresa and gestured for the woman's arm. Mira stole furtive glances across the room as her mother rubbed the woman's arm and tied a delicate braided bracelet of byssus around her wrist. "Receive this gift," she said, "offered from the sea and from the Father above, that it might remind you that you're protected and blessed."

Mira hummed along with the familiar chanting song her mother quietly sang. She caught Teresa's eye and smiled at her. It dawned on her that for the first time, she didn't have to fight the urge to rush from the room, putting distance between her emptiness and another woman's obvious fertility. The ugly vine of envy had unfurled itself from her heart and left it free to feel happiness for someone else.

Zaneta rose from her chair. "Let me get you some raspberry tea. I think I remember that's good for pregnancy. I haven't had the occasion to brew any for some time."

Teresa glanced at Mira, who rolled her eyes at the thinly veiled comment. She shrugged and shook her head at Teresa. *Mothers,* her gesture said. *What can you do?*

After Teresa had gone, Mira adjusted the colors of threads on her oleander spindle while her mother cleaned up the saucers. "Why must you do that?" she asked.

The dishes clattered in the small pedestal sink as her mother washed and rinsed them. "I don't know what you mean."

"Yes, you do." Mira laid the spindle on top of the weave. "Badger me like that about having a baby."

Zaneta dried her hands and turned to face her. "I wasn't *badgering* you, Mira. You're so sensitive. Maybe hinting a bit."

"I got the hint a long time ago, Mamma. You need to stop."

"You've been married several years now."

"And?"

"What exactly are you waiting for? Is it just to spite me?"

Mira threw her hands in the air. "Oy vey! Yes, Mamma. That's it exactly. Dante and I have deliberately gotten pregnant over and over and then ripped our hearts out with each miscarriage solely to have the satisfaction of spiting you." Tears sprang to her eyes, and she hastily wiped them away. Her mother's mouth fell open, and she continued.

"Oh, you didn't know? Why would you? Did you ever notice that I was quiet or sad? That I managed to be absent when expecting women came to the door? Did you ever ask or just imply I wasn't trying, wasn't doing enough?"

"You should've said." Her mother pressed her lips together. "To let me go on like that was cruel."

"Of course, that's my fault, too." She laughed, the sound bitter and brittle. She shook her head then. If she'd learned anything, it was that her mother's responses were at least predictable. "Just stop," she said, holding up her hands. "I'm asking you to stop. If we don't have children, it wasn't meant to be. It's not my choice, though, so enough with the blame. I guess I can't expect you to understand. You've never felt this kind of pain."

Her mother's hand gripped the towel she still held, and her eyes darkened like a storm rolling in. She stood erect, but Mira thought she saw the faintest quiver in her mother's chin. She'd never seen her mother show a weakness before, certainly not actual tears.

"You know so much?" she spat. "You have no idea what I've carried. All I've sacrificed to keep our tradition and line alive, and of course—*of course*—the only daughter I'm given in a pit of ruin would be its undoing. Will I never stop being punished?" Zaneta put a hand to her throat as if her voice had betrayed her. She threw the towel to the ground and stalked out, leaving the door to slam behind her.

Mira's arms were tired of hefting her imaginary shield to deflect Zaneta's arrows. She'd become adept at fending them off. Dante had given her a new way of seeing herself, making her shield stronger. Yet every once in a while, like now, an arrow met its mark. Zaneta thought of her as a punishment? She'd come from a pit of ruin? She trembled with the effort it took not to howl like an animal releasing its pain. In the terrible silence that Zaneta had left in her wake, it struck her that—still—the blame lay at her own feet. Still, her mother had never said she was sorry.

Chapter 28

Dante leaned in to kiss Mira's neck as she sat near the window in her studio, the perfect place for the autumn Mediterranean light to stream in over her loom. She shivered. Even after twelve years of marriage, he still gave her butterflies.

"How's the work today?" he asked, placing a brown sack on the table near her. She smelled the almonds and knew it must be from the bakery near the port.

Mira arched her back and stretched her arms behind her to ease the ache in her shoulders. "Bene, bene," she said. "I'm doing a veil for Tess Grenaldi and after that, back to the tapestry for Santa Croce."

Dante shook his head. "I still think it's odd that a Roman Catholic church asks for an altar piece from a Jewish weaver who uses ancient arts."

"That church happens to be built on top of one of the earliest synagogues in Italy, and byssus weaving isn't about taking sides. It's been used in both Jewish and Christian vestments."

Dante kissed her again. "Carry on, then, dear. I'll leave it to you to mend the historic rifts of religion while I tackle that roof leak."

"Don't fall," she warned. "There are only so many rifts I can mend in one day."

Mira watched as Dante climbed the ladder to the studio's roof, his legs passing her window as his feet stepped higher until they disappeared and she heard his footsteps above. Though math was more his specialty, he did his best to keep things working around their small house. The studio, though, had been a true labor of love. After Mira and her mother's explosive falling-out, Mira had marched home, her face flushed and her apron wet from tears. That had been Dante's line in the sand.

"No more," he'd said. "I won't stand for it. You're not working over there anymore. You can't keep getting torn up like this."

"I'm a water woman, Dante," she'd sobbed. "That's our workshop."

"We'll build a new one," he'd declared. "Starting tomorrow."

Building had been the easy part. Assembling the dyes, plants, and materials had been quite another task. Mira waited for a day when she knew Zaneta would be at the market, and she'd let herself into the workshop. She gathered everything she might need—tools, samples, cloth, and a few of the rarer dyes that she couldn't easily replicate immediately—leaving plenty for her mother's use. If Zaneta wanted to keep the line of water women intact, she couldn't begrudge allowing Mira something to work with.

Her father had heard noises and come to investigate. "Mira, you've come back." He was relieved, she could tell, but as much as she hated to disappoint him, she'd shaken her head.

"Just to gather a few things. From now on, I'll work from my own home, Papà. This space is too cramped for two of us."

Luccio had looked at her sadly. "I know, Mira. This is probably for the best. Your mother—"

"Don't make excuses for her, Papà."

"She told me about your . . . your difficulties," he stammered. Luccio was of a generation where men didn't speak of female matters. "I'm so sorry, cara."

Mira squeezed her father around his neck. "Thank you." She shrugged. "I have Dante, and he's more than enough."

Luccio looked at the spools and plants in Mira's baskets. "What will you do for a loom?"

"I'm not sure yet," she'd admitted, tracing the scarred wood of the familiar ancient beast. "This one holds so much history. It's the only one I've ever used."

"Leave that to me," he'd told her. "I owe you at least that."

She'd taken his offer for what it was—a request for restoration. Her father was a man of few words, but she could tell what he'd been trying to say was that he was sorry both for what had happened between her and her mother and for whatever part he'd played in his daughter's exodus.

A year later, after putting in long hours after school, tiling, sanding, and ensuring Mira's studio was snug and full of light, Dante walked her outside their kitchen after the last laborer had driven away. He led her, blindfolded, down the stone path that wound from their back door to the door of the studio. She hadn't been allowed in for the last two weeks of its construction, and she'd been giddy with anticipation of finally having a space of her own.

Dante had opened the door and guided her inside, where the comforting smell of dyes and the warm scent of wool and cloth hung in the air, mixed with fresh paint and cut wood.

"Now?" she'd asked, one hand on her blindfold.

"All right. Go ahead."

She'd whipped off the blindfold to find the space full of people shouting "Sorpresa" and toasting her with raised glasses of Vermentino. Carmina's family was there, and Signor Donetti with plates of his cookies. Mira saw several women she'd gifted with byssus over the years and a colleague or two from Dante's school who'd come to see the project that had taken all his free time and energy over the past year. The inside walls had been freshly whitewashed and hung with tidy shelves holding spools of thread organized by color. She recognized Carmina's hand in such efficiency. There was a sink along one wall, handy for rinsing tools and for the constant fresh water needed for washing the byssus. Tight lines of rope had been strung across one corner near the windows where she could hang flock to dry.

Dante had framed a series of photos and arranged them on one wall. He'd captured images of their favorite places on the island: the rocky shore where she went to offer her song to the sea, a grand view of the water from one of the high points on the island, one of the nuragic ruins bathed in sunlight and shadow, and the isolated lagoon where the byssus grew. Mira's eye fell on one other that she didn't recognize at first; it wasn't from Sant'Antioco. When she realized what it was—a photo of the cove where she'd led Dante out into the sea on their Sicilian honeymoon—she'd met his eyes and blushed, smiling. The studio couldn't have been more perfect.

"Thank you! Thank you!" she'd gushed. "It's perfect. I can't wait to get to work here." The gatherers had parted then, opening like the Red Sea and drawing Mira's gaze to the window, where her father sat on an olive-wood stool in front of a beautiful loom, a loom of her very own. "Oh." Mira's hand flew to her mouth, and her eyes welled with tears.

Her father had risen and ceded his seat to Mira, and she'd run her hands over the loom's parts, the upper and lower crossbeams between which she'd be able to weave her own worlds of creation, the spindles and distaff and bobbins that had been sanded smooth by her father's hands. It was beautiful, made of juniper wood and pieced with the precision of an engineer, a perfect replica of the one she'd used all her life.

"Papà," she'd said. "Papà." Those were the only words she'd managed to croak before she dissolved into tears. Luccio had hugged her tightly.

"I hope you like it," he'd whispered. "It should last a good long time. Be worthy of passing down someday." Then he'd stopped, stricken by what he'd said. "I—didn't mean—I'm sorry," he'd sputtered.

"It's all right, Papà. I know what you meant. Thank you for this. I'll treasure every minute on it."

The only one absent that night had been her mother, but even that couldn't have spoiled Dante's surprise. Mira had her own byssus studio, her private space where she could work and receive visitors, where she could create and sing and weave. After everyone had gone and all the glasses and cookie crumbs had been cleared away, Dante and Mira had gone for a chilly walk on the shore near the byssus lagoon beneath a smile of yellow moon that reflected in golden waves of light on the dark water. Mira drew Dante's hands to her waist and tilted her chin to look up at him in the pale moonlight.

"Dante Barone, you'll never be able to top that studio." Mira kissed him. "Thank you."

"It makes my heart happy to see you so happy," he'd told her. "I'm especially glad you recognized the photos on the wall."

"There was that one I couldn't place at first," she'd teased.

"Let's see if we can jog your memory." He'd taken Mira's hand and turned to the sea, but she shrieked, swatting him.

"It's too cold. We'll freeze!"

"Maybe January isn't the best time for swimming under the moon. Let's go home."

They raced each other along the shore, sand flying from their feet, and burst breathless and flushed through the door of their house, casting their clothes in a hasty pile on the yellow wood floor.

With Dante hammering on the roof of the studio, Mira walked outside for some fresh spring air and nibbled a handful of dainty amaretti cookies. She should ask Dante to stop bringing these home, Mira thought. Either that or she needed to swim a bit more each day. She was getting thicker around her middle. Approaching thirty, she no longer had the metabolism that she once did. Mira toyed with her long braid, noting that it, too, had a few wiry strands of gray twisting through the plait.

A movement caught Mira's eye, and she looked up to see a flock of dark-brown swifts dancing in the currents high above. The pale outline of the moon was still visible, the faint gray shape no match for the sun's glare in the blue sky. She sighed. Absently, Mira stared at the moon, wondering at its faraway partnership with the tides she knew intimately here below. The pressing nudge of a thought tugged at her as she brushed the sugar from her fingers, the last of the cookies eaten. She'd long ago stopped measuring her own body by the moon, but now, she thought, what if?

She glanced up at Dante, shielding her eyes against the sun. His strong back was bent over as he tacked new tiles to the roof. "I have to run an errand," she called. "I might be gone for a while."

He waved in response, intent on his task. "Keys are on the hook. I'm almost done up here. I'll clean that grouper you brought, and we can have that for dinner when you get back."

In a fog, Mira took the keys from their hook by the door and started the car. She headed toward town, but instead of following the easy, winding road to the port, she detoured and took the faster route that led to the land bridge and the larger island of Sardegna. She wanted a market where she would be less likely to be recognized, though even on the big island, as they called it, all the locals knew one another. This couldn't wait until after the weekend when the clinics opened. Mira thought she might burst before then.

She skipped the nearest market and opted for one on the eastern side of the island, where most of the tourists gathered. It was offseason, which meant diminished crowds, but it would have to do. Mira parked and sat in the car for a minute, gathering her courage and trying to remember what breathing felt like. She only had to wait behind one other customer, and when it was her turn, she pushed the pregnancy test across the counter, along with a bottle of water and a packet of the biscotti Dante liked with his coffee, as if they could camouflage the issue. She managed a tight smile as she gathered the items and hurried to the car.

Once inside, the old mix of hope and disappointment flooded back so vividly, it was almost as if she could taste it on her tongue. She couldn't make it back to the house without knowing, but neither could she go back into the market and use the restroom. She felt like a guilty teenager skulking around. Instead, Mira crossed back over the land bridge to Sant'Antioco and pulled over near a sandy path shielded by scrubby forest. She ducked into the brush and worked her way far enough from the road where she wouldn't be seen. She spent enough hours outdoors that taking care of basic needs as they arose was common. She told herself that was all this was.

A pair of red deer bounded through the trees about twenty feet from where she squatted in the brush, holding the white stick beneath her, and Mira nearly toppled over, but she gripped the test stick like a lifeline. Gathering her dignity, she marched back to the car, poured water on her hands and shook them dry, and waited. *Positive.* Mira's hands trembled on the wheel as she drove the rest of the way home. How many years had it been since they'd last been through this? She'd thought they were done, that she was past even having to be mindful of this chance. Once or twice, Mira had thought to ask her mother about her own experience—how old had she been when she'd stopped bleeding—but they'd never talked of such things before, and they surely wouldn't now. Her stomach lurched as memories from all the other losses flooded back. How could they have been so careless?

The savory smell of fresh breaded grouper fingers met Mira before she even opened the door to the house. The sun had almost set—she'd been gone longer than she thought—and the once pale moon had gathered strength and now glowed white across the water's surface.

"What?" Dante asked as soon as he saw her face. His hands froze over the pan of fish strips. "What's happened?"

Mira sank into a chair at the table and slid the market sack over to him. She clutched the half-empty bottle of water and biscotti in her hands. Dante snatched up the bag and looked inside. He pulled out the test and stared at it for a full minute, not saying a word. His brow furrowed as he looked at her in confusion.

"I couldn't believe it either," said Mira, her voice ragged with emotion. She stared down at her hands. "Oh, I got you some biscotti."

Dante turned off the stove and shoved the pan off the heat. He knelt on the floor beside Mira and laid his head in her lap, his arms around her waist. They stayed like that while darkness fell, lengthening the shadows on the walls until finally the whole kitchen was cast in shades of charcoal and gray.

Chapter 29

Arrested hope is a feeble-winged bird hopping about on earth instead of tasting the wind and clouds as its nature demands. On an endless loop, Mira reminded herself, as the weeks passed and she waited for the pregnancy to end, that it meant nothing, would come to nothing. Although she was further along than she'd ever been before, fourteen weeks now, she kept her heart prisoner in an airless chamber, out of the reach of hope or the slightest pangs of anticipation. It was like eating handfuls of sugar and denying the tongue's sensation of sweet, forcing instead the thought *sour, sour, sour*. Frankly, it was exhausting. Mira slept more than she ever had in her life. It was easier than the constant warring going on inside her.

Dante was cautious and attentive. Mira could tell he worried about her, hovering and watching her at the loom when he was home from work.

"Maybe you could let Zeta do the dyeing this time?" he asked.

"Everything we use is natural, plant based," Mira replied, shrugging. What did it matter?

"Have you told her yet?" he asked once her belly grew large enough to be noticed. "Or your father? Even Carmina?"

Her shoulders slumped. "Telling just means untelling. Let's just leave it. I wear a loose bathing suit and tie the basket around my waist when I swim. No one's said anything. Soon, we'll leave off swimming, so I won't have to explain." He brought her lemon tea, goat's milk, her favorite pecorino sardo with sea-salted crackers. She wanted to tell him to stop, but she knew it was his way of coping, helping.

Late summer was rainier than usual, and they kept indoors, with Mira often draped under a blanket, staring out the window while her tea grew cold, an idle hand tracing her swelling abdomen. When she wasn't napping, she frenetically worked at the loom, weaving magical scenes of nuragic gondolas ferrying women beneath a phasing moon. Carmina called a few times, concerned Mira might be sick, but Dante put her off enough so that she quit. All couples went through rough patches, and Dante hinted this was one of theirs and they needed some space.

One evening after dinner, while Mira washed their dishes at the sink, she froze, letting the water overfill a glass until it spilled onto the floor.

"Mira?" Dante set down the plate he had dried. "Is everything okay?" She turned the water off and burst into tears, and Dante pulled her close.

"Should I call the doctor?" he whispered. He'd been walking on eggshells, she knew, waiting for Mira to signal what she needed.

"No," she cried. "It's never lasted this long before." She pulled away and grabbed his hand. "I thought I'd imagined it, but this time it was real." She wiped her nose with the dish towel and put Dante's hand on her side. "*There.*"

A swish and a flutter, and Dante pulled his hand away, his eyes round. "Was that . . . ?"

Mira nodded. It was the first time either of them had felt a baby move. Before, she'd miscarried long before any quickening. He put both hands on her belly, waiting. They were rewarded with another kick and tumble large enough that they saw Dante's hand move.

Dante opened his mouth to speak, but Mira put her hand to his lips and shook her head. *Don't voice it,* her heart screamed, *don't say it out loud. Don't let yourself hope*. He understood, but he hugged her close. Mira felt the change in him, the energy that buzzed through his body into hers. He hadn't been quick enough; hope had escaped its prison.

Autumn was getting underway, bringing with it a respite from the lagoon, so Mira no longer saw her mother almost daily. They'd forged a fragile peace but were nowhere close to sharing secrets. Mira was bigger and clumsy, and her back ached from having to lean across her belly to reach the loom as she worked. Carmina visited for the first time in ages, her youngest son with her, bearing soup and bread for the friend she believed to be recovering from a stubborn illness. When Mira opened the door, the folds of her dress and apron weren't enough to hide her secret. Carmina grasped Mira by the shoulders and stared full into her face.

"How could you not tell me?"

Mira hugged Carmina to her, surprising herself with the relief that came with the news. "We assumed there would be nothing to tell, and then time got away." They both cried openly. Mira was doing more and more of that these days; her emotions tumbled out so frequently, Dante could barely keep up. "I'm sorry. I should've. I just didn't dare—"

"When?"

"I'm seven months."

"Your parents?" asked Carmina.

Mira sheepishly picked at the folds of her apron. "We'll tell them. Dante's wanted to for a while, but I've had to warm up to it. All the added pressure."

"A baby, Mira!" Carmina beamed and squeezed her friend's hand. "After all this time."

Her parents were almost as shocked as Mira had been by the news, and they stood in stunned silence for several seconds before her father shouted and broke out the wine. He pumped Dante's hand and slapped him on the back and hugged her, gingerly avoiding her middle. Her mother clasped her hands together, and her thin lips opened into a smile. Then she ducked out of the room and left the others to their celebration. Mira shot a glance at Dante. Her reaction was anticlimactic, but at least they'd received a smile, no small grace, given the cold war that had been stewing between them for years.

Just as they were sitting down to wine and antipasti, with hot tea for Mira, her mother entered the room and sat beside her.

"Your brothers have given us grandsons to spare," she said. "Not a girl in the bunch."

Here it is, thought Mira. *I can't just have a child; it has to be the right sort.* Even if Johann's and Isaac's wives had produced girls, they wouldn't have technically been in a direct female line. Zaneta startled her by taking her hand. "For you," she said, pulling a bracelet of byssus from her pocket. She tied it around Mira's wrist and whispered the familiar prayer. It was lovely, delicate but impossibly strong: *"Like a woman,"* Zaneta used to say. Embroidered with the tiniest Hebrew letters, even in the dim room, the bracelet seemed to draw light to itself to display its golden shimmer. Mira perched her glasses on her nose and examined the delicate threads more closely to make out the word. *Blessed.*

"Do you know," she breathed, running her fingertips over the bracelet, "this is the first piece of byssus I've ever owned?"

"You've never asked," said her mother.

Before Mira could respond, her father interrupted. "It's stunning, Zeta. A treasure."

"Thank you," she said, giving her father a pointed look. "I know what it took to make this. The stitching is perfect."

Satisfied, her mother nodded and met her eyes. "For a healthy child, a quick delivery, and a daughter."

Chapter 30

One Sunday evening in November, Mira and Dante shared a light supper since Mira hadn't felt much like eating. She stood over the crib in the small nursery, running her fingers over the soft blankets and imagining the life the three of them would have, how they would cherish this unexpected gift. Dante had fashioned an enchanting mobile from driftwood and fishing line. Suspended from it hung pieces of oyster shell, the mother-of-pearl changing colors in the early evening light shining through the window. He'd mixed in other things, too: sand dollars, colorful blue and gold glass fish from one of the shops at the port, and white stones polished smooth by the ocean.

When the mobile began to sway, the stones and glass clinking, Mira turned to shut the window. She didn't remember having opened it, especially not when the evenings had begun to carry a chill. But it wasn't open at all, and as she reached out a hand to steady the mobile—the glass fishes weren't meant to knock about so roughly—Dante rushed into the nursery behind her.

"Mira!" He grabbed her from behind and staggered as he pulled her into the doorway. Still, she was confused—it wasn't like Dante to hurt her like that—and why were the books jumping on the shelves, the baby's rattles, lying in the crib, sounding as if they were being shaken by an invisible hand? He held her arms so tightly she thought she might find marks in the morning. When she heard plates shatter against the floor in the kitchen, the fact of the earthquake finally dawned on her, and she crouched low, shielding the swell of her belly with her arms. Though it seemed endless, the worst of the shaking couldn't have gone on more than a few minutes, and when it was over, only a few broken plates and a crack in one window were the result.

Dante rose to his feet, and his gaze swept around the main room. "More than a little rumble," he said, "but not too bad. I'll get a broom."

But Mira remained on the floor, braced against the doorframe. It wasn't over, not yet. Somehow, an equal tectonic shift was occurring inside her, threatening to shatter everything. A vise tightened around her middle until the pain became so sharp it took her breath. Mira moaned, her eyes wide and frightened. This wasn't how they'd planned it. She'd imagined a warm bed, soft lights, and Dante soothing her through the process. The room's edges darkened, and flashes of silver danced in Mira's vision. Strangely, they reminded her of the phosphorescent plankton that sometimes floated in with the ocean on the night tide.

Miles away on the mainland, fires broke out in Naples from broken gas mains, and authorities scrambled to rescue hundreds in the rubble of collapsed churches and apartments. But Mira was oblivious, gripping the dashboard of their Fiat as Dante raced to the hospital in Cagliari. Later, they learned that while the quake struck hardest in Potenza, damage had occurred all along the coast and the Bay of Naples as far south as Sicily. Reports filled the news: the worst to hit Italy in over fifty years, hundreds dead or missing, hospitals filled to capacity. Mira was moved twice to different rooms to accommodate injured people ferried from Sicily to Sardegna.

After the birth, both quicker and involving much more pain and blood than Mira had anticipated, the three of them huddled together in a knot of exhaustion and gratitude as hospital staff dashed back and forth down the corridor outside their room with more urgent concerns than the arrival of a healthy baby girl. Mira wept. It was as if a faucet had unleashed an endless flow of all the sorrow and quenched hope she'd had for over ten years and mixed them with a tidal wave of happiness and love so great she couldn't contain the rush of it.

"Should I call someone?" Poor Dante, his system wrecked by adrenaline, stared at her with a helpless expression. "Are you in pain?"

No, no. Mira shook her head, covering the baby with the thin blanket the nurses had wrapped her in. The edge of it was already soaked with her blubbering. Carmina had warned her about the exodus of emotions that might occur when the hormones readjusted, but Mira knew this was something else. She patted Dante's hand and lay back, letting the tears leak out of her eyes onto the pillows. She tried to reassure him.

"It's simply—everything: joy at holding her, grief—again, does it ever go away?—for those we lost, both happiness and terror at being a mother and wanting more than anything to do it right, to do it *well*. If I'm honest, and"—she laughed, aware of the spectacle she made—"I might as well be, it's also because my own mother fell so woefully short at making me feel loved. What if I—oh, Dante, what if I ever make our daughter feel anything close to that?" The tears gushed faster.

Dante squeezed her hand in his and spoke to her in the professor voice he likely used with his unruly students. "Mira. Listen to me. You will be, no question, the best mother there is. No one has wanted this more, planned for this more, and been more grateful for this gift than you. Even if you tried your hardest, you couldn't mess it up. Look, she already looks at you like you hung the moon."

Mira gazed at the infant in the crook of her arm. One of her tiny fists waved in the air, and the other opened and closed like an anemone in the current. A small finger caught on Mira's byssus bracelet, and the baby's hand impulsively closed on it, grasping by reflex. When she caught Mira's eyes, she stared, blinking against the light.

"See?" said Dante. "She's already drawn to the sea silk."

Mira didn't even hear him, so mesmerized was she by Daniella, her flat button nose, her impossibly long lashes and sandy hair like her father's, and the tip of her pink tongue that poked in and out of her bow mouth. Safe in her cozy nest of motherhood, she forgot all about the earthquake's portent. Such augury was for old-world witches and had no place in Mira's heart.

Chapter 31

Those first weeks and months with the baby blurred together in a haze of exhaustion and endless feeding, napping, and crying—for both Mira and Daniella. When the days stretched longer and warmed, Mira spent as much time as possible outdoors, walking along the shore, pointing out creatures in tide pools, soaking in the salt and spray from the ocean and the warmth from the sun that seemed to renew her from a bone-deep place. She let Daniella splash her toes in the sea and pat the sand with her chubby hands. Squinting against the brightness, the tiny girl laughed at the birds and the waves.

Gradually, the days fell into a rhythm where Mira slipped out early to sing and pray on the rocks as the sun rose across the sea. If there was time, she'd swim and check on the mollusks in the lagoon and walk back to the house, where Dante would be feeding Daniella a breakfast of scrambled eggs and fruit. After he left for school, Mira took her daughter to the studio and let her play in a sunny spot under the window while she spun or wove or mixed dyes. All the while, she sang the byssus songs in all their languages so that Daniella's ears would know them as her own. She chatted and narrated her work, the loom projecting great shadows on the wall as its bars clicked and moved. Daniella was spellbound by the shadows and the way they flickered in and out of the light, and she'd gaze at them until she fell asleep.

Their island was changing. With the warmer weather, more and more tourists showed up at the port, poking around in the few shops, crowding the reliable local cafés to the point that the families who lived there were no longer guaranteed a table. Small inns and seasonal businesses sprang up along the coastline, catering to tourists and the lire they brought to local pockets. Mira preferred to stay home or wander her secret spots along the shore when fewer people were likely to intrude. Dante liked the extra bustle, though, and he'd stop in town on his way home from teaching to catch the latest news and meet people from interesting places. Recently, he'd come home excited to have met a team of archaeologists from a university in Roma. They were collaborating with other universities to excavate and study the Bronze Age nuragic ruins on the island. So little was known about the odd beehive-shaped structures and the people who'd lived there, and the team had been eager to hire locals to map out the area. They'd already begun staking out digs. Sardegna's regional government was certain the extra buzz would mean more visitors, drawn by the unique area.

"Perhaps so," she'd said. "Is that all anyone wants now? More people, more lire?"

"More people to admire the byssus," he countered.

"It's not something to be sold."

"Not to sell. To learn about."

Mira had twisted her mouth. She wasn't sure about that. It wasn't like they kept their byssus work a secret, but displaying it to people who would think of it as a souvenir seemed to cheapen it somehow. She thought of the pescatore families she'd known all her life. Some of the younger sons had started offering fishing trips to tourists, letting them pull in octopus traps or hook a dorado or tuna. She'd seen them posing for their fancy Kodaks at the quay, holding their catch up as they grinned from ear to ear, and it made her sad, somehow. It felt like auctioning their craft and knowledge to the highest bidder. She and Dante discussed it often.

"Is the alternative better? The rest of the world progressing while families here work so hard in the mines or the sea just to scrape by?"

"It may be that we'll all eventually have to get on the train," she admitted. "But I'll probably be in the caboose, looking back at what we're leaving behind."

"Fair enough, love," he said, kissing her on top of her head. "I'm just as happy to stay here with you on the shore, waving as the train goes by."

~

At least twice a week, sometimes more, Mira would answer a knock at the door to find her mother, who happened to be passing by and thought to deliver an extra spool, or some thread ready for weaving, or some other equally flimsy excuse to see Daniella. Mira was cautiously glad of it—at least they were speaking, and she noticed that for the privilege of spending time with her granddaughter, her mother seemed capable of withholding criticism, at least for an hour or so at a stretch. Probably because when Daniella was present, Mira dissolved into invisibility. Zaneta breezed into her home or studio with a glance and a greeting, her eyes combing the usual spots for Daniella—her baby seat, the braided rug in the living room, Mira's arms. After that, all conversation was directed to Daniella: *"Tell Mamma you want to come to Nonna. That's it, dear."* Before Daniella reached six months old, Zaneta had given her granddaughter byssus bracelets and tiny rings, embroidered pillows, and dainty bonnets.

"She's turned into someone I don't even know," Mira mentioned to Dante one night over dinner. "Daniella could reach for one of the fish on her mobile, and my mother would act like she'd landed on the moon."

Dante was careful with his words. "Isn't it—*good*—that she praises her granddaughter?"

"Well, I guess," she conceded. Mira tore a hunk of bread from the challah loaf and dipped it in olive oil. "But I could weave the *Mona Lisa* in gold and she wouldn't bat an eye. Daniella manages to clap her hands, and the angels come down from heaven."

"It sounds like—"

"Don't even say it, Dante. I know where you're going. I'm not jealous of my own daughter. I did *manage* to give birth to her, though, and I'm not totally failing at raising her. *And* I'm still carrying all the responsibilities of a water woman." As she spoke, she gestured with her hands, splattering drops of oil on the table.

Dante captured one of her hands as it fluttered. "I haven't told you enough how amazing you are at balancing everything, have I? How your daughter and I both appreciate you and all you do?"

"It's not that. I just wish . . ."

"I know." He squeezed her hand. "Maybe the only way she can say it to you is by doubling up on the baby. It's like another chance to love a version of you all over again, better this time."

"It comes naturally for me with Daniella. Why is it so hard for her with me?"

Dante shook his head and spread his hands. "*I* love you."

Mira softened. "Despite all my crazy."

Daniella banged a spoon on her tray and shrieked. Dante clasped a hand to his heart in feigned shock and mimicked Zaneta's voice. "Will you look at that, Mira? She's clearly a musical prodigy."

Mira laughed and threw a bite of bread at him. "She can sing while she weaves." She wiped Daniella's hands and face and lifted her out of her seat. "Shall we go for a walk on the beach before bedtime?" she cooed. "Time to go give our song to the sea, my sweet."

Daniella rubbed her eyes with her fists and yawned. "I can keep her here if she's too sleepy," offered Dante.

Mira threw a shawl over her shoulders and tucked a blanket around Daniella. "Nonsense. She wants to go to the shore. We always do, and she can fall asleep on the way home."

~

One rainy afternoon in September, when the usually blue sky was covered by a blanket of white and gray clouds, Mira strapped the baby to her chest and set off for a walk along the shore. She'd made sure to wrap Daniella snugly to keep the cooler breeze from giving her a chill. She laughed at the way Daniella stretched her small hands up toward the open umbrella she carried. The child seemed determined to touch this strange new roof that spun round in circles. Mira didn't have a destination. She simply loved being outdoors, no matter the weather.

Her feet brought her to the familiar cove where she came each morning, but this time she kept walking.

"Where shall we go, Dani? Up the shore? Do you think we can find some flamingos?"

Her daughter seemed to consider the question and babbled back in imitation, one hand gesturing as if making a point. Mira laughed. She saw so much of herself in Daniella, even down to mannerisms like this. It's funny, she thought, how parents search so intently to find themselves in their children, from the moment they're born. *She has her mother's eyes, her father's chin. See how she walks? It's just like her father. How she smiles with those dimples? Her mother's likeness exactly*. She'd done it herself on many occasions.

She wondered what her own mother had made of her. Had she found any similarities between them? Had she noticed her black curls or her tendency to chew the inside of her lip when she wove and seen it as confirmation that, *yes, this one is mine*? When they stood together, people sometimes remarked that they saw the resemblance, but if it hadn't been for the byssus, she wondered if anyone would know she was Zaneta's daughter. Her friend Carmina had shaken her head more than once, bewildered that Mira could be so different from her mother. Mira was kind, she'd said, and easy to talk to, an encourager and fun to be with, but a friend had to say such things, didn't she?

Mira brushed the top of Daniella's head with her hand as the rain fell harder. The wonder of her existence still struck Mira with a forceful blow sometimes, this child they never thought they'd have. She and

Dante had stood over her last night as she'd slept, sharing whispered thoughts about their daughter.

"What do you think she thought of her first taste of octopus?" Dante said. "That face she made." He'd chuckled softly so as not to wake her.

"When she starts walking, the chickens better beware," Mira had said with a laugh. "If you could have seen how fast she crawled trying to catch them. Fearless."

They'd wondered together if she'd be quick with numbers, like Dante, or have a creative streak, like Mira.

"Maybe neither," Dante had stated. "She could be something totally unexpected, a surprise to us both." He put his arms around Mira's waist as they'd gazed down on her. "I want to show her everything, to see what she makes of it all."

"We already know what her life will be like," said Mira. "She's the daughter of a water woman. Someday she'll learn to weave and tend the byssus."

"What if she doesn't?"

The question had seemed so preposterous, so unaskable that Mira had laughed as it hung in the air. But as she'd watched Daniella's chest rise and fall, her tiny fists flung out on either side of her, the thought lingered. This was the only child she'd ever have, her heart's desire. If she grew to be a teacher, say, or a shopkeeper, would she love her any less?

A sudden memory. "When I was five, my mother and I sat on a bench by the port. We were watching a pescatore thigh-deep in the waves. 'Watch the line he casts out when something takes it. See how it pulls tight?' she told me.

"I remember the way the pole's tip curved as the man pulled against the fish he'd snagged. He'd take a few steps backward. Reel and pull, reel and pull. I'd wondered what creature fought against the man: A small shark? Maybe a whale or even a mermaid? At that age, my imagination ran wild."

Dante laughed. "It still does, cara." Mira swiped at him and went on.

"My mother told me, 'If you tried to hold on to that line, it might cut your hand, it's so tight. If you run a finger down it very carefully, when it's taut like that, and listen very hard, you might hear a sound, like a bow across a violin. If you touch it while it makes that hum, it will travel down your finger, up your arm, and right into the middle of you.' She pointed a finger at the center of my chest and smiled, as if to say, *Wouldn't that be grand?*

"But something about that description unsettled me, though at five I couldn't say why. The thought of being connected to a sound or a song that might pull me out where my toes no longer touched the sand was frightening. 'I hope the fish gets free,' I told her. 'Maybe he can swim very hard.'

"She asked me why I'd want that to happen. She said the fisherman would be sad. 'But the fish wouldn't,' I told her."

Dante had stepped closer and wrapped her in his arms. Daniella had stirred in her crib, her small legs kicking out. The little mobile made of glass fish tinkled faintly as a breeze wafted in from the open window. Here was their little fish, Mira thought.

Mira remembered the time before she'd taken the water oath, her brief wonderings about a different life. Had she not followed in her mother's footsteps, she was sure, Zaneta would have had little use for her. What had she ever been besides a placeholder, the next in line?

Daniella started to cry as the sky opened up. The umbrella's feeble shield no longer kept them dry with the rain coming sideways. Mira closed it, tucked Daniella's head beneath her own chin, and sprinted for the rocks ahead. Thankfully, the tide was out. Sometimes that meant shelter in the rocks.

"It's all right, Dani," she soothed. "We'll be out of this wind in a minute."

Just as she'd hoped, there was a small opening between two of the jutting fingers of rock, and she scrambled into the entrance as best she could with one hand on the baby and using the other for balance. It was a sea cave, damp and dark, but at least out of the wind and stinging rain. Daniella's cries echoed inside and seemed to scare her into even louder wails.

"Look, figlia," she coaxed, swaying from side to side with a motion all mothers seem to innately adopt. "What's inside here? What can we see?" Distraction. It always seemed to work where her curious child was concerned.

Mira always carried with her a pouch and a handful of tools in case she happened upon plants or sea life worth gathering. Fortunately, Dante had insisted she carry a flashlight with her as well, after one too many evenings when time had slipped away from her and she'd arrived home after dark. She pulled it from the pouch and switched it on. Immediately, Daniella quieted, and the damp cave felt more hospitable. Mira reminded herself to tell Dante he'd been right about her carrying it.

"A starfish." Mira fixed the light on a pool of water near the ground. "What a pretty orange. And there's a purple one."

She ventured farther in. The cave seemed drier nearer the back, safe from the reach of the high tides. Mira wondered how she hadn't noticed this opening before. If she had, she'd probably been too busy with her work to go exploring, and it was in an out-of-the-way part of the shoreline.

"Ninna nanna, ninna oh. Questo bimbo a chi lo do?" Mira absent-mindedly sang the lullaby as she swayed. Daniella had ceased her squirming, and Mira aimed the flashlight so that the light fell near the ceiling, lighting Dani's face, her eyes round and expressive. She loved how long and soft her daughter's lashes were and the way they made her deep-brown eyes even bigger. Mira softly rubbed the baby's back as she nestled against her. Her eyes followed the light as it reflected, hitting something that was not rock.

Curious, Mira edged closer. There, on an overhang up near the ceiling, something was wedged. It looked like a box with a metal latch. That's what the light must have picked up. Mira stood on her tiptoes and stretched out her arm. She could almost reach it. She was clumsy and off-balance with Daniella's weight across her front. Her pouch! She untied the bag from her waist and cinched its opening tight.

Again, she rose up on her tiptoes, and this time she swung the pouch in an upward arc, intending to knock the thing loose. She missed and tried again, experimenting with distance. This time her aim was better, nudging the box toward the edge of the stone where it rested. One more blow and she'd have it. With her last swing, the box tumbled off the ledge and landed on the damp floor as Mira yelped in victory.

"What do you think this is?" she whispered to Daniella. "Someone's hidden treasure?"

The baby babbled in response, her eyes tracking the beam of light across the floor like a cat. Mira stepped carefully, wary of falling with Dani strapped to her. She knelt on the floor, the light aimed at the discovery.

The box was old; she could tell that much. And unique: made of oleander, with a lovely clasp corroded from the constant salty mist that filled the cave. The bottom was etched with lines, and as Mira peered closer, she could tell it was a map. A map of Sardegna, how lovely! The tumble had marred the surface here and there, but otherwise, it seemed intact. Mira ran her fingers over the lid, appreciating the woodwork. Despite the corrosion, with only a little effort, she was able to pry the clasp free.

Astonishing. Mira sat back on her heels, trying to fathom what she'd found as her heart leaped in her chest. The box was full of familiar items: byssus, dyes, small glass containers of dried flowers, and thread in various stages of processing. Her fingers brushed through sepia photos captioned with dates penned in spiky handwriting. A bundle of letters tied with faded purple ribbon. Mira feared handling them in this damp place lest they fall apart.

"Oh," she breathed when, poking further, she found a wondrous handheld loom in the shape of a lyre, meant for weaving the smallest of byssus creations. And at the bottom of the box, wrapped in layers of leather and cloth, lay what clearly was some sort of ancient script. Mira unrolled it and recognized some of the Hebrew letters, but her knowledge of the language was rusty.

Daniella's warm breath tickled Mira's neck, and she glanced down to see that the child had fallen asleep. The find meant nothing to her, and the sound of the rain falling outside the dim, quiet cave had been enough to lull her into a nap. Mira shut the box and refastened the old clasp. She rose to her feet, cradling Daniella in her sling with one arm while lifting the box in the crook of her other. She peered out at the beach. The rain had tapered off. She couldn't wait to get back to the house, where she could examine everything in a dry, lit place. How long had this box been wedged in the back of this sea cave? Who had put it there, and why had they left it? Obviously, the owners had been water women, given the contents. She had so many questions, and the only one she could possibly ask was her mother. Mira adjusted the weight she carried and set off across the wet sand toward home.

Chapter 32

Mira and Dante sat across from each other in her studio, the contents of the box spread on the table between them.

"How old do you think this is?" Dante asked. His voice was a low whisper so as not to wake Daniella, still sleeping against Mira in her wrap.

She shrugged. "Here's a photo from 1911—a wedding photo, and another dated 1925. It looks like the same couple but with four children. I don't recognize any of them. I've never seen a little loom like this, but it would certainly be handy for small weavings."

Dante picked up the sheaf of letters. "These are postmarked before 1920," he said, sifting through the envelopes. He squinted at the faded handwriting. "Mira."

"What is it?"

"The names. These were written during the first war. Letters sent between Johann and Allegra Renda."

Mira's head jerked up. "My grandparents? The ones my mother never talks about?" She took the letters from him and slid one out. *"My dearest A,"* she began, then stopped. "This box must have belonged to them. I must bring these to my mother."

Dante was already gathering the photos and byssus items and placing them back in the box. He kissed her on the forehead. "I'll drive you," he said. "It'll be quicker."

~

Mira waited outside her mother's byssus studio until the pair of older women who'd been visiting left. She nodded to them on their way out the door, the little string of shells and bells jingling against the glass panes.

Zaneta had already turned her attention back to the threads she had soaking, and she only turned when Mira shut the door behind her. Her face registered surprise. She didn't often come by for unscheduled visits, especially in the middle of the day. Her mother brightened as she took in her granddaughter's sleeping form, always happy to see Daniella. Then Zaneta's eyes fell on the box Mira held down by her side, and she took a step backward, as if struck.

"Where did you get that?" She pointed. Her jaw fell, and she raised a hand to her mouth.

"I found it this morning. In the back of a sea cave." Clearly, her mother recognized it. "You've seen it before."

Her mother smoothed the front of her apron, trying to regain her composure. "My father made that," she said. "We hid it before—" She broke off. "My mother wanted us to put it in the cave for safekeeping."

"You knew it was there?" Mira asked. She pushed aside cards of thread and assorted jars on the worn table and put the box down. Her mother's eyes never left it. She stepped forward and placed a hand on the carved lid.

"Yes. I helped put it there. We all went together. Mamma said just in case. Things were very uncertain with the war. My brothers had gone to fight, and I think they still thought there might be a way we could get out." Mira stood silently, hardly daring to breathe. She watched as tears ran down her mother's cheeks. Her mother never spoke of her parents or the war. She'd always dismissed Mira's questions with an impatient wave, saying it didn't matter, couldn't be helped.

Slowly, her mother's hands found the clasp. She was like a blind woman, exploring the box's surface by touch, her fingers lingering on the carved etches as if she might read some hidden message from her father there. She opened the rusty clasp, its leather strap faded with age and mold, and tipped back the lid.

Something in the air of the studio changed. Mira saw a breeze ripple through the thin muslin curtains at the window and felt it across her neck, although it was midday and still as a stone outside in the bright sun. She knew her mother had felt it, too. She'd shuddered as if a chill had passed through her. Mira imagined ghosts unleashed around them both, swirling around the legs of the byssus loom, whispering through the bunches of tied herbs hung from the ceiling beams.

"I never imagined it had survived," her mother said. "I assumed it had disappeared like everything else. I never even went back to look for it."

"It was a good spot," Mira said. "It was only by chance I was there and my light fell on it. If it hadn't started raining . . ."

"Who else but you should have found this? It wasn't chance," her mother said. Then she sat hard in the wooden chair by the table, the wedding photo in her hand. How many years had it been, Mira wondered, since she'd seen a photo of her family? All of them had been lost or destroyed in the war. Mira's father had told her that much, that although he'd tried to watch over it, the family home had been rifled through, sentimental objects tossed outside as kindling for bonfires. He'd managed to right most of the rooms afterward, hoping they'd return, but most of what documented the Renda family's existence had been destroyed.

"These are my parents." Another shudder of her shoulders, and she glanced around the room again. Mira wondered if she hoped to see specters conjured by opening this door to the past.

Another photo. "And here. Avi, Lev, Marta, and Dahlia with them. This was before I was born." Her mother clasped the photo to her chest, her eyes closed. Mira had so seldom heard her mother mention her past. Although she knew the names of her aunts and uncles, Mira couldn't remember the last time her mother had uttered them aloud.

"Mira," she said finally. Her voice was a strangled croak. "I thought I would never see their faces again." It was almost a thank-you.

"There's more," Mira offered. She sat herself, one hand cradling the curve of little Daniella's body. "Letters between your mother and father from the war. I didn't read them."

"Her handwriting." Her mother smoothed the envelopes with her hand.

"There are byssus things."

"Yes," her mother said, laying the letters aside for later. "Mamma wanted to preserve some. I had some things with me that day, too. In the bag she carried." Her mother was far away now, her eyes staring at something Mira couldn't see.

Mira picked up the little lyre-shaped loom and held it out to her mother. "I've never seen one like this," she said. "It looks hand carved, like the box."

Again, her mother's hands went to her mouth. "My father made it," she managed. "He was so good with a piece of wood." A crooked smile at the memory. "I had one like it."

"You did?" Mira was surprised. "I've never seen you use it. It would be so much easier for small bracelets and things."

"It's gone," she replied. "I lost it in the ruins."

Mira opened her mouth to ask a question, but her mother dug deeper into the box. "Here's some of the smaller weavings my mother did," she said. "Thread, dyes . . . here's a picture. This is me as a baby." She actually chuckled. "Mamma's wearing the apron she always wore for dyeing. You can see the stains." She showed it to Mira.

"It's just like the one you have," Mira said. "And mine."

"I made them from memory." She nodded.

"Do you know what this pouch is?" Mira pulled out a small drawstring purse made of byssus and carefully pried apart its opening.

Her mother took it from her and tipped its contents into her hand. "Locks of hair. And these slivers of something hard." She examined them under the light. "They look like fish scales, but why they'd be worth saving like this, I don't know."

"They must have meant something special to your mother. There's no note to explain."

"She expected to return. She would've explained it herself."

"There's this at the bottom," Mira said, carefully pulling out the leather-bound scroll. "I couldn't read it."

Zaneta's brow furrowed as she unfurled the barest portion. "It's Hebrew. And very old from the looks of it. I don't recognize it."

Daniella roused, squirming and blinking her eyes. Mira pulled her out of the wrap and snuggled her close. She would be hungry and soon expressing her opinion about that.

"Mira." The spell, whatever it was, had been broken. Her mother left the scroll on the table and stood. "See to Daniella. The box has waited this long."

The baby wailed in earnest, her little face reddening. Mira loosened the laces of her black vest and lifted the white blouse she wore beneath it so that Dani could nurse. As she latched on, Daniella butted Mira with her face and smacked at her with an open hand. Waiting wasn't one of her best skills, especially when a meal was past due. Mira smiled down at her daughter as she felt the tingle of her milk letting down.

"Goodness, figlia, you act like you've never been fed before." Across the room, Zaneta peered out the window, although the expression on her face told Mira she wasn't seeing the sky or the strawberry and olive trees in the yard. As Daniella quieted and settled into her lunch, Mira seized the opening.

"Mamma," she began. "Can you sit? Will you tell me about all this?"

Zaneta's trance broke, and she wiped her eyes with the palms of her hands. They were weathered, Mira noticed, etched with deep wrinkles and spotted with age. She glanced down at her own hands cradling her daughter, and a memory rose. Mira traced the familiar scars between her thumbs and forefingers on each hand. Identical marks shaped like the number seven from when she'd gleefully held up a blue crab she'd caught at age six to show her mother. No matter what she did, it had always been with an eye toward her mother. Zaneta had been busy with other things, gathering seaweed in her basket, scolding Mira's brothers, and she'd finally turned toward Mira to see her clutching the creature around its middle, holding it up like a prize.

Look at me! Here I am! See what I did. Wasn't this good? When the crab hooked its claws into the tender flesh near her thumbs, Mira's smile had remained glued in place, even as her eyes filled and blood trickled down her arms. When her mother had turned away, she'd flung the crab back into its tide pool and watched it scuttle beneath a rock with a spray of sand. The marks on her hands had faded into the odd-shaped scars she still bore decades later. Lucky sevens, Carmina had called them, and Mira had never said otherwise.

To Mira's surprise, Zaneta leaned over her, placed a hand on her shoulder, and stroked Daniella's soft cheek with a finger.

"You're good with her," she said. "You always know what she needs."

Mira laughed. "She *tells* me."

Zaneta fixed her dark-brown eyes on Mira's own. "You listen," she said, a tremor in her voice. She turned back to the open box on the table. Mira smelled the salty damp it still carried from the cave.

"I know about the water women, the weavers," Mira said. "We say their names in remembrance before the byssus harvest. But there's a missing piece. I don't know what came before *me*. I don't know about you."

"Why these questions?" asked her mother. "Because of this box?"

Mira shook her head. "It's not the box." She shifted Daniella to her other side. "It's Daniella. I think I want to know where I come from so I know where I'm going. Because now I'm taking someone with me."

Her mother seemed to consider this while her mouth worked and her hands twisted the pocket of her apron.

Finally, "You may not like what you discover. The past can be a treacherous place. Here lie dragons," she mumbled. When Mira looked at her quizzically, she added, "Old maps sometimes have that written on the edges. In places no explorers had been, it was like a 'traveler beware' beacon. There might be dragons or sea monsters, or you could even sail right off the edge of the world."

"Or," she offered, "there could be treasure or mermaids or byssus."

Her mother sighed heavily. "Persistent as a barnacle."

Mira handed Daniella to her mother to burp as she straightened up her blouse. She spread a blanket across the floor and scattered some wooden spools and spoons for Daniella to play with. The back door opened, and her father breezed in, a sack in his hands.

"Mira." He beamed. "And little Daniella, too! Lucky, I brought some amaretti with me from the quay." He unrolled the fresh cookies from the paper they'd been wrapped in and placed them on the table. "What's this?"

"A box I found today in a sea cave," Mira explained.

"It belonged to my mother," Zaneta added. At that, Luccio ceased his business with the cookies and his hands stilled. Mira noticed the sharp glance he gave her mother. "I was about to tell Mira about her grandparents."

"I'll start the Moka pot," he said, and the grateful smile her mother gave him made her appreciate her father's presence. He'd always been a sort of buoy for her mother, a bobbing, reliable lifeline that kept her from sinking. He filled the pot with water and strong coffee, removed three plain white cups and saucers from the kitchen shelves, and added a plate for his sack of amaretti for good measure. With her father here, the remarkable box Mira had found, and their granddaughter playing nearby on the floor, maybe some of the questions she'd had for so long would finally find answers.

Chapter 33

Their coffee cooled in the cups her father had poured as the three of them sat around the box at the table. Mira didn't really know what she'd expected to hear after a lifetime of her mother's refusal to speak about her family. She supposed somehow her grandmother must have been a shrew or a harsh woman, judging by her own mother's moods and exacting demands, but the woman her mother described was nothing like that. Zaneta described a happy childhood—a large, warm family and a busy life in the community of weavers. Their work had been revered and honored. They were renowned, tapestries and other pieces requested from faraway places—for churches, dignitaries, altars, and burials of important people.

The pictures in the box gave Mira a glimpse of aunts and uncles she'd never seen and heard little about. There'd been two sisters who had often looked after her mother as the youngest, teaching her letters, sharing their hair ribbons. Her two brothers had been typical boisterous fishermen, tossing her about like a bundle of nets to make her laugh. They were strong, Zaneta recounted, always joking and making mischief that had her father laughing and her mother shaking her head.

A strange calm seemed to have come over her mother as she sifted through the long-hidden memories. Mira found herself holding her breath and keeping still, making herself smaller, as if that would keep her mother talking. She was reluctant to ask questions, though she was burning with them. Now and then, her father reached over and draped an arm on the back of her mother's chair or nodded encouragement to her. He'd known them, too, in his way, and he smiled at her recollections as if to remind her mother that her memories held joy as well as pain.

Mira studied her grandparents' wedding photo while her mother described how hard they worked, how their home—the very same house her parents lived in now—was always full of visitors, family, and women from their community because of her mother's position. She was a maestra, her mother said, wise and adept at weaving the byssus. She was their historian, keeper of the few records they had and some of the oldest weavings of byssus still in existence.

The box held some of these pieces, wrapped in layers of linen and tissue paper for safekeeping, labeled with what her mother said was the spiky handwriting of Mira's grandmother. As Zaneta told it, her mother was proud to have been able to read and write and made sure her daughters knew the skills as well. In their rural Sardegnan island town, literacy wasn't always a given for the residents, especially the women, but school had never been a question for Mira. Her own mother had seen to that.

When Daniella started to fuss, her father pushed back his chair and picked her up. He made silly faces at her and let her grab at his beard as he walked her around the small kitchen.

Zaneta pulled the sheaf of letters across the table and untied the worn ribbon that bound them. "These I've never seen," she said. "They wrote to each other while my father was a soldier in the first war." Slowly, she read through them, placing them in order when she was finished. "I can hear their voices in these letters. Certain phrases he'd use or ways she'd pronounce a word. I've often thought what I'd give to hear a real recording. If only we'd had those tape machines they have now. In some ways, though, you always carry your mother's voice in your head, you know?"

Mira gave her mother a rueful smile. Yes, that she certainly knew.

Luccio broke in. "What do you say, Mira, if I take Daniella for a walk down by the quay? We can watch the catch come in."

"Would you like that, Dani? A walk with Nonno?" She handed him the small bag she'd packed and gave her daughter a kiss.

"Back soon," he said, closing the door. Mira heard his deep voice singing nonsense songs to Daniella as they headed down the path. Her father made a perfect nonno, and she loved seeing them together.

"Would you like to take a walk, too, Mamma? We could go down by the shoreline and breathe the air."

"All right," she said. "I'll bring this scroll with me."

The shore wasn't far, and they followed the worn path through the rocks and grass until the sea came into view. Her mother was quiet, obviously lost in the thoughts and memories the box must certainly have stirred up. Mira's shoulders relaxed at the sight of the water. She felt more at ease here than anywhere else. Together, they walked to the water's edge, kicked off their sandals, and let the water wash over their toes. The tide was out.

"There's a good flat rock." She pointed. "Let's sit there and you can translate the scroll."

Zaneta tucked the folds of her long skirt around her legs and unrolled the leather binding. Mira hiked her skirt to her knees and let her feet trail in the shallow water of the tide pool along one edge of the rock. The paper of the scroll wasn't like anything Mira had ever seen. Yellowing and stained from what she imagined must have been the fingers of generations past, she could see that someone, at some point, had mounted the fragile original onto a firmer surface to help preserve it. She wrinkled her nose as she caught a woody aromatic whiff as the sea breeze swept across its surface.

"It's Hebrew," her mother said. "You should have studied more."

"Probably," Mira admitted. "I could do it, but it would take me longer. You just read it."

Smoothing the first page, her mother read "*Letter of Berenice Agrippa*" and stopped short. "Do you know what this is?" Her mother sat up straight and thrust the binding at her. Her hands were shaking.

"*The* Berenice?" Mira asked, her mouth hanging open. Hers was the first name they recited when they chanted the litany of weavers who'd come before. The first-century queen who'd brought the knowledge and weaving of the byssus thread to Sardegna.

"Who else? It has to be."

"What does it say?" Mira urged.

Her mother cleared her throat and began to read:

> *Letter of Berenice Agrippa,*
> *Princess, Widow, Traitor, and Exile. I've quite a list of monikers, depending on who tells the tale. Now, my daughter Titia, at my life's end, I tell you the story so you can weave traces of it through the fine byssus garments and tapestries your fingers create. All of us build a life from the material we've been given. The trick is to know which patterns need embellishing and which should be abandoned or removed. For us, Titia, and our daughters to follow, our strength comes from being bound to one another through the sea and creating beauty. That's the legacy I leave. That, and you, my dearest.*

"Amazing," Mira breathed. "It's the beginning of everything."

Her mother's eyes scanned the text. "She says her father, Marcus Agrippa, Herod I, was king and in the line of her great-grandfather, Herodes Magnus, Herod the Great. She was taught to read and write, even then. She writes of the byssus. How her mother taught her. Not much has changed since then. It sounds like what we do still."

"What else?"

"This bit is faded, hard to make out. It's something about her brother Agrippa being called to the palace. Another brother, Drusus, falling from a horse. Here, she goes on."

> *Mother prayed with him endlessly until he died, while my father ordered the animal killed, one grieving via silence and the other rage. For months, palace mirrors remained draped in black cloth. We ate our meals without seasoning and barely left our chambers, far more than the days of shivah required. Mother and I wove our sorrows into the most beautiful tapestry, cliffs dashed by an angry sea teeming with fish. A lone vessel teetered on those broiling waves, and when the breeze caught the edges of the cloth, it appeared that the sea actually rose and dipped with the wind.*

Mira nodded along. Weaving her own emotions into the cloth felt familiar. She knew that lone vessel well. She'd woven plenty of her own.

Zaneta traced the text with a finger. "Here, she recounts her marriages. She was a young bride the first time, then widowed by sixteen. Married again to an uncle, another king, and once more widowed by twenty, with two sons. Then to live with her mother and brother, now king."

"By twenty?" Mira marveled. "Not quite the same as our slow, simple island life, is it?"

"She had no say. It was for politics and alignments. She was literate, though, and a princess."

"We've always called her Queen Berenice," Mira noted. "How did she become a queen?"

"Ah. Here it is. She says. She married a king named Polemon. That's where her title comes in." Zaneta mumbled to herself, scanning the parchment for highlights, occasionally reading bits aloud.

> *I was able to offer my brother reasonable counsel. Unlike my husbands, Agrippa turned his ear to my words and thought them worthy. Others fuel rumors, Titia, that your uncle and I had an unholy union, a thought borne of*

jealousy rather than truth. He didn't marry, it's true, but he hadn't need: plenty of temple concubines were available to him. I often accompanied him on official trips. On one occasion, together we heard the court testimony of a Roman Jew named Paul, one who had been a follower of that Nazarene, Jesus. Imagine! The defendant, Paul of Tarsus, dared to try to persuade Agrippa to become a follower also. Agrippa was amused by the man's folly but impressed by his courage.

Here's where the story turns, Titia. Mother died, and with her, my spirit. I took a Nazirite vow, abstaining from wine and even shaving my head. As is the custom, I wore no shoes and kept my nails untrimmed, and in this state, your uncle and I faced Judea's Jewish rebellion. You've never lived in Roma, my dear, so you will not know what it looks like when the Romans decide to display their power. It's terrifying, yet many Jews mistakenly thought they could somehow resist. A fool's game. What means did they possess against such an empire?

Here, her mother stopped. "It's so much like the war," she said, her voice husky. "What means did we possess against such an empire as the Germans?"

"That's what they tell us in school, Mamma. History repeats."

Zaneta sucked in a deep breath and forged on.

The scenes in the streets broke my heart. Debased as I was, under the conditions of my vow, I sought audience with the procurator to plead their case. I have never witnessed such atrocities before or since. With my bare feet in pools of my people's blood, I begged for his mercy. Something in the soldiers hardened. I felt it when it happened, as if the whole room had gone cold. One of them turned his eyes on me. What a sight I must have been, with my shorn head and tearstained cheeks. No queen was I, to him. I fled then. It took me a full two days to stop trembling.

Mira's mother lay the parchment in her lap and looked out at the horizon. Mira sensed a shift in her. Something about Berenice's words had resonated deeply. In a sense, they were all kindred spirits, sharing their lineage, but this seemed to connect in a different way with her mother—a memory that Mira wasn't privy to. She wanted to probe but was afraid to break the spell.

Agrippa and I tried to persuade our people to comply, but they'd suffered immensely under the Romans. Our own community hated us for trying to dissuade them, deemed us traitors and worse. We had to flee finally when they burned our home, and from that point on, the Jewish people—those in my own community—set their hearts against me.

Say what you will, but we found sympathy with the Romans. Not all of them were murderous beasts. So it happened that Agrippa and I were invited to a banquet, where we were decidedly in the minority. Who do you think the man at the table's head was? Your father, Titia. That was the night we met. I'd never before felt so enlivened by a presence, though he was at least ten years my junior. I, a twice-widowed Jewish queen, fell in love with Titus, the very Roman ruler sent to suppress my people's rebellion. If you had seen him: blue eyes lit from within and shoulders chiseled from stone. After the banquet, he sent for me, and I knew when the attendant knocked on my chamber door that I would go gladly.

> *The Jews hated us both for it. The Romans hated him for stooping to consort with me. Not even a year after Vespasian was installed, Titus—my Titus—helped sack Jerusalem and destroy the temple. How could one heart hold both complete sorrow and utter love at once? That was my lot. I was rent in two.*
>
> *The last time I returned to Roma, Titus was under such pressure from the Roman public. Our love fell to dust, and he sent me away. That's how, Titia, we ended up here, in exile, without family or fortune, but with all the time necessary for plying the sea's gift, the very thing I'd wished for long before. Titus couldn't have guessed I carried you within me as I left.*

Here, her mother grasped Mira's hand and held it fiercely. She'd stopped several times while reading to catch her breath. To Mira's astonishment, her mother wept openly, her words strangled as she read.

"What is it, Mamma? What's upset you?"

"I wish I'd read this years ago," she whispered. "I should've looked for the box. I had no idea her life held such things as mine."

Mira nodded. "I know the war must have been impossibly hard."

Zaneta looked at her then, her eyes full. "It's not just that," she said. She seemed about to say something else. Mira could see her lips trying to form words, but something still kept her from speaking them aloud.

"This last," her mother said. "Let me read you this last part."

> *My daughter, you were God's final gift to me, my restoration. He allowed me to raise you in this place, surrounded by water, where the sea thread is plentiful. The weaving overflows from my grateful heart that our names and craft will go on, that my mother's skill, and mine, continues through you.*

You've learned all I have to teach you, and your fingers are deft at the loom. I tell you the truth, Titia. Though this thread is precious and our weaving skill a gift, it will never be stronger or more precious than you. Its gift has been to teach us daily, as we work at the loom, how immutable is the link between mother and daughter. Should there come a day when the byssus disappears or no more hands are left to weave its magical golden threads, nothing can erase the love I carry for you, or that my own mother carried for me. No destiny of vocation trumps that, my dearest. The spirit of it will live on as long as mothers have daughters.

Chapter 34

As Zaneta gently placed the missive back inside its leather cover, neither spoke. Mira turned her head and stared out at the sea. Pieces of the letter came back to her with a force that took her breath away. *Should there come a day when the byssus disappears or no more hands are left to weave its magical golden threads, nothing can erase the love I carry for you, or that my own mother carried for me.*

Her whole life, Mira had shouldered the weight of centuries, as her mother reminded her again and again. But Berenice's words seemed to say their craft and calling had never been truly about the byssus itself. Undeniably beautiful and singular, its gift was weaving community and closeness among women, especially during times when women had been valued only for their usefulness to the men they served. For her, Mira saw, it had done just the opposite; her mother's resting everything on the byssus drove them apart rather than creating the closeness she'd craved.

Mira's mother finally broke the silence. "I've heard pieces of her story over the years, but I didn't know all of it. Not like this. I'm going to have to read it again and again. Her words carry so many lessons." She stopped and looked at Mira, holding both her hands. "I should have told you those things, too, figlia. *You* are strong and precious. Despite how harsh I may have been."

Mira's face crumpled, and she couldn't hold back her tears any longer. She bowed her head and let them fall into the sand at her feet. "Thank you for saying that, Mamma." They stood that way for a moment, and then, because affection and sentiment were awkward, Mira spoke.

"I can't believe it survived all this time in that sea cave."

"Why didn't I look for the box?" Zaneta shook her head. "So many other things were lost, looted, and destroyed during that time that I never gave it a thought."

Mira rose from the rock and offered her mother her hand. "Let's walk back. The sea air probably isn't the best condition for a two-thousand-year-old letter. I imagine Papà may need a rest from Daniella, too."

Mira waited while Zaneta tucked the binding inside her vest and then helped her off the rock. Seeing the cracks in her mother's veneer, the buried emotions she'd long suppressed, opened a window for Mira to glimpse the woman her mother really was. Mira found herself softening at her mother's vulnerability, and for a moment, she could see beyond her own hurt to what she must have survived. Mira was proud of her for that, grateful she'd endured. She glanced out toward the horizon, and the swell of the waves brought a sudden sensation of dizziness. Thoughts reeled in her head, and Mira imagined herself tumbling in the waves, buffeted like an empty shell. How might her life have been different, she wondered, not for the first time. What if she could turn back the clock to before the war, to a life where she knew her grandmother and aunts and where her mother could have been free of her dark moods and wounds?

Mira paused and looked over her shoulder as a diving bird broke the sea's surface like an arrow. She noticed her footprints trailing behind in the sand, parallel with her mother's, tracks that seemed to chase them. She thought about Daniella. What would her own daughter wish, someday, about *her*? What might she wish Mira had set aside or freed herself from? Would Daniella want to move to Milan or Florence, a landlocked city far from the sea? Maybe weaving the byssus would seem too old-fashioned or simple a life for the more modern world she would grow up in. Mira let that possibility settle on her heart for a moment like a bobber on a fishing line, feeling the ripples of emotion it created and seeing what sort of beasts it might snag lurking beneath the surface. A faint surge of panic rose, but it dawned on her that it wasn't because *she* felt panicked about what Daniella might become. No, she knew some part of her was bracing for the blow of her mother's reaction.

Curious, Mira thought. Did she filter everything through that emotional sieve? Isn't that what children do? She remembered times when she'd visited Carmina, chatting and drinking a bit of espresso while her friend's children played nearby. Inevitably, one of them would tumble or knock into something, and their immediate reaction—before any tears or even that first intake of breath—was to glance at their mother. Mira remembered joking with Carmina about it.

"It's like they're checking your face to see whether they should cry or not," she'd said, laughing. "Don't they know if they're hurt?"

"Sure they do," Carmina had said. "But my reaction tells them how bad I think it is. If I smile and give them a quick dust-off and send them on their way, somehow they believe they're tough, and they get right back at it. If I gasp and look horrified—and there have been times, especially with the boys, where that's been warranted—they're afraid, too, and the wailing starts. At some point, they figure it out and judge for themselves. They'll quit looking to me."

Mira wondered if, in some ways, she'd ever stopped looking to her own mother. Maybe the difference was that Carmina's children, she knew, had learned their mother loved them through scrapes and tears, failures and successes. Her love seemed to be a given, as assured as the sun rising every morning. Mira's sun was less reliable. She'd always needed to check the horizon to be sure its rays were still there.

Mira and her mother could see the house in the distance. Her mother had been unusually quiet on the walk home, but then, Mira supposed, she'd been lost in her own thoughts, too.

"What's going on up there?" her mother spoke, pointing to the house.

A strange car was angled in the yard. Who would have driven out this way? A visitor curious about the byssus?

Her mother stopped abruptly, her voice sharp. "It's the polizia," she said.

"Something's happened," Mira said, thinking immediately of Daniella. She lifted her skirts and sprinted toward the house, praying with every step that her daughter was safe.

Mira burst through the back door, sandy and breathless, her eyes blinded by having been in the bright sun. "Papà?" she called.

She heard Daniella's happy squeal before she saw her, and she turned toward the sound, her arms already outstretched.

"Mira." Her father handed Daniella to her, and she held the girl close and breathed her in, her wild imaginings banished. Finally, she registered the two polizia seated at the kitchen table, as if it were a normal occurrence for such officials to stop in for coffee.

"Where's your mother?" her father asked. His smile was strained. He was not himself.

"On the way," she explained, gesturing down the path. "We saw the car and it scared me." Mira patted Daniella, who was pulling on her braid and trying to chew the end of it.

"Sorry to alarm you, Signora," one of the officers said, rising. "Everyone is all right."

Her father held up a finger. "Give me a moment, please, while I go find my wife. Please, enjoy the coffee."

In the uncomfortable silence that followed, Mira smiled and glanced around the kitchen, seeing it as she imagined the officers might. Sparse and orderly, plates and cups stacked on the open shelves that lined the walls. A crusty loaf of bread cooled on an olive-wood cutting board near jars filled with dried beans and spices. The large, weathered box they'd looked through earlier had been moved from the table to a shelf in the main sitting area. A few dishes lay strewn in the sink, left from breakfast. Thin curtains fluttered at the window above. She could see down the path where her father and mother were walking back toward the house, her arm in his, deep in conversation.

"Here they are," Mira offered, bouncing Daniella on her hip. "She wasn't far behind me."

One of the officers—probably the senior of the two—stood as her parents entered the house.

"Signora Mazza," he said with a nod of his head.

Mira noticed her mother's uncharacteristic stiffness, the way she clenched her jaw, making the sinews in her neck stand out, how her dark eyes darted between the officers, sizing them up. Her father still held her mother's arm looped in his own. His large hand covered hers, and he stood slightly in front of her, as if protecting her, it seemed.

Zaneta didn't speak. She merely inclined her head as an inquiry.

The officer coughed, and Mira felt some compassion for the man. She'd been in his shoes before, knew how uncomfortable it could be when faced with her mother's unflinching assessment.

"You may know," he explained, "the Italian authorities have been in cooperation with the university to study the island's nuragic ruins, to try and learn more about their history and such."

Her mother shrugged slightly, twisting her mouth to suggest she was waiting to hear the relevance.

"In so doing," the officer continued, "one of the field teams has discovered what they believe may be some sort of temple."

"There's no telling what's under all the brush up there," the second officer piped up. "It's miles of untouched and half-buried structures. Now they think if they dust things off a bit, the mystery of it all may bring the tourists in. More business for the shops and such, right?"

"I'm a pescatore," her father said, "and my wife weaves the byssus. Our place is by the shore, so we don't really go up inland."

"Well, Signore, it's your wife's hobby that we're interested in, actually."

"Hobby?" Mira almost winced at her mother's acidic tone.

The younger officer stepped in. "Art," he corrected.

"Yes, yes." The senior officer waved his hand, impatient to come to the point of their visit. "Yesterday, when uncovering the ruins of this temple, they happened to find the remains of a body."

Mira wrinkled her nose in distaste. What had any of this to do with them?

At this, her mother turned toward the window and reached to pour herself a cup from the Moka pot. She added no honey or milk, just sipped it strong and black.

"How terrible," her mother said, turning back to the visitors. "Why is it you're here telling us all this?"

The younger officer stood and stuck a hand in the pocket of his uniform. When he pulled out a small lyre-shaped handheld loom, Mira sucked in a breath. She'd seen another just like it only this morning, in the box she'd discovered in the sea cave, the box that had belonged to her grandmother. Zaneta had said she'd had one like it, one she'd lost in the ruins. Her eyes darted to her mother's face, but before she could say anything, her father caught her eye.

The shake of his head was almost imperceptible, but Mira recognized in his eyes that look that told her to hold her tongue. She and her father had communicated in these silent ways her whole life, with her father acting as mediator between his wife and daughter. *Careful,* he was saying, *don't make things worse. This will pass if you swallow your words, stuff down your emotions, and control your tongue.* Mira knew it was her father's way of trying to protect her from her mother's unpredictable moods, but it always seemed to her to have been one-sided. *She'd* been the one learning to stay calm and bite back retorts while her mother had been allowed to strike with her words; rage and slam doors; or retreat to dark rooms, sometimes for days at a time.

"This was found with the remains. We were directed here, told you might shed some light."

"Have they been identified?" her mother replied, skirting the issue. "These remains?"

The second officer consulted a notebook he pulled from the same pocket that had held the loom. “Dog tags say Jan Fuchs. German.”

Her mother’s eyes narrowed, and her words were terse. “A German soldier, then. There were many here during the war.”

The senior officer regarded her. “Military-issue weapon with him. Listed as a deserter. But this?” Again, he asked, handing it to her. His actions seemed casual, Mira noticed, but his eyes never left her mother’s face. He was gauging her reaction, the same as she was.

Mira watched as her mother casually turned the small loom over in her hands, watched her swallow hard and measure her words before she looked directly at Mira and said, “I’ve never seen this before.”

Mira’s senses sharpened, and the room seemed to narrow into focus. Her father’s shoulders relaxed the slightest bit. The curtains fluttered at the window, and the squawk of jackdaws fussing outside echoed in her ears. Her mother was lying. It dawned on Mira that the last time officials had been to this house was probably during the war, when they rounded up the families in their community and took them all away. Not all, she corrected herself. One remained. Mira knew that much of the story, but with the arrival of this loom and her parents’ reaction, there appeared to be more to it. Her mother stood in her kitchen, eyes leveled at the officer, her raised, defiant chin devoid of even a trace of a quiver.

Zaneta shrugged and handed back the loom. Her father said, “You must know, Officers, that this area was—” He paused and chose his words carefully. Even this long after the war, only a tenuous trust had been forged between the people and the authorities. “Deserted,” he continued. “It was a largely Jewish community. Hardly anyone remained. I myself saw many of the homes in this area looted, and—if this object is associated with weaving, as you seem to imply—it could’ve been stolen from any of them.”

The senior officer nodded while the second man jotted notes in his notebook. Daniella, who’d been squirming in her mother’s arms, finally lost patience and let out a shrieking wail. Mira needed to take her home. She wanted to be fed, and she probably needed changing.

"And you, Signora?" the younger officer addressed her. "Can you tell us anything about it?"

Flustered, Mira tried to shush Daniella and busied herself with gathering her things. "I'm sorry, but no," she said. "All of that was before I was born. I don't know what more I could say than my mother has."

The polizia seemed satisfied and mumbled their appreciation as they left. Daniella ushered them out with her high-pitched cries, her face turning red.

"I've got to get home," Mira said, heading out the door after them. "Daniella is about to rival Mount Etna."

"Of course." Her father waved her off. "Poor nipotina. Go, go."

As Mira set off toward home, the polizia car stirred up a cloud of dust as it disappeared down the road to town. She glanced over her shoulder at her parents' house and, through the kitchen window, saw her father and mother wrapped in a tight embrace. Even over the din of the relentless jackdaws, Mira thought she heard the sound of her mother sobbing.

Chapter 35

Talk in their small town the next few weeks was of little else—at the bakery, at the quay when the boats came in, at the post office, and when friends gathered for coffee. So little seemed to happen on their sleepy, isolated island that the discovery of a soldier's remains and—even more curious—the weaver's loom in his possession was fodder for all sorts of speculation. Families of shepherds had lived on the island for as long as anyone could remember. Couldn't the loom have been used for woolens? Perhaps, but a more salacious possibility was that it had come from the island's other weavers, its water women, whom some saw as secretive and keeping to themselves. It hadn't been so many decades ago that the word *strega* had been lobbed at them.

Truly, most of the island's families had weavings they'd asked for, pleaded for, some of them, hoping to be blessed, wishing to be fertile or married or happy. That was innocent enough. When faced with desperate yearnings of the heart, not many would shy away from the thinnest bracelet of golden thread if it meant fate might turn her face favorably toward you. But the water women were no longer a bustling community. There were only two, a mother and daughter, who kept up the craft despite all that had happened in the war. When soldiers came to wipe out your people, who knew what you might be capable of, even quiet, gentle neighbors you spoke to in the streets of town.

Mira knew what people were saying, the outrageous stories being spun for entertainment. Her friend Carmina tutted and tsked, disgusted with the opinions and conjecture, and she told Mira so.

"Ridiculous," she snorted. "To think that you or your mother would have anything to do with such a thing. I wish those historians, or whoever they are, would backfill all the ruins with beach sand."

Mira wanted to agree. Since finding the box in the cave, she'd been so preoccupied, Dante had started to worry about her. She'd told Carmina about the box and the letter from Queen Berenice, but she hadn't told her all it contained. "I'm not worried about it," Mira said. "Tourists will begin to arrive soon, and all that will be forgotten. People are just bored and eager for a good story."

Her friend wasn't mollified. "Why must they always pin things on—" She broke off.

"Jews are the usual suspects," Mira said with a sigh. "Don't you remember learning that in Signora Campolo's history class?"

"Yes," Carmina replied. "You challenged her then, and we should challenge people now."

"I'd rather it blow away with the sea breeze."

"Mira, I've never seen you so dismissive! Where did all your spirit go?"

Mira only smiled and nodded toward the nursery. "Daniella captured every last bit of it, and I don't begrudge her at all. How my heart doesn't burst, I'll never know."

It was a constant wonder to her. With each passing week, she delighted more in how Daniella changed and in the new things her daughter learned. Mira was insatiable when it came to Daniella. Sometimes, when Mira held her close and the wispy down of Daniella's hair brushed her cheek, she felt she could literally consume the child whole. All so unexpected, she experienced a dizzying seesaw sensation of the two of them being somehow the same person and at the same time separate and unique. Mira didn't have the words—or the sort of relationship—to ask her mother if she'd felt the same with her as a small child. She couldn't imagine that she had. Her mother had never been connected to anything so strongly as she was to the byssus, she believed. She'd been willing to bend Mira to its existence, so long as the skill would continue.

She hadn't spoken to her mother since the day they'd found the letter, the day the officers had confronted Zaneta at the house. When she called or stopped by, her father only shook his head and reported she hadn't been feeling well, was resting, even in the middle of the day—the usual fare of Mira's childhood. She'd tried to broach the subject with her father, but as close as they were, he was not, after all, a weaver. He knew their work but didn't really understand the bond they'd sworn to the sea and its craft. Her father's first loyalty had always been to her mother. If she had any secrets, he would not speak them.

"You've heard what people are saying?" she'd asked. "That the soldier was somehow associated with us, the byssus weavers. One of us was his friend and helped him hide? Or the opposite—one of us was responsible for him being at the bottom of that well."

"Yes, yes." He nodded. "It means nothing. You know what they did to the families in this community, Mira, your own grandparents, aunts, uncles. They were all lost. What weaver would have willingly helped one of them do anything? It was so long ago, how can anyone know the truth of it? People will talk. You know how people can be."

"Of course," she'd agreed. She considered how to ask the questions she had. "You saw what was in the box I found."

He nodded.

"You don't think it's curious that the little loom in the box is almost identical to the one the polizia brought here?"

"Curious, yes. Definitely."

Mira heaved a sigh. "Mamma said she'd lost one in the ruins, but I didn't know what she meant. Then, we found the letter and got distracted. I have to wonder, Papà, is it—" she started to ask.

Her father held up a hand. "What you want to ask is understandable, Mira. But whatever the answer is, it doesn't change anything.

Makes nothing better or worse. Maybe it offers you some *explanation* of your mother, but it won't change the definition of her. She is who she is."

~

Mira gave up trying to ferret out answers about what might have happened in her mother's past. Those doors had obviously been shut and locked. No further officials appeared in anyone's kitchen, thrusting "police evidence" in their faces. Zaneta was no more willing to unspool stories of her childhood or her family than she'd ever been. It was as if, by clutching the memories close to her chest, her mother must have felt that was her only way of protecting them, these people and this time that she'd somehow let slip from her grasp. Mira sighed in frustration. Her mother had been about to say something after reading Berenice's letter; she just knew it. But even as moved as she'd been then, she couldn't bring herself to open up. By holding so desperately tight to what was, she'd never had open hands to receive much else: joy, appreciation for her—the daughter she did have—or an openness to anything but the byssus as her one path and a singular focus.

Soon enough, just as she'd told Carmina would happen, the tourists trickled in. The nuragic ruins up in the island's interior were a curiosity for visitors while they picnicked among the wild horses, and rumors about the bones of a German deserter added to the place's intrigue. Her mother eventually emerged from her room and took up the byssus work again, as if she'd just been away on a short trip. Nothing much changed.

Except Daniella, who seemed to change daily and was growing like wild myrtle. Mira often lost herself staring at Daniella as she played happily on the floor, puzzling out, as all parents do, what parts of herself she could claim in her daughter: the way she wrinkled her nose when she concentrated on grabbing at something, the curve of her chin. Dante would say their daughter's love of color and textures had come from Mira. There were other things, too, Mira noticed. Sometimes when Daniella refused to settle before a nap, pushing against her chest with her little balled-up fists, Mira fought the surge of worry that rose. She recognized it as the same feeling she'd felt as a child watching her mother wrestle with her moods.

In moments like these, Mira brushed her daughter's unruly hair from her damp forehead and gave her what comfort she could—her embrace, her soft, singsong voice. Daniella's moods were her own, and with Mira's guidance and assurance, she'd learn to tame them. Nothing was as predetermined as she imagined. Persistent ocean waves, she knew, could wear away even the deepest etchings in stone.

~

Later, when Daniella took her first tottering steps, arms akimbo for balance, Mira would absently raise a hand to her heart as it swelled to bursting with pride. When Daniella grew old enough to swim in the sea and wander on the shore, pointing out the swifts and gulls, Mira wanted nothing more than to know what was churning in her young imagination. What stories was she weaving? When Dani learned something new—mastering sums her father practiced with her—she delighted in it for its own sake, because she was proud of herself, not because it satisfied Mira.

~

Mira and Dante talked about it late at night, his breath warm on her shoulder. She stroked the scratchy stubble of his beard and whispered her fears to him.

"Do you think Dani is all right?" she'd ask, still sometimes second-guessing her ability to mother her well.

"Of course," Dante reassured her. "She seems content."

"You should have seen her when we were gathering plants near the wetlands today, amore mio. The flamingos are all gathered, nesting behind the beaches. We came upon them suddenly, and her face lit up. It was magical. She just dropped the basket and stared. They were so noisy with their squawks and calling, and then they must have realized they were being watched. All at once, a giant pink cloud rose up from the water. Thousands of them, so thick we felt the wind from their wings. Daniella just stood there with her mouth open and her eyes wide as saucers, drinking it all in. It was gorgeous."

"You see? She's happy."

"I remember the first time I saw the flamingos, probably five or six, not much older than she is now." Mira's hand stilled on Dante's chin. "It was the busy season for the byssus, and Mamma seemed almost frantic at the time with so much to do. I was to carry the baskets while she gathered the plants for dyeing. She seemed so angry. We didn't have time to pause and watch the birds."

Dante reached an arm up to Mira's hair. "Love," he said with a sigh. "Your mother carries so much guilt about being the only one left in her family that there's no room for happy things like flamingos. She feels like she has to carry everything—the past and the future—on her back, and most of the time, it seems to me she added that load to you as well."

Mira was quiet. "Just the way she used to look at me sometimes when she was in her moods. It felt like she was always assessing me for something, sifting through me, trying to find some quality or aspect. I don't know if she ever saw what she was looking for, or if she did, whether it was good or not." Her thoughts were all over the place that evening. "What she told the police—that loom they found in the ruins was hers. Do you think she had something to do with that soldier? His being in the well?"

Dante let out a long breath. "Your mother is a small woman. I don't think she'd have the strength to overpower a soldier, if that's what you're saying. It was wartime. A lot of people saw and did things they were probably ashamed of later. It had to have been horrible. I'm glad we weren't around for it."

"So if she did have something to do with him . . ."

"Then what's done is done. She probably had no choice, and I, for one, wouldn't blame her for it, given what she had to have been through. What I do blame her for is letting the fallout from it bleed all over you. And you haven't done a thing." He kissed her neck. "You've got to quit handing your mother the keys to your kingdom, amore."

Mira rolled over to face her husband. He was right, of course. He reminded her so often that she was a different person now, with her own family, her own daughter, and her own path to walk. As he pulled her close, the salty musk of him filling her senses, Mira had not one thought of her mother or daughter at all.

Mira

1994

Chapter 36

While it was still dark, Mira slipped from beneath the covers of her warm bed where Dante slept on, unburdened. Accustomed to padding about in the dim light before morning yawned itself awake, she slipped into her black swimsuit, threw a light tunic over her head, and secured her belt around her waist. She let the door close with a soft click after she pocketed a hunk of cheese to nibble on the way. Mira stood in the damp, waning night, letting her skin adjust to the cold. The yellow moon hung low in the sky, casting its pale light on the path, while scattered stars still winked above. Closing her eyes, Mira drew a deep breath of the bracing salt air. She ate a bit of the sharp cheese and started her pilgrimage, barefoot, to the shore, mirroring the quiet of the night, chanting and singing barely above a whisper. Some might have described her walk as lonely, but not her: she was surrounded by the siren call of those who'd come before, the long, winding line of water women like her. Her mother was recovering from a recent illness, and Daniella was living at her university in Venezia, far off in the north, so she'd have the cove to herself. She relished the solitude.

At the moment when the sun's rosy fingers stretched over the peaks of the twin islets to the west, Mira's lips ceased their chant. She'd reached the shore, where the water lapped ceaselessly at the smooth gray and white rocks. Mira picked her way through the stones, the soles of her feet calloused and toughened by over forty years of treading on this surface. The water was brisk, not yet warmed by the sun, and small crabs and schools of fish scuttled and darted away from her steps. She waded deeper, letting herself sink into the water, bending her knees until the Mediterranean Sea closed over the top of her head like a secret hatch. This was her favorite bit: when the sea took over and carried her body, weightless in the pull of its current. Mira stretched her arms wide and gave herself to the water's tug, her tanned face fanned by her floating hair.

It was spring—late May—and time to harvest the sea. Mira surfaced for a breath and dove again, gaining ground as her strong arms pulled through the water, feet kicking an even, measured pace. Her destination was the familiar protected lagoon where the sea lapped the rocky shore. Another breath, another dive. An icy stir of anxiety nudged Mira's stomach. Visions had visited her again in the night, and they flashed through her mind now: the lagoon bed decimated and empty, bits of fishermen's nets snagged on the remains of the shells.

Mira exhaled a stream of air through her nose, and bubbles rose to the surface. The lagoon had the protection of the Italian government, the coast guard even now likely anchored nearby. The noble pen shells, though they looked tough enough, were actually quite delicate and endangered by pollution and overfishing. Mira understood this well; the legacy of the water women faced extinction, too. This was the source of her worry and the visions that disturbed her sleep. Mira's lungs burned as she pushed her six-minute limit of holding her breath.

Breaking through the surface, Mira gasped and treaded water as she gulped the air her lungs craved. In the time it had taken her to swim the quarter mile, the sun had already risen above the horizon, the rosy-pink dawn fading to the promise of another bright day. The calls of seabirds searching and diving for their breakfast reached her ears, and she turned toward the shore. It was a short distance around the island's curve to the lagoon. She spotted the white coast guard vessel bobbing just inside the lagoon's mouth. Mira raised a hand in greeting and received the brief blast of an air horn in reply. She was a woman of few words; the standard exchange signaled the whole of their conversation. She pressed on and swam toward the boat, forcing down her mother's urgent voice that echoed in her head like a beating drum, still, after all these years, the voice that repeated the same words: duty, reverence, faithfulness. *"Say it with me, Mira. Again. You mustn't forget."* The voice was softer now, more of a whisper than a shout, but old habits surface now and then.

The sea grew shallower, and its current relaxed as Mira swam through the lagoon's entrance, swaying green seagrass and the occasional orange or purple starfish visible beneath the transparent waters. Unclipping the short scalpel from the belt she wore around her waist, Mira planted her feet in the seabed and sank her toes in the sand, the field of mollusks fanned out in front of her. This was why she'd come. Her purpose was as clear as the crystal water that buoyed her. Mira nodded to the pair of men who sat watching on the boat's bow with their hands shading their eyes against the sun's glare, banished all other thoughts from her head, and began her work.

Chapter 37

The small, whitewashed house was as quiet when Mira returned as when she'd left. It was midmorning, and Dante would have left hours ago to join his students. He would have made an efficient breakfast of black coffee and bread spread with prickly pear jam before gathering his satchel and glasses. Dante was as reliable as the clock that kept time on the stone mantel, the clock that he routinely wound and oiled. He didn't believe in retirement and still taught statistics and calculus during the spring and fall at the university in Cagliari.

Mira untied her belt and laid it and the pouch it contained atop the wooden kitchen table. Dante had cleaned up, but he'd left her a note: *Asparagus and fava in the fridge for lunch. Don't forget to eat.* Mira smiled and walked to the back of the house to their bedroom, where the bed she'd deserted was tidy, the hand-stitched quilt tucked tight beneath the pillows. She stripped off her tunic and the swimsuit, damp and stiff with salt, and stepped into the stone-tiled shower. She'd dived for hours, a solitary figure surfacing and disappearing again like a dolphin. Now, her muscles tired and her skin tight from the sun and salt, Mira stood beneath the shower's warm, fresh water and let it stream the length of her body. It took longer than it once had to bounce back from hours of labor, even such a labor of love.

Later, after wringing the moisture from her waist-length hair and dressing in a fresh, dry cotton dress and sandals, Mira sat at the table to examine the day's harvest. Curtains fluttered at the open windows, ushering in the spring warmth and fresh air, and Mira pushed her heavy-framed glasses up her long nose and swept her hair up off her neck in a thick twist. She teased open the drawstring on her pouch and tipped its contents into a bowl of clean, fresh water. It was a tangle of shell-encrusted, algae-covered string, almost like the cast-off salted nets tossed aside by the fishermen once they were past mending. Mira's fingers dipped and swirled the mess again and again in the water, pulling off shreds of algae and carefully scraping tiny shells from the surface of the byssus. After a few hours, she'd tossed and refilled the bowl's contents at least ten times, with most of the debris removed from the prize underneath. She studied the jumbled remains that sloshed in the bowl and hummed a song of thanksgiving in Hebrew.

As often happened, her thoughts drifted to Daniella, and Mira wondered what her daughter was doing at her Venetian apartment. It was just after noon, and she might have just awakened. She'd become a night owl, that one, abandoning their early-morning routines in favor of late-afternoon classes and later-night studies, a scholar like her father. Neither she nor Dante had been surprised when she'd laid out her plan to leave for school and a broader world. The byssus and quotidian life on their island felt provincial and safe, and their bold daughter was after more than that.

If Mira was honest, she admitted to being equal parts disappointed and proud. She admired la audacia of Daniella, and it was partly her own fault, raising her with loose reins, that she'd chosen to forsake the byssus. But perhaps *forsake* was too strong a word. Daniella was immersed in the Department of Antiquity and Literature, and although it was early days—she was young and only just starting in her field—she'd already made a name for herself with her publications based on the letter of Queen Berenice. While she wasn't a weaver, the byssus still had a hold on her in its own way.

The telephone's jangle interrupted Mira's musings, and she realized she'd been lost in thought, absently swirling the byssus in the bowl. She dried her dripping fingers and picked up the phone.

"Pronto."

"Signora Barone?" Mira didn't recognize the voice, but it sounded official. "Mira Barone?"

"Sì, sì."

"This is the Ospedale Civile in Cagliari. Your husband, Dante, has been in an accident. You need to come, please."

Mira was grateful she was seated. "What kind of accident? How is he?" Her voice rose in pitch with each word.

"Automobile. He's stable for now, but you need to come."

"Certo! I'll get there as soon as I can." Mira hung up and collected her purse and keys in a scramble. Dante had their car. How would she get to the hospital? *Carmina,* she thought, quickly dialing the number of her friend. Only when Carmina had assured her she was on her way did Mira allow herself to think.

Dante had to be all right. Her hands trembled as her imagination rambled. Mira glanced at the mantel clock and calculated what time it would be three hours from now. Once the byssus was harvested, it had to be rinsed and transferred to clear, fresh water every three hours. If she went to the hospital now, she'd have to be back by six. With no car, she'd have no way of getting back and forth on her own.

Mira caught herself and was horrified. Dante had been hurt. Nothing was more important than that right now. The byssus would have to wait. Having Daniella had taught her there were more important things than the byssus, a thought she once would never have believed. Carmina's tires crunched on the gravel outside, and Mira placed her hands on the bowl, muttering a hasty prayer. It was the best she could do. She grabbed her purse and headed out to her friend's idling car.

Wringing her hands in the passenger seat, Mira explained the little she knew to Carmina.

"They didn't say what had happened?" Carmina shifted gears and zipped around a tour bus. "Il fastidio," she growled, glaring at the groups taking pictures of the coastline, heedless of the local traffic.

"Only that it was a car accident. Dante is so careful, I can't imagine." Mira pressed a fist to her mouth.

Carmina pulled up to the emergency room entrance, and Mira climbed out, blowing her a grateful kiss as the glass doors slid open. The bright artificial lights shone cold against the white tiled corridors and floors. An antiseptic tang stung Mira's nose as she hustled to the front desk.

"Dante Barone?" she asked. "They called about my husband?"

The young, blond nurse nodded and stood. "This way, Signora," she said, her voice as crisp as her white uniform. "He's awake." She led the way down a series of hallways that made Mira dizzy before stopping at the doorway of a patient's room and ushering Mira inside.

"Dante?" Mira whispered. He lay in the hospital bed, his bandaged head propped on pillows. His tanned face had been cut in several places, the stiff ends of stitches poking through spots of dried blood. His handsome nose was bruised across the bridge. Mira noticed his broken glasses lying on the bedside table. Already, his eyes were blackening with bruises. He turned to look at her and groaned.

"Sorry, love," he managed. "Rotten timing."

"Don't think about that." She waved a hand but glanced at the clock all the same. Of course he would think about her work, despite everything. Sweet Dante. "What happened?" She dropped her things on the floor and took his hand, careful of the IV that snaked from his arm to the hanging bag of fluids.

"I was on my way home from class, and some young Tom on a Vespa swerved right in front of me. It was on the coastal road. I was between a bus and a drop-off, and when my tire went off the edge, the whole car went with it."

"Dante!"

"I was lucky. You should see the car." He winced. "Or maybe you shouldn't."

A middle-aged man in a white coat knocked on the door and entered without waiting for an answer. "Signora Barone?" He shook

Mira's hand. "This one was lucky they didn't have to fish him out of the sea."

"People keep using that word. I'm not sure I'd call what happened lucky," said Mira.

"Could've been much worse, I mean. As it is, in addition to all these bumps and bruises on the outside, your husband has some significant bruising on the inside that we're keeping an eye on. I don't like the look of his spleen, for one. We're going to keep running some tests, but surgery is a real possibility."

Mira nodded, taking it all in. Dante shrugged, clearly sleepy from whatever was in the IV. She'd be here. She'd make it work, even if the byssus went unattended for a season. Mira's stomach growled so loudly her eyes widened in embarrassment. Dante, half-asleep, patted her hand.

"You didn't eat the asparagus and fava, did you?" he chided. "Who will look after you while I'm gone, tesoro?" Mira shrugged. She knew the answer: no one had ever looked after her like Dante.

Chapter 38

By the time Dante was released from the hospital, his bruises fading from purple to green, Mira had freshened up the spare room for Daniella, and Carmina had stocked their kitchen with hearty meals for his homecoming. Mother and daughter flanked him as he walked stiffly from the car to the comfortable chair Mira had moved to the main room for his benefit.

"I'm not an invalid," he groused, a good-natured smile playing on his lips.

"You've had *surgery*, Papà," Daniella pointed out. "You're going to need help for a bit. Don't be such an uomo macho."

Mira raised an eyebrow at her daughter. Her time at the university had granted her liberties they weren't used to. With Dante ensconced in his chair, Mira gave him his medication, and they let him rest. It would be a couple of weeks before he was back to teaching, the doctors had told her. He would need care and rest, and she would gladly provide that.

Daniella had come for a bit of moral support and for reassurance that her father was out of the woods, and Mira was grateful for the time with her.

"Will Nonni be coming for dinner?" Daniella asked as she poked through the wrapped dishes in the refrigerator. "Zia Carmina has left enough for the whole neighborhood."

"I can ask them if you like," Mira said. "I'm sure they'd love to see you while you're here. Nonna might like to hear what you're working on at school."

Daniella brightened. "I didn't have the chance to tell you yet." She glanced into the other room as Dante's snoring rose in volume, and she lowered her voice to a whisper. "I've been selected to present at the antiquities conference in Roma this summer. A professor from the archaeology department there is leading a group to the nuragic ruins this spring, and they think some of my research on the origins of the byssus and Berenice might tie in."

"That sounds important," Mira said.

"I don't know where it'll lead. You know how digs can go." Mira, in fact, didn't know. She knew as much about archaeology as outer space. "It may be nothing, but I'm excited to be included."

"Maybe Nonna can add some perspective?" she offered.

"I've tried to get her to tell her stories, especially since her mother was the historian of the weaver community. With her memory slipping, and a lot of things being lost or destroyed in the war . . ." Daniella shrugged. Mira sighed. Her mother's memory was indeed fading. She and her father had both noticed some disturbing lapses lately. Trying to flush her glasses down the toilet, constantly opening drawers in the studio and taking all the items out for no reason. Twice, her father had awakened to find the bed empty and the front door open, her mother trying to unlock the fenced yard. They were worried she'd wander toward the sea in the night. She'd kept most of this from Daniella. What could she do but worry?

~

The two of them spent the afternoon puttering around the studio and catching up. Mira loved seeing Daniella as a woman apart from herself. She was amazed at her daughter's confidence and assured manner. She'd grown into a beauty; her dark hair and brown eyes seemed to reflect the

Mediterranean light so that she almost shone as she bent to pick a bouquet of wildflowers for the table. For Mira, it was a dizzying sensation watching her grown daughter, this person who had come from her in the most intimate ways yet sprang forward with her own uniqueness, beauty, and purpose. She was in constant motion. There was no pinning her down to define her as *weaver* or *scholar*, *daughter* or *signora*. Daniella was a shape-shifting work in progress, and it was both thrilling and a little startling to behold, given the molded expectations of her own life.

A great bustle entered the house when Mira's parents arrived. Daniella jumped up to kiss their cheeks, while Dante gave a wave from his seat. Mira helped her mother with the threshold—steps were more difficult for her these days—and took the steaming dish from her father's hands. He shrugged and exchanged a look with her. The food was unnecessary, but of course, they would not arrive empty-handed.

A bottle of Cannonau was uncorked, and glasses clinked as they laughed and settled at the table. As Mira always did, she dipped her fingers in the red wine and flicked the drops across the white tablecloth. It was a sign of hospitality so that the guests would be comfortable enough not to worry about spilling or finery. There were more important things when gathered together for a meal.

Mira was grateful to Carmina for her delicious spread of seafood fregola and culurgiones, the dumpling pasta stuffed with potatoes that was Daniella's favorite. With some vegetable soup and crusty bread, no one went hungry. Dante joined them for as long as he was able, and then they helped him to the back porch, where they sat to watch the moon rise.

Zaneta was doting on Daniella, offering her sweets and more wine, nudging her to indulge, asking her about her studies. Mira marveled at their interaction. It was as if all the urgency surrounding the byssus and its care had vanished when it came to Daniella.

"You know what I thought the other day, Dani?" her mother said. "What you're doing at school with your research is also a kind of weaving. Have you ever considered that?"

"What do you mean, Nonna?"

"You're telling the story of us. You're tracing our history. What do we say about telling stories? You're weaving a tale, spinning a yarn, following a thread, like we do when we're at the loom. It's kind of the same thing, but different, no?"

Daniella laughed. "Yes, I see that. I'm a word weaver or a history weaver, and you're a thread weaver, but it's all about the byssus either way."

Zaneta shook a crooked finger at her granddaughter. "You can't escape it, my dear. It's in your blood one way or another. I'm just happy you're happy."

Mira doubted her mother would have seen it so generously had it been Mira's desire to break the line of byssus weavers. Somehow, when it came to her granddaughter, Zaneta was much more openhanded and relaxed. The rules were less rules and more suggestions. Mira had often expressed her astonishment at this change of character with Dante.

He'd made a joke of it to calm her down. "Don't you think if Abraham had been asked to sacrifice his *grandson* instead of the petulant teenager Isaac, the story would have played out completely differently? No way they would have made it to the altar that day. That's how grandparents are when they have all the benefits and none of the responsibility."

"Nonna, do you know of any connections between the weavers and the nuragic ruins?" Daniella asked. "That may be something I'm starting to look into for some of my research. Because of the things I've published so far, I've been asked to join a research team."

Zaneta waved her hand and smiled. "Oh, the German soldier, you mean? I gave him the mad honey and pushed him into the well." She shrugged and reached for her wineglass.

A hush fell over the room, and Luccio cleared his throat with a nervous laugh. "Zaneta, amore, I think we've had enough wine, don't you? Think what you're saying." He took the glass and shook his head at Dani. Mira sat frozen in the dark, her hand gripping Dante's leg. *What did she just say?*

Zaneta gave Luccio an annoyed look and pulled her wrap closer around her shoulders. "It's not the wine, dear, you know that. The Allies were days away, and time was up. I had to survive so the byssus could go on."

"Nonna?" Daniella put her hands on her grandmother's and leaned to look into her eyes. "You mean during the war?"

She nodded. Talk of those days used to be taboo, guaranteed to bring on one of her headaches or days of depression. This time, she laughed. "Yes, of course, dear. When the whole community of weavers, all those in the Jewish neighborhood, were taken." She leaned in and whispered loudly to Dani as if it were a great secret. *"Killed."*

Mira couldn't move. Something riveted her to her seat and rendered her unable to stop her daughter's questions.

"What else?" Daniella probed. Her grandmother, goodness knows, had never been so forthcoming.

"He insisted I weave for him, small things he could peddle on the quay. I used the last of the byssus my mother had saved to make a golden swastika that he *sold* to an officer in town. Byssus can't be sold—you know that. And it was never meant to weave things of evil."

"Of course not, Nonna. That must have been terrible."

Mira suddenly remembered the earthquake the day Daniella was born, how she braced herself between the beams of the doorway. Something in her was bracing like that now. She felt as if the ground might just give way beneath her.

"I used that little loom, Mira, you remember? Like the one in the box? I had one just like it that I'd use to weave little things and then pick apart and weave again. It got so lonesome and tedious all those months."

Months? She'd known her mother had hidden during the war, but her imagination had always had to fill in the details. She hadn't known where or for how long. She'd lived in the ruins for months? Questions swirled in Mira's head, but she feared asking them might stop her mother's words.

"Dani," her father interrupted. "Your nonna is tired, confused."

"I'm not," she barked. "I see it like it was this very morning. I knew then I was of no more use to him. The byssus was gone, and I couldn't very well dive for more. Then I saw the bees, and that was my gift. We ate fish and honey that night. Well, one of us did." She paused, her eyes unfocused and far away. "Then, he was in the well. But the little loom had fallen in, too. I was very sad about that."

Mira stared at her mother. She'd known it. On some level, she'd known something like that had happened when the police had visited all those years ago. And her father had been right. What difference did knowing make? Her aged mother had no idea the story she was recounting was even shocking. She was still her mother. How awful it must have been, being trapped there with someone like that after her family had been taken away. She might have done the same thing herself. Who could know how you'd react when faced with those circumstances?

Her father stood and started to gather their things. "It's late," he said. "Dante, you're probably exhausted on your first night home."

Mira saw the look on her father's face, the lines of worry. Perhaps he'd kept more from her about her mother's state than he'd let on. She would have to speak to him about that soon. Clearly. Her mother stood as well, balancing against him for support.

Mira rose, kissing her father on the cheek. "Thank you for coming, Papà."

"Mira, Mira." Her mother laughed and patted her father on his arm. "No, don't you see? Your papà is at the bottom of a well."

Chapter 39

All the air left the room. Even the muslin curtains at the window stilled. Something held Mira's arm, anchoring her to the ground, thankfully, or else she might have floated away, through the ceiling and tiled roof, up into the night sky she knew to be flecked with stars. There was Papà, staring at her with his wide green eyes brimming with tears. Daniella, still in her chair, her mouth agape and eyes fixed on her mother. Her mother, undisturbed, fussing with her bag and shawl, as if she'd just announced the butcher had a sale going on lamb this week. And Mira somehow saw herself from above, looking as she must have to everyone else in the room—one hand at her throat, her face drained of color, blinking slowly like she'd had too much wine.

Ah, she thought from where she drifted, dizzy, above the house. *Well, of course.* Fragments of memory wafted past, feathers carried by an invisible wind. Moments from her childhood, arrows her mother had loosed. They were tangled with memories of Daniella as a baby, Mira holding her close, watching her toddle on the shore, Dani glancing back at her to be certain she was still there. *Always, my love, always.* It was a strange timeline, backward to her own beginnings and forward to Daniella's, Mira suspended in the middle, holding the golden thread connecting them.

Mira watched the thread reach far into the sky above and knew by heart the names of the other mothers, all weavers, who held their own length of the cord. Through her body, vibrations resonated from the line as they tapped it, playing it like a fiddle. Below her, in the kitchen, she watched as the cord unspooled from her and reached its gossamer tendril around her daughter, its filament a vine seeking purchase.

No matter the fate of the byssus, they were all connected, their pasts sending ripples into futures down the line. Mira watched as Daniella stood and walked to her, felt her daughter's arms encircle her neck and her warmth as she hugged her close. The vibration suddenly stopped. Mira let out a long breath she hadn't known she'd been holding.

Through a dull pounding, which she realized must have been her heartbeat thrumming its slow measure in her ears, Mira heard her name.

"Mira? Mira, look at me."

Dante. It was Dante who'd been grasping her arm, Dante trying to pull her back down from the stars to the kitchen. His face was white with pain. He shouldn't have been exerting himself after the surgery.

Once more, the floor beneath her feet was solid. She was back in the kitchen, surrounded by her family.

"It's all right, Dani," she said, returning the hug. "Really, Dante, you need to sit down. And, Papà—" She smiled, reassuring her father, whose face looked shattered, not on his own behalf—clearly, he'd suspected—but for her. "I'm okay. It explains a lot, actually. Something I think I'd known had been brewing for a long time. But it doesn't change anything. You're my papà. The one I've always known and loved. The one who built me the beautiful loom that I treasure with all my heart."

Luccio swiped a hand across his eyes and sniffed loudly. "Let's get you home," he said to her mother, clearing his throat, but his eyes were locked with Mira's, speaking volumes without saying a word. Perhaps they would make time for that later, but Mira wasn't certain she needed anything else filled in.

~

A few days later, apparently satisfied that her parents could manage, Daniella returned to Venezia. Carmina drove her to Cagliari to catch the ferry to the mainland while Mira stayed with Dante. She wasn't yet ready to leave him alone in case he needed her. Daniella had arranged for a friend to pick her up from the airport, and she promised to call when she reached her apartment.

Mira brewed some coffee and set two chairs outside the front door in the small garden. As the afternoon faded into dusk, she and Dante sat together watching the sky's palette of lavender and rose fade into the horizon. The cozy house was once more theirs, and although they'd welcomed having Daniella home again and were grateful for neighbors and friends who'd stopped by to say hello and leave a loaf of bread or a round of cheese, a comfort settled upon them as they returned to their quiet party of two.

"Want to talk about it?" Dante asked. He sipped his coffee and stretched his legs out in front of him on the grass.

Mira sighed. "My German heritage, you mean? I don't really see how it changes anything. I'm still me."

He reached a hand across the space between them and rested it on her arm. "That's all I want."

"It makes a lot of sense of things I grew up with. How she sometimes looked at me. Her moods. I thought it was losing everyone in the war, but there was more to it."

"None of it was your fault. You know that, right?"

"Of course." She paused. "You know, when we were together, reading Berenice's letter for the first time, I thought then there was something she wanted to say. She couldn't do it, not until she wasn't in control of her memory anymore. There was a lot in Berenice's story that I see now."

She smiled at him. "I've been thinking. This morning, before Daniella left, I was boxing up some weavings of byssus I'd done. She wanted to take some back with her to be photographed."

He nodded. "It's fantastic that your work will finally receive some attention from outside the island. It's art. It should be shown."

Mira shrugged it off. Fame had never been a weaver's aim. "In case something should happen to the craft, that's a good thing, I suppose. It won't be forgotten."

"Dani may be going a different way, but she might someday have a daughter . . ." Dante trailed off.

"Whether she does or not, it's for her to work out. That's what I started to say. I happened to look up and catch my reflection in the window. For a second, I thought it was Dani standing behind me."

"The older she gets, the more she looks like you."

"You think so? But she's not me, and she shouldn't be."

"Since you found the box with your family's photographs in it, I actually think you look more like your grandmother. I just hadn't seen it before."

"Hm. Really?" Mira smiled, considering.

The phone rang, and Mira rose to answer it. "That'll be Daniella, I hope."

"I'm home, Mamma," the voice on the line said, and Mira knew it was true. Home, for Daniella, was no longer Sant'Antioco.

"Brava, amore. Your father and I were just having some coffee in the quiet."

"I can picture you. Outside in the garden? I'm so glad Papà's going to be okay."

"He'll be back to teaching as soon as he can. Thanks for the call and for coming, even with . . . well, everything. Probably with all your resources at the university, you can dig up all sorts of new family history if you want. I'm happy with mine as is, though, Daniella."

"All right, Mamma. I understand."

"Oh, I tucked something in with the byssus when I was wrapping it up for you. I love you, piccina."

"Love you, Mamma. Ciao."

~

Daniella hung up the phone and twisted her long brown hair into a messy bun. She had laundry to do before going back to work in the morning. Her grandmother's story had no bearing on the research the team would be doing with the nuragic ruins, but imagined scenes played in Daniella's mind all the same. She'd have to keep her personal life separate from her work, although in her case, that was a tricky task. For centuries, the byssus had braided their work into their personal lives. Who was she to think she could unlink the two?

She turned to the box that held the wrapped byssus pieces. Daniella was excited to show the university curators actual examples of the material itself rather than photos gathered from museum displays around the world. Some of these were newer, intricate miniature tapestries her mother or grandmother had wrought. Some she remembered from her childhood. Her mother had included a golden scene of fishing boats anchored near the quay. Daniella heard the cries of the gulls in her head and could conjure the smell of the sea.

What had her mother added to the box? She dug through the cloth and found, at the bottom, a handheld mirror. It was the one that had lain on her mother's bedroom chest for as long as she could remember. Beneath it lay a note in her mother's handwriting. She swept aside the suitcase that crowded her bed and sat.

Dani,
Knowing your grandmother's story changes nothing about us. You're as beautiful, smart, and loved as ever. I hope that's what you see when you look in this mirror. It's what I see when I look at you. Although you came from me, you're uniquely you. It's been one of my greatest delights to discover you as you've grown up.

I see now your grandmother saw me as a reflection of her, but not because I looked like her or followed the byssus path. You know how she can be. She wanted a flattering reflection, one that didn't also remind her who my father was or stir up memories of her family that were simply too painful for her to face. One that she shaped and directed to please her.

Berenice's letter has taken you in an unexpected direction. For a time, I was sad about that. But I see what you're doing with the letter, your research—it's bringing preservation of the byssus in a different way, one that's no less important. Byssus or no, Daniella, wherever you are, whatever you're doing, you're loved.

~

Daniella held the letter to her chest for a moment. She was both grateful for her mother's words and sad that Mira hadn't heard or felt that herself. Lifting the mirror, Dani studied her face. She was tired from the travel, her hair a mess. During the week she'd spent in Sant'Antioco, she'd run into so many neighbors and friends who'd known her as a child. Over and over again, she'd heard them remark, "You look so much like your mother"; "You're your mother's image twenty years ago"; "My goodness, I almost thought you were Mira."

It was true. Same eyes, same mouth. It used to irritate Dani to hear such things when she was younger, in school. This time, though, it buoyed her heart. If she resembled her mother—in looks or her strength or capacity for love and forgiveness—she could do far worse.

"Grazie," she'd responded all week, with a smile. "Grazie."

AUTHOR'S NOTE

While the story of Allegra Renda, Zaneta Mazza, and Mira and Daniella Barone is fiction, it is set in a real place within an actual historical timeline. I first learned the word *byssus* from a tweet some years ago and quickly fell down a rabbit hole delving into its origins, unique qualities, and history. My grandfather was a deep-sea fisherman, and the allure of magical and unknown things beneath the ocean has sparked my imagination since I was a child.

Textiles, however, had never really been on my radar. I couldn't have told you the difference between toile and tulle. My late mother (the fisherman's daughter) was an accomplished seamstress, and despite her best efforts, I can in no way replicate her quilts, dolls, clothing, curtains, or pillows. In a pinch, about the only useful handiwork I can manage is to sew on a mean button. The irony of suddenly being fascinated by cloth, weavers, looms, and thread is not lost on me. The idea of skills (or values or ways of life) being passed from mother to daughter (or not) is part of my own life story and certainly found its way into these pages.

Sardinia (or Sardegna) is a small island that lies off the west coast of Italy in the middle of the blue Tyrrhenian Sea. D. H. Lawrence's *Sea and Sardinia* (1921) was useful for early impressions of the place from a visitor's perspective. Both world wars affected the island's residents. In the second war, the island's Jewish community was leveled. Sardinia's strategic location made it a frequent way-stop for troops engaged in fighting on the fronts in Africa, Greece, and Italy itself. In one instance, to heighten the story's tension, I collapsed the historic timeline of actual air attacks in Cagliari and Alghero in February and May to allow the women to hide the oleander box in the cave in January.

By the mid-1940s, Sardinia was the most malaria-ridden region of Italy, with thousands of acres of wetlands lying beyond its beaches. As part of the Rockefeller Foundation Sardinian Project (1946–1951), over ten thousand tons of DDT were sprayed over an area the size of New Hampshire. The island was used as a test site in 1944, with DDT sprayed directly inside homes and on residents themselves. Black-and-white photos exist of children sitting on their beds while men in protective suits spray the chemical throughout the room. While this effectively eliminated the plague of malaria from the island, there were high mortality rates for children under age five. Shepherds, fishermen, and beekeepers blamed huge losses on the spraying, and many residents continued to experience persistent fertility issues.

Sardinia is unique in many ways and different from the mainland of Italy. Although it's now frequented as a vacation destination—its beautiful beaches and impressive cliffs on the public's radar—it still maintains much of its culture and ways of life, with traditional dress, food, and employment in fishing, farming, and mining. The nuragic ruins remain largely a mystery, with no written records yet discovered. The name is derived from its iconic structure, the nuraghe, a tower-fortress. More than seven thousand of these nuraghes pepper the Sardinian landscape. I took the liberty of imagining they could have been used as a hiding place during the war.

The *Pinna nobilis* giant mollusk is an actual creature that thrives in warm Mediterranean waters. It was classified as endangered in 1992 and is protected by European law; it's illegal to harvest it in the Mediterranean today. Byssus, or sea silk, is an incredibly unique, real textile. It's been referenced in the Bible. King Solomon was said to have appeared "shining in public," perhaps in robes woven from byssus. Some have surmised that the curtain of the temple itself was woven from byssus, along with altar cloths and the garments of the

Levite singers. It's believed to have been found over ten thousand years ago in the Middle East, passed through the tribe of Levi and brought to Sardinia by Princess Berenice, the great-granddaughter of Herod, during the second half of the first century. By 500 AD, the silkworm was introduced to Europe, and the use of byssus declined. As with many lost arts, only a few remain who care for and weave the lightweight thread that shines like gold in the sun.

Allegra, Zaneta, and Mira are not meant to represent actual, real-life figures, although weavers of sea silk did and still do exist. I fashioned their lives to toy with the question of what might happen when knowledge, craft, or a profession that's been handed down for generations comes to an end.

ACKNOWLEDGMENTS

So much linguistic midwifery goes into putting a book into readers' hands, and although it's not quite as painful as *actual* childbirth, there may have been some wailing and thrashing about all the same. Now that it's here, the travails are (mostly) forgotten, and I'm once again grateful to have been part of the process.

I'm indebted to the thorough, kind, and professional team at Lake Union, chiefly editor Nancy Holmes, who connected with the weavers in a personal way, but also the art department for rendering the cover design, and copy editors and proofreaders who tracked down (in Italian!) each oversight. Thanks also to Cate Hart, my persistent agent, who patiently drummed her fingers and tapped her feet, waiting for this manuscript for a long time.

Always, I'm humbled by the way my husband, Bob, and the rest of the "Blaylock Battalion" encourage and celebrate with me over the words I string together. I'm so lucky our lives are woven together, and our family's tapestry is my favorite masterpiece.

And Reader, I'm thankful for you spending time in these pages when you've no doubt got plenty of other things you could've been doing instead. You're who we're all aiming for. If you've connected in some way to these generations of women, if you're a mother or a daughter and something resonated, I'd love for you to leave a review or drop me a note.

BOOK CLUB QUESTIONS

1. In the context of the story's framework—potentially losing an ancient art—a larger question arises. What other burdens might we as parents (mothers in particular) lay on our children?
2. What consequences might a parent's expectations and disappointments have on their daughter (or son)?
3. Which is more pressing, our duty to those before us or our responsibility to those who come after us? Ties to community or family, or individual freedom? The culture you're born into might change your answer.
4. Are there things worth keeping (saving) from old ways of doing things? Is it worth it to keep teaching a language, for example, to preserve a heritage? Are there elements of tradition, faith, and family history that should be preserved, or is it better to adopt new ways of thinking and doing for the sake of the youth?
5. Many people feel a deep attachment to their home (or homeland) and would feel a great loss if they had to leave. Have you ever experienced that? Is there a spot of land or a region of the country you're deeply drawn to?

6. Do you think Daniella's work in Venice was a good enough way for her to carry on the line of water women?
7. If you'd been in the line, would you have taken the water oath, or would you have wanted to have options?
8. Did you have a favorite character? Allegra, Zaneta, Mira, or Daniella? Why?

ABOUT THE AUTHOR

Photo © 2019 Dawn Harrison

Bonnie Blaylock is the author of *Light to the Hills*, winner of the Porch Prize for fiction. She lives with her husband on a small farm near Nashville, Tennessee, where they keep donkeys, chickens, and bees. For more information, visit www.bonnieblaylock.com.